Blood,

Fire

and

Ice

By C. Edgar North

Blood, Fire and Ice by C. Edgar North

Special thanks to Linda and Bruce who gave me the idea and to Diane for putting up with my time-outs for writing. C. E. N.

ISBN 9781631922275

Contact: *cedgarnorth@gmail.com*

Prelude

August 20, 1962 Beaufort Sea near Prince of Wales Strait

The United States Nuclear Attack Submarine, *SSN Orca,* was following the route charted by *SSN Sargo* and *SSN Sea Dragon* the previous year. Submerged the entire way since departing Bangor, Maine, it had entered the Arctic Ocean from the Atlantic side, negotiating through Lancaster Sound passage between Greenland and Baffin Island, then through Prince of Wales Strait into the Beaufort Sea. The sub was equipped with special Upward Looking Sonar and pressure sensors that could "read" the depth and structure of the ice pack above, and it had an updated version of the North American Aviation N6A-1 inertial navigation system that enabled accurate navigation underwater. The route had been used only twice since the *SSN Nautilus* made the first underwater foray to the North Pole in 1958.

Following the course plotted by *Sargo* and *Sea Dragon*, the sub had transitioned out of Prince of Wales Strait after a six-hundred-mile passage from Baffin Bay. The sub was cruising at a depth of one hundred thirty feet along the relatively shallow continental shelf of the Arctic Canadian coastline, heading for deeper water. The sub's sonar was showing a depth of over one hundred feet of water beneath the keel – ample room – and the charts showed the sea floor would soon be sloping deeper. The navigator felt the sub was a comfortable distance from the pack ice above, varying from six to twenty feet thick, and the sea floor one hundred feet (about 17 fathoms) below. Just the same, they weren't in any hurry. Although capable of far more speed, the sub was cruising at a leisurely seven knots. When they got off the continental shelf, they would increase speed.

Lieutenant Commander Bernard "Barney" Cross, officially the navigator, was standing watch as Officer of the Deck (OOD). An Annapolis graduate now ten years after his commissioning and subsequent training at the submarine school in Bangor, Maine, he was renowned as one of the best navigators in the submarine service. At thirty-three years old, he was happy with his lot in life

3

and proud to be on patrol in waters that had only recently been explored. He was standing over the chart table, holding his slide rule in his right hand and gently tapping it in the palm of his left. According to the internal navigation system and sonar soundings, he was right on course. Right on time. Perfect. They would be in deep water at the continental shelf drop-off in sixteen hours.

On the far side of the control room, Chief Petty Officer Rob Cartwright was standing behind the sonar and hydrophone operators. After briefly talking to Seaman First Class Tyler Ross, the hydrophone operator seated at a small console facing the port side bulkhead, CPO Cartwright turned and shouted across the control room, "Sir, we're getting something unusual on the hydrophones."

Barney took a few steps to cross from the chart table to stand beside Chief Petty Officer Cartwright. "What have you got Tyler?" he asked Seaman Ross.

'It sounds like bubbles, sir. Lots of bubbles. It's getting stronger fast."

"Put it on your speaker; let's hear it." A loud rumbling came out of a speaker on the bulkhead above Seaman Ross. "Wow!" He turned toward the seaman, Jerry Rose, at the sonar. "Jerry, got a fix on this?"

"Sir, it's dead ahead but spreads port for a mile and starboard for half a mile. It's hard to tell for sure, but it seems to be about fifty miles distant and we're closing on it."

Barney turned to Chief Petty Officer Cartwright, "Summon the captain to the control room. Reduce speed to four knots. Maintain depth and course."

"Aye sir." As he reached for the intercom phone, Chief Cartwright turned to the seaman at the throttle console. "Reduce speed to four knots." He received an immediate acknowledgement – "Reducing speed to four knots." He then keyed the microphone for the speaker system. "Captain to the control room, Captain to the control room."

Meanwhile, Lieutenant Commander Cross made a note in the sub's navigational log.

Captain Ken Jessup, a twenty-three year veteran of the silent service, was sitting in the mess with some off-duty sailors, enjoying an old movie, *Son of Paleface*, a comedy starring Roy Rogers, his horse Trigger, Bob Hope and Jane Russell. He was well-known for an unflappable temperament and his ability to motivate his crew. He excused himself and made his way to the control room. When he entered, he said, "Captain is taking the Conn." Then he turned to Barney. "What's up?"

"We're getting an unusual disturbance on the hydrophones and sonar. Sounds like a lot of bubbles. Range seems to be fifty miles and we're closing on it dead ahead. It seems to cover a wide path to port and starboard. I've reduced speed to four knots but maintain depth and course."

He turned to the hydrophone operator. "Tyler, put the sound on speaker. Let's hear it."

Seaman Ross turned a switch and all listened for a few moments. Then Captain Jessup said, "Interesting. Jerry, what have you got?"

"I've got a range on the bubbles of, now forty-seven miles ahead spreading port as far as a mile and starboard about half a mile before diminishing."

"OK We'll play it safe and sidestep the disturbance. Barney, plot us a course to take us around the starboard extremity of the bubbles."

"Aye sir." He plotted the course and gave the first new direction heading to the helmsman, then turned to Captain Jessup. "At current speed, we stay on this heading for ten hours then change heading to triangulate back to original."

"OK. We're going off the established course slightly. Keep alert."

Ten hours later, they were passing over the extremity of the disturbance. Bubbles were slight but the hydrophone operator noted they were passing over some. The watch had changed with Captain

5

Jessup as Officer of the Deck. Commander Dean Jones, the second in command of the sub, was off watch, asleep in his bunk. Barney had come to the control room for the course change.

Barney changed course, triangulating the sub back toward their prescribed path. Depth below the keel had increased slightly, now one hundred fifty feet. The ice scanning sonar indicated they had exited the ice flow into clear water on the surface with no ice showing for over one hundred miles in front. This encouraged Captain Jessup to increase speed to seven knots. He turned to Barney. "Looks as if we've passed it."

A few moments later, the hydrophone operator shouted and took his headphones off. "Sir, bubbles. Very strong!"

The sonar operator shouted, "Sir, we're in a field of solid bubbles. I can't get a reading. We're surrounded by bubbles."

Captain Jessup calmly said, "Reduce speed to three knots. Maintain course and depth. What's our depth?"

"Sir, no reading on depth."

"Must be the bubbles interfering," said Barney.

"Agree. Let's hope we pass through this quickly."

A few minutes later, no one was prepared for the jolt as the sub struck something, causing the sub to heel over thirty degrees to starboard, tilt upward twenty degrees and come to a grinding halt. Everyone standing was thrown forward; those seated at consoles on port and starboard sides of the control room were thrown sideways. As he was thrown forward, Captain Jessup managed to grab a stanchion and stop his momentum. Chief Petty Officer Cartwright was hurtled on top of Seaman Ross and badly gashed his forehead on a wiring panel. Barney was thrown sprawling on top of the chart table but he managed to stop by grabbing one end of the table.

"Stop engines," Captain Jessup ordered the helmsman, who responded immediately while climbing back into his seat. A grinding noise could be heard beneath the keel as the sub settled.

6

Captain Jessup grabbed the microphone above him for the speaker system. "All hands to emergency stations. All hands to emergency stations. We've grounded. Rig for emergency. Close all compartment doors. Assess damage."

The depth gauge began to operate, showing they were grounded at one hundred twenty feet. Barney noted the gyrocompass and inertial navigation system were functioning.

"Sir, the bubbles are reducing."

Captain Jessup looked around, noting two people in the control room were nursing severe cuts to their heads and one was holding his left shoulder as if it had been dislocated. He turned toward the man on the diving planes who was holding his shoulder. "Fred, are you able to handle the controls?"

He grimaced and nodded. "Sir, the controls are stiff. I'm having trouble moving them with my shoulder out. The diving planes may be damaged." Captain Jessup said, "Barney, take his place for now." He then called over the speaker: "Corpsman to the control room."

Barney helped the seaman to his feet, propping him up against the chart table, and replaced him at the diving plane controls. "Sir, the dive planes are very stiff but I'm getting some response."

During the commotion, a pharmacist's mate had arrived and was tending to the wounded in the control room. Crew members, including the second in command, Commander Dean Jones, who had been off watch when the sub grounded, arrived and assumed their positions in the control room, relieving some who had been injured and doubling up in action station mode. Commander Jones, an Annapolis grad, was a seventeen-year veteran of the silent service, renowned for his cheerful demeanor and Dale Carnegie-schooled ability to win friends and influence people. His leadership qualities and proven ability had him in line for a promotion to a sub of his own.

Captain Jessup toggled the intercom. "Damage control report. Forward torpedo room first." Quickly, in order starting at the bow, damage control leaders in each compartment reported on the condition of the hull, machinery and crew. They reported no leakage and no broken pipes; the reactor and propulsion systems seemed fine. Twenty-five of the crew had sustained injuries from being tossed about in the grounding, mainly cuts – some needing stitches – and bruises. Nothing more major than a mild concussion, a displaced shoulder, a broken wrist and the cook had burns on his left wrist from scalding coffee.

Captain Jessup called the sonar operator. "What does the ice monitor say about conditions at the surface?"

"No ice above sir. All clear."

"OK, let's take her up. Blow ballast and trim for an even keel." They could feel the sub lift off the seabed and level out. "Sonar, any obstructions in front of us now?"

"No sir, all clear."

They could feel the sub rise and straighten out to an even keel. Once he felt they were well clear of the shoal, he said, "Set speed ahead three knots. Same course. Trim and hold at fifty feet. To Barney, he said, "How are the diving planes responding?"

"Stiff but responding."

Finally Captain Jessup had time to fill in Dean Jones. "Dean, looks as if we grounded on an outcrop that was behind a stream of bubbles. It wasn't seen on the sonar as the bubbles obscured the readings. Thought we were clear of the bubbles but they popped up again all of a sudden, right under us. Everything was clear before the bubbles popped up again."

"Have we sustained much damage?"

"So far, only the diving planes may be damaged."

"Sir! Bubbles are surrounding us again," shouted the sonar and hydrophone operators, almost in unison.

"Blow the ballast, we're surfacing." Captain Jessup toggled the speaker system and alerted the crew. "Now hear this, we are surfacing to assess damage. We may have sustained some damage to the diving planes." He turned to Dean Jones. "I want you to lead the hull assessment. Organize a team of hull technicians with divers. You know the drill. Even though it's summer topside, we're probably near or below freezing." As he could feel the sub respond, angling upward, he called out, "Up periscopes!" With dual periscopes, both captain and commander could reconnoiter at once.

"No depth indicator showing," Barney called out. "Probably due to the bubbles."

They felt the sub surface and level out. There was no time to reconnoiter from periscope depth, but both Captain Jessup and Commander Jones conducted a 360-degree-long range sweep of the surface, thankful for the long daylight hours in the Arctic that time of year. Commander Jones, proceeding to do a close-in sweep, said, "There's a huge stream of bubbles surfacing off our port side, about half a mile away."

Captain Jessup refocused his periscope. "I see it." He turned periscope watch over to Barney. "OK Dean, assemble your team."

It took a good twenty minutes before Dean and his men were dressed and ready to go "topside" through a hatch near the bow in the torpedo room. As they exited the hatch, they could feel the cold as the chill factor was boosted by a twenty-knot wind blowing across the hull. They could see the display of bubbles about three hundred yards away visibly churning the water and producing a vapor cloud. It seemed the line of bubbles stretched for about half a mile. Dean had two divers dressed and they were soon in the frigid water inspecting the hull while other technicians carefully inspected the hull above the water. Shortly, the divers reported back that the hull was sound. Some protective sound-deadening coating had been scraped off around the keel on the port side. There was slight damage to one propeller blade. However, the port side forward diving plane had been bent.

During the inspection, the sub had been drifting slowly toward the bubbles. It had closed to within two hundred yards of them when the wind died, and the five men remaining on deck noticed a smell of gas that was rapidly getting stronger as the vapor cloud from the bubbles began to drift toward the sub. They began to cough and retch. One passed out and fell overboard. Another doubled over as he crumpled to the deck. And another, coming to his aid, crumpled on top of him and passed out. The fourth man, farthest from the hatch, held his breath and ran toward the hatch, only to succumb within three feet of the open hatch. The fifth man made it into the hatch, trying desperately to pull the fourth man in with him. He passed out on the ladder and slid into the torpedo room, collapsing at the foot of the ladder. While two of his mates on the deck below jumped to his aid, a sailor ran up the ladder and, holding his breath grabbed the unconscious fourth man, bringing him down the ladder in a fireman's carry. When he got to the deck, another sailor ran up the ladder and, holding his breath, closed the hatch. Although a little gas vapor had come down the hatch, the torpedo room crew managed to contain it to the torpedo room by closing the door to the next compartment and venting through a valve in the hull with positive pressure.

Sailors performed CPR on the two unconscious men while the chief of the torpedo room was on the phone reporting the incident to the control room. Commander Jones arrived quickly and organized a rescue party with breathing apparatus to go on deck from the diver's air lock and bring in the others. Regrettably, despite resuscitation efforts, four were dead.

Captain Jessup reported the incident to Sub Command and was ordered to abort the trip and bring his damaged vessel back to Bangor, Maine.

The incident remained a naval secret. The cause of the grounding remained a mystery for a few years until scientists discovered that methane gas, in the form of solidified methane hydrate, is present in large quantities in many places on the continental shelf of the Arctic Ocean and that there is an extremely active zone in the Beaufort Sea. As water temperatures change ever so slightly upward during the Arctic summer, the methane is disturbed, some of it shifting from frozen to gaseous state, bubbling to the surface and pushing a mound of frozen methane and earth up through the permafrost layer at the bottom of the ocean. Often, this creates pingo-like mounds rising from the ocean floor, similar to the pingo mounds of permafrost pushing up on land in the Arctic that had been discovered by early Arctic explorers. Hydrographic surveys show tall new mounds, as much as three hundred feet high, that have pushed up over a short summer season. It was presumed *SSN Orca* encountered a rare eruption of methane hydrate that quickly pushed up a pingo-like mound.

Through the ensuing decades, the submarine service continued regular cold war patrols of the Arctic, especially with ballistic missile submarines, but a lesson had been learned the hard way to avoid the shallows of the Arctic continental shelf and the presence of methane hydrate deposits.

After a number of additional voyages over the next three years, Captain Jessup was reassigned to a desk job in the Pentagon. Both Dean Jones and Barney Cross eventually rose in rank to command ballistic missile subs.

Chapter 1

<u>August 10, 2012 Beaufort Sea</u>

The ship was anchored offshore from the Canadian Arctic Ocean port of Tuktoyaktuk, situated on the eastern side of the riverine delta where the Arctic Ocean is blessed with the nutrients of the mighty MacKenzie River. The farewell party was being held in the main mess of the venerable icebreaker. The summer open ice season was drawing to a close and half the scientists aboard would soon depart to be replaced by another group who would conduct various research activities while the ship wended its way back through the Eastern Arctic, eastward and southward down through one of the Northwest Passages skirting Baffin Island and the Hudson Bay to its home base in St. John's Newfoundland.

The departing research team of twenty men and women were nationals from Japan, Russia, the USA and Canada who had participated for the past six weeks in a variety of jointly sponsored studies on climate change and Arctic geology. This was the tenth summer season in the Arctic that the team members had worked together. Over the decade, they had witnessed first hand the effects of global warming in the ecologically sensitive Arctic and could point to significant results from their diverse studies which had been and continued to be published in learned scientific journals worldwide.

Ten members of the departing team were Japanese, from the University of Sapporo, while the other ten comprised six Canadians, three Americans and one Russian. The bar, located in the Officers' Lounge, was open and many were well into their second or third rounds when the lead scientist, Robert Berubé, tapped a spoon on his beer glass to call for silence and attention. Robert, a slightly stooped six foot two, thin as a rail at one hundred seventy pounds, and a professor of hydrology from Trois Rivieres University in Quebec said, "Ladies and gentlemen, thank you for your attention! It's thank-you time! First, let's have a great round of applause for the crew of our ship, the Heavy Icebreaker, *RCS Louis Riel,* who have been the perfect hosts. Many of the crew have been with us since we began our experiments ten years ago and for us, returning to the ship is always like returning to home and old friends. Of course, special thanks today must go to the galley crew who have provided such a delicious buffet! I propose a toast to the crew and the ship!"

This solicited a polite response from all. "Hear, hear! To the crew! And to the ship!"

"Our research has been jointly sponsored and would not have been possible without the significant financing provided by Japan, the United States, Russia and Canada. We must thank Japan and our sterling Japanese comrades for their most significant contribution as we would not be here without their generosity in paying for the fuel for the *Louis Riel*. I propose a toast to our generous Japanese sponsors and to our excellent colleagues from the University of Sapporo!"

The non-Japanese present in the room loudly responded "Hear, hear!" to which the Japanese members held their glasses in front of themselves with two hands, bowed, raised their glasses above their heads, bowed lightly, then sipped their drinks with the others.

"We must also give credit to America and Russia who funded our provisions for the voyage, and to the Canadian government for funding the Canadian science team, providing the *Louis Riel* and its excellent crew."

Another round of "Hear, hear!" was followed by more clinking of glasses and sipping.

"I think we all agree that our research this year was most productive! May I call on Professor Iawama to say a few words?" He looked toward Professor Iawama and bowed.

The bow was returned and Professor Iawama stepped forward to take the portable microphone. He bowed again to his audience and said, "Domo aragito gozayamus!" Then, after bowing again, he spoke to the audience with the slight Western American twang that reflected the years he had spent obtaining his doctorate at Texas A & M . "I thank you all, such good friends and colleagues, for helping to bring our research to fruition! I think we can rightfully say you have helped show how to put a collar on a tiger! In our experiment, we have been able to safely extract and contain methane hydrate from the permafrost – a first for the world and a huge step to viable commercialization. We could not have gotten so far so quickly without all your expertise! Thank you one and all!"

This solicited a big "Yea" from the audience.

"We have vast deposits of frozen methane hydrate – call it methane calthrate if you will – in Northern Japan, in the waters around Hokkaido and our northern outer islands, and now we have the key to capture and commercialize them! We can liberate Japan from its dependence on oil imports for centuries! As you have helped determine, the Arctic permafrost, both on land and in the sea, holds sufficient methane hydrate – just that which we have identified on our voyage, with much more territory yet to be explored – to make all of North America fuel independent for over four hundred years! I am pleased to announce that the Government of Japan has agreed to provide near unlimited resources to the University of Sapporo to advance commercialization. We will begin drilling within six months off northeastern Hokkaido."

Cheers all round.

"Thank you for your help. As we are in full collaboration, you will take the benefits of this research back to your respective governments and research institutions and I wish for you all as much success as we have in pushing forward with commercialization. I look forward to seeing you all in the near future and to further collaboration."

Cheers all round. Iawama-san returned the microphone to Robert.

"Our charter flight will be arriving within the hour to take us to Edmonton to make transfers to our respective homes and institutions. Captain Ferguson says we have a half hour before we will be transported to the airport. So, in the meantime, drink up!"

Edmonton International Airport, Canada (YEG)

While waiting for their connecting flights, Norma Jensen's to Victoria, Robert Berubé's to Quebec, both were sitting at a table at

14

one of the airport's in-transit restaurants. Norma, with a PhD in biosciences, five foot nothing and one hundred twenty pounds on her fifty-seven-year-old frame, was sipping an iced tea. Robert was playing with his iPod, reviewing his e-mail, when he let go a string of expletives. "Sacre' nom de cochon! Merde! Merde! Merde! Les etourdis! C'est impossible!"

"My goodness, Robert, what's got you so excited? You seldom swear! Did you know that in India it's a sign of sophistication if members of parliament can swear in English rather than in their mother tongue when they get excited?"

"Our funding has been removed! Our research project has been shut down!"

"What?"

"My office manager received a letter today directly from the Prime Minister's Office stating that the National Science Council has been ordered to withdraw our funding effective immediately. We are to turn over all our research notes to the Canadian government and are placed under the Secrecy Act – we cannot discuss our findings!"

"You're kidding? This applies to all of us?"

"I am sure you will also be notified soon. Merde!"

"Those of us who are on tenure at a university may not be laid off, but the people at the federal research institutes who can't easily transfer to another project will be out of work. This is a catastrophe!"

"That goes to show the short-sightedness of our current federal government. They're dominated by the oil patch. This looks and smells like a sell-out to "big oil." I've always said Quebec should be separate from the yahoos of the West!"

Chapter 2

Darkness in the jungle. Dark and dank in the bushes. A rainfall had raised the stench of the vegetation but the rain had ended and now the trail was slightly illuminated by a half moon. His men were in place, well concealed on each side of the trail where they had been waiting for the past hour. They had planned their ambush position well, having selected a spot where the trail passed down through a small ravine which afforded a line of fire down onto their quarry from ten feet above. The vertical sides of the small gully could contain those trying to scramble off the trail. The men were positioned with one at each end of the trap plus four more midway, two along each side of the trail on the high ground. A scout was positioned farther down the trail in deep cover to provide early warning when the quarry was approaching. The men were well equipped with MP5 assault weapons and two-way radios. They wore camouflage and night vision goggles.

All heard three clicks in their earpieces alerting them that their quarry had passed the scout. It was followed a few seconds later by, "Five in the lead and six behind plus our six in the middle." This was acknowledged by two clicks from the leader. They waited.

The scout clicked three again then said, "Five rear guard three hundred yards behind." This was followed by two clicks from the leader and, "Scout and back door take the rear guard. Ed and Sid assist when finished here." Two clicks repeated as each man acknowledged. They waited.

They watched as the single file procession entered the kill zone. Five armed rebels in front, six hostages tied together by rope, then six armed rebels. They waited until the last rebel was well past the back door and deep into the middle of the trap. Almost simultaneously, the middle soldiers opened fire, first cutting down the quarry on each side of the hostages as the others took out the startled remainder. It was over in seconds. One of the soldiers shouted to the hostages, "Get down and stay down and stay still until we get the rest of them." They hugged the earth. One of the soldiers ran down the line of fallen rebels placing double-tap shots into the head of each. There could be no survivors. No time. The others would be coming up fast, attracted by the shots. They were undisciplined; they'd run to the noise.

In the interim, the solders regrouped with two moving to the back door off the trail to support Mike, the back door man. Two approached the hostages and cut them free, then jumped to either side of the trail taking defensive positions when they heard the remaining rebels noisily running towards them. Almost there. They waited.

As predicted, the remaining rebels ran into the trap zone and were mowed down. Two tried to run away back the way they had come but were cut down by the scout. All received follow-up double tap shots to the head, just in case.

Paddy, the squad leader, came up to the hostages. "OK fellas, up you get. No thank-you's yet, please, until we get you safely back to the platform. You've got a bit of a walk in hostile territory yet, then a boat ride."

With one man as advance scout, they worked their way back up the trail for a few hundred yards, then branched to another. On the way in, they had left "tell-tales" on that trail which the scout located and checked to see if anyone had passed by. Half a mile of trekking brought them to a very small cove on the river where they had left three fast inflatable boats and the coxswains as a rear guard. They made it safely into the estuary, then into more open water and back to the oil production platform about ten miles into the open but fairly shallow water of the delta. They were warmly greeted by a welcoming group when they tied up at the boat dock of the platform. Paddy was the first off and was greeted by Jon Larson, boss of the oil platform. "Well Paddy, you did it again! Great going! Anybody hurt?"

"No. Just the rebels. We made examples of them – no man left standing. The village they came from will be mourning for quite a while. That should teach them that messing with your men is not healthy."

Paddy West was a senior partner in Xtractions Inc. based in Calgary, Alberta, Canada. His firm specialized in extracting people in danger from political, climatic and medical upheavals ranging from coups to floods and plagues, and in solving international business problems in developing countries – such as disputes over ownership of mineral resources in an unstable political climate. They would use force, bribery and intimidation, whatever was necessary and the client could afford. One of Xtraction Inc.'s major revenue sources was the sale of emergency extraction insurance for individuals working in difficult countries. A major revenue stream came from being on retainer for various large oil and mining interests. Yet another revenue stream was entitled "specialty services" for specific projects – things others didn't want to be associated with.

Paddy was thirty-nine years old, an ex-British SAS commando who had served twelve enjoyable and action-packed years. He was a big man, six foot three, two hundred thirty solid pounds, electric blue eyes, crew-cut brown hair on a large oval face, reconstructed but broken again large nose, size fourteen shoes. He was neither handsome nor ugly. When relaxed, he had a smile with full teeth, which women liked, and a keen sense of humor. He could be gentle or rough. He had no conscience, no remorse when it came to killing. He had never married, wasn't too keen on women trying to tie him down. In Xtraction Inc. he tended to gather a crew of like-minded people. A lot were former British SAS but some came from US and Canadian Special Forces – he had picked up some Canadians from a commando unit that had been disbanded when they were deemed too rough, unacceptable for peacekeeping purposes. They were mercenaries in a way – for hire by corporations treading internationally in unsavory climates.

"I've got the chopper standing by," said Jon Larson. "We can have you and the hostages at Port Harcourt airport in half an hour. There's a company jet waiting, with a doctor and nurse aboard. I also got a call from your corporate HQ. You're wanted for another project. Your team is to stay here, with Fred replacing you. You're to fly out with the hostages and get off in Curacao for a briefing. The plane will go on to Galveston with the guys you rescued."

"OK," Paddy replied. "I'll change and pack while your people attend to the rescued – food, showers, change of clothes. An hour?"

"OK."

Curacao

Not only was the boardroom opulent, but the view of Willemstad was awesome. He always marveled at the colorful Dutch-influenced buildings of Punda. He had been waiting five minutes, enjoying the view and the excellent coffee the receptionist had provided. The door opened and he was greeted by a tall, thin gentleman with swept back, un-parted, long stringy brown and grey hair, and horn-rimmed bi-focal glasses focusing blue eyes. With a white shirt and red tie complimenting a navy blue suit, he looked comfortable in the chilly air conditioning. They shook hands, firm grips. He said, "Paddy, welcome! I hear you did an excellent job rescuing the hostages in the River Delta. That's the third time this year alone, isn't it?"

"Thank you Chairman Van der Zalm. It went well. You'd think the youth of the Niger River Delta would learn not to mess with the oil industry."

"They feel they have a good cause. High unemployment, displacement, poor education, boredom and the Nigerian government not sharing the oil wealth with the region. As well, the oil industry has run roughshod over the land, with acid rain ruining the soil, and hydrocarbons polluting the water. It's only recently we've started to clean up our act and that's mainly only because we've found markets for the natural gas and sulfur we were wasting. If I were there and young, I'd be tempted to join them."

"Maybe."

He motioned Paddy to be seated, then began, "You and your firm, Xtraction Inc. have been providing a very useful service to the oil industry. Your ability to rescue hostages, bring out our people from difficult spots in case of emergency and nip sabotage in the bud is most valuable. You did a great job getting our people out of India when we had that cholera-typhoid scare last year. You quickly eliminated those saboteurs who were blowing up the pipeline in Angola. We, that is, the Global Association of Refiners and Petroleum Poducers, for whom I speak as chairman, are greatly appreciative. We look forward to a long, continuing relationship."

"Thank you, Chairman. Always available for you."

"Something, ah, delicate has come up, for which we seek your services."

"Delicate?"

"Yes. Our industry has prided itself on being able to control supply to some extent. We've been fortunate to have increasing demand, especially with the developing tigers of China and India demonstrating a huge thirst for oil. That has pushed up prices, as supply has been paced slightly behind demand. We've been able to lobby major governments effectively and that has helped, such as delaying tighter emissions regulations and slowing the mandates for better fuel mileage in vehicles and alternative means of propulsion. Until recently, natural gas delivery was nearly matching demand and that complemented our industry where we have invested heavily to capture more of it at the wellhead to supply a ready market. We were able to delay new technologies that would enable easier extraction of natural gas from coal seams and by fracking oil deposits, but those resources have now come online, resulting in an oversupply and plummeting prices in North America. Thankfully, the coal industry is taking most of the hit with the drive to replace coal with gas for electricity generation. In the past, we helped build the image that nuclear power was undesirable.

"Now, there's a new threat in the form of methane hydrate extraction and we'd like to delay it for a while. The biggest problem we have is the Japanese who are seeking ways to get away from imported oil dependency. Russia, Canada and the US are also making headway with the Japanese in extraction technology – yet they feel less urgency in development right now as their natural gas is so bountiful. They've had a joint research program for the past decade and now claim a technical breakthrough. It means multi-billions to us if we can stop or delay harnessing methane hydrate extraction.

"Add to this the issue of global warming. We are accused of significantly contributing to this in a variety of ways from processing of hydrocarbons, to wasting natural gas by flaring it off during oil extraction, and we get part of the blame for consumption pollution – too many cars creating smog etc. Methane hydrate and the potential for the release of huge amounts into the atmosphere through warming in arctic regions is a significant developing issue. It can draw public attention to focus on inhibiting the contributors to global warming and that means we'll be targeted and that our bottom line could be affected."

"And how can I and my company assist?"

"Assist in the delay process. We have lobbyists who can be effective in Canada and the USA but Russia and Japan are another question. The Committee would like you to nip the problem at its root – take out or stifle the people responsible for the breakthrough. If we can't stop it, we want to obtain and control that processing breakthrough and delay implementation. And we don't want attention focusing on global warming. "

"Let's discuss my fee."

Paddy decided to spend the night in Curacao, and visit the infamous "Le Mirage" – the government-approved brothel by the airport. Next day, he was heading home to Calgary and planning his next moves.

Chapter 3

<u>Winnipeg, Manitoba</u>

Portage and Main, Winnipeg, Manitoba, is one of winter's coldest, windiest downtown corners in any city of Canada but tonight it was early autumn, warm and clear, with no wind and few pedestrians. There was no excuse for anybody to have been struck in a marked crosswalk by a car accelerating quickly from behind the pedestrian, turning on a red light and knocking the body flying some thirty feet under the wheels of an oncoming transit bus. The car sped off. There were a few eyewitnesses – but each gave conflicting descriptions of the car and driver. The police called it a hit and run, probably by joy riders in a stolen car, as the car was recovered the next day in a desolate part of the rail yards – burned out but with extensive damage on its front grill. It had been stolen in one of the suburbs two days before.

<u>Sausalito, San Francisco Bay</u>

It was a beautiful evening, just after the rush hour. Victor had walked the short distance down the hill from his bay view condo to the marina, as was his routine ever since he returned home from the Arctic. The wharf finger, old Ollie Olsen, was a fixture at the marina. His was the first boat on the wharf at the foot of the gangway, an old fifty-foot wooden-hulled displacement cabin cruiser which had seen better days. Ollie had greeted Victor and they had exchanged some small talk about the beautiful fog-free autumn weather. Last Ollie saw of Victor, he was walking farther down the dock to his twenty-six-foot sailboat, the *Mary Rose.* The harbor police boat responded to a report of a sailboat out in the bay circling aimlessly, apparently not under command, and found the *Mary Rose* running in circles under power with no one aboard. The body of Victor Wong was found the next day floating at the edge of the tidal swamp north of Sausalito.

<u>Toronto, Ontario</u>

Marie LeCourt, as was her routine at the end of the workday, came down the escalator onto the crowded loading platform of the Yonge and Eglington subway station. She walked toward the rear of the platform along its edge, as she had found it was easier to push through from the side, rather than be directly in front of the train's doors when they opened, as one was often pushed back by passengers trying to get off. It was rush hour, after all, and Torontonians were not too courteous when clambering for their public transit ride home – even for those exiting the train it was a push with people jockeying for an advantage, pushing, trying to board and crowding personal space to nothing. Marie fell sideways right onto the tracks and the electrified third rail just as the train was exiting the tunnel and braking. She didn't have a chance. She was decapitated by the front wheels and electrocuted. No one saw her being pushed by the big guy or noticed that he faded into the crowd and up the exit escalator. Marie LeCourt was cursed by thousands for bringing the North-South Yonge Line to a stop and fouling up their homeward commutes.

Sapporo Japan

Since his return from the Arctic, Kenji Ube' could not get enough of baseball. His team, the *Nippon Professionals,* were into the playoffs and tonight would be one final step to the pennant – if they won. He was on his way to the game, walking to the Sapporo Dome, about two blocks distant. As he crossed the street, he was hit by a car which sped away. Although three people caught the license plate, police determined the vehicle had been stolen the week before. Fortunately, fellow pedestrians rendered effective first aid and Professor Kenji Ube' wound up in hospital in serious, but stable condition with multiple fractures.

Victoria, British Columbia

"Oh my God! I can't believe it! When and how did it happen?" Norma was almost screaming into the phone, nearly hysterical. Her husband Carl, still holding a tea towel he had been using to dry the dishes, was rushing into the room, drawn by Norma's near hysterics. She turned to Carl and half covered the phone with her hand. "It's Robert. Jayson Metcalfe was killed while crossing the street at Portage and Main in Winnipeg."

23

Carl said, "My God, another one! What's going on here?"

Norma spoke into the phone, "That's three of us gone in less than three weeks – all by accidents. This is beyond coincidence. What, are we cursed?"

Robert Berubé, on the other end of the line said, "I'm getting the same feeling. First, it was the fall off the platform in front of the subway train that claimed Marie LeCourt in Toronto, then Victor Wong fell off his boat and drowned while sailing in San Francisco Bay."

"We should go to the police!"

"I did, but didn't get anywhere. I went to the Quebec Provincial Police – the QPP, who were polite and took the information, then referred me to the RCMP. The RCMP took my information and contacted the Ontario Provincial Police – the OPP – and the Metro Toronto Police who hold the view that Marie's death was simply an accident. Jayson died in Winnipeg, another police jurisdiction and, of course, Victor is American and died in San Francisco. There doesn't seem to be any interest, or any police jurisdiction capable of linking the deaths together. The RCMP certainly doesn't seem to care – even though they are all linked with the northern research."

"Victor was American. What about the FBI?"

"I'm trying to make an appointment with one of their people in the Consulate in Montreal, but I'm even afraid to travel from Troi Riveries to see them in Montreal. I hope I can talk to someone over the phone."

"Do you think, if I spoke to anyone here in Victoria, it might help?"

"I doubt it. You haven't been hurt or had any near accidents yet?"

"No. All is normal."

"Perhaps I'm just being paranoid. I'm checking with all the other team members to see if anything unusual has happened. I e-mailed Iawama-san and he replied that Professor Ube' was hospitalized from a hit and run traffic accident. Since receiving my e-mail about the three deaths, he went to the police and they are treating the incident with great seriousness and are providing security – even planning to move all the researchers to a secure research facility. Apparently, their government people are going to talk with the Russian, American and Canadian government people to bring attention to it all."

"Now you're scaring me! Since the Canadian government shut our project down, maybe they're after us! I doubt that, of course – not Canada – but someone of influence who can pull strings to get our funding cut off may be behind everything."

"You mean, someone who would not benefit from our research?"

"There are some very powerful people in the oil Industry."

Chapter 4

Hector Skog, Supervisory Special Agent, FBI Counterintelligence Division, Washington, D.C., was summoned to the office of his superior, Special Agent in Charge Elaine Winter. Hector was a career special agent who joined the FBI a few years after graduating with honors in law at Georgetown University then being called to the bar in New York, where he started his career as a junior lawyer in a major law firm. He had served with merit in various departments and capacities in the FBI's offices in St. Paul, Utah, Miami, Chicago and now, Washington, D.C. He was happily married to his Swedish-American wife of twenty-five years and they had produced and raised two girls and a boy who had made their way through college and scattered across America. As empty nesters, Hector and Harma had moved into a fixer-upper row house on a very trendy up-and-coming street between the U. of Georgetown Hospital and the infamous Watergate apartments. They spent much of their spare time renovating the condo. They had been successful in "fixing and flipping" properties and were looking forward to putting their newly modernized condo on the market next year and socking some more capital gains into their retirement funds.

When Hector entered Elaine Winter's outer office, her secretary motioned him to her office door. "She said to go right on in when you got here," said Dan.

"Thanks," Hector replied. He was 53, a handsome, well-built man with blue eyes and a clean-shaven face reflecting his Norwegian-American heritage. He was wearing a custom-tailored blue wool blend single-breasted suit, accented by a white shirt and light blue Brooks Brothers tie. He knocked on the inner office door and entered, finding Elaine at her desk signing a document. Elaine was fifty-something, a trim woman with an auburn pageboy complemented by very light makeup and a tailored suit. Every time he saw her, Hector found it hard to imagine that she was a diamond-level expert marksman (marksperson in the vernacular of the new FBI) and held a black belt in karate. She looked up and said, "Hi Hector, thanks for dropping in. I've got something for you." She picked up a file from her IN basket and brought it over to the low coffee table which was surrounded by a few comfortable chairs. She took a seat after motioning to a chair for him. She pointed to the coffee carafe on the sideboard credenza. "Fresh coffee if you wish."

"No thanks," he replied. "I'm coffeed out right now. You got something interesting?"

"Maybe. Pierre LeBois, our person in our consulate in Montreal, sent in an alert that I would like you to dig into. Apparently, some scientists engaged in a multi-country Arctic research project have died a short time apart and in different locations. Two Canadians, and one American died in separate "accidents" within three weeks of each other shortly after returning from a research project in the Arctic. One died in Winnipeg, another in Toronto and one, an American, died in San Francisco. There was also one Japanese badly injured in a hit and run in Sapporo. Their team leader, a Canadian by the name of Robert Berubé, living in Trois Riveries, Quebec, believes strongly that there is a linkage and is fearing for his life.

"Apparently, the team has been coming together for the past ten summers to do some research in the Arctic. The research has been jointly sponsored by Japan, USA, Canada and Russia. This summer, there was a breakthrough discovery − a method of safely extracting methane gas from its frozen state in the permafrost. This has generated excitement in Japan as they are highly dependent on imported oil and they have the potential to tap large fields of frozen methane on the seabed in northern Japanese waters. I haven't yet heard how the American and Russian governments have reacted but the Canadian response was very quick − they immediately ceased all funding of their people and have forbidden their scientists from sharing their findings. In fact, they terminated the employment of some of them. And that action came directly out of the Prime Minister's Office."

"Interesting! Also an improbable string of coincidences. There may be something significant."

"As one of the deceased is American, we'll investigate. That's Victor Wong, a tenured professor at Berkley. There are two more

27

Americans of the team, Stephanie Lees at the University of Alaska in Anchorage, and professor Hayden Kincaid at the University of Oregon. All three have been funded by the Willard Institute for the Advancement of the Environment. It's based here in D.C. and the contact there is a Ms. Thelma Kenny, the CEO."

"I'll initiate contact right away. Does this have a high priority?"

"Yes. Just in case there's something to it, let's try not to lose any more American researchers. You can authorize Alaska and Oregon offices to provide protective surveillance – even sequestering – if they deem it relevant."

Back in his own office, Hector was quick to initiate a conference call with senior officers in Anchorage and Portland, explaining the situation and requesting priority contact and investigation with the professors. He then called San Francisco and requested an in-depth investigation into the death of Victor Wong. Once that was underway, he called Ms. Kenny at the Willard Institute. Her office assistant was able to slot him in for a visit in the next hour. He decided to walk over as the institute's office was only two blocks away. The institute was on the third floor of a non-imposing building and seemed to occupy the whole floor. He was greeted by a receptionist and taken down an inner hall to a small meeting room. He accepted a coffee and a few moments later Ms. Kenny entered and introduced herself. She seemed to be in her early forties, over five foot eleven in medium heels. She was immaculately dressed in a gray business suit, which Hector felt must have cost a fortune, matching shoes and very expensive jewelry – a solid gold diamond-encrusted Rollex watch and a large diamond-dominated pendant with a thick gold setting and chain. She also wore a huge diamond ring on her ring finger. "Special Agent Skog? I'm Thelma Kinney. How can I help you?"

Hector explained the situation, to which she responded, "This is most alarming! We have yet to be notified of Victor Wong's death – but that is reasonable if it is less than a week ago, as we only receive monthly progress reports from his office. He was due to send in a synopsis of his Arctic trip – in fact, he was due here to present it at the end of the month. The same goes for Hayden Kincaid and Stephanie Lees. Mind you, I got emails from all of them on their return from the Arctic stating the team had great success with their methane hydrate extraction process and they were looking forward to making their formal presentation at the end of the month. This is alarming! Have the others been contacted? Is there a way we can get them protected?"

Hector was impressed with her growing concern. "Our offices are contacting Mr. Kincaid and Ms. Lees as we speak. We'll provide protection if they want, set up some monitoring and we'll try to get to the bottom of this. But I have some questions. How significant is this research and how and why is your institute involved? And, of course, who is behind this – if indeed it is not a string of coincidences? And then, can you describe this joint venture with Japan, Canada, the USA and Russia? And, of course, who are you – the Willard Institute, that is?"

She frowned, thought a bit, and said, "All good questions. Let's start with the Willard Institute. It's a registered philanthropic organization with a huge endowment whose mission is to fund basic and applied research to advance environmental protection. We are very much concerned about global warming – even though it is not a fashionable concern in many political circles in America."

"In Canada?"

"Even less fashionable right now with their current federal government and an economy in some regions dominated by huge revenues from energy exports, especially oil and gas – much of which, such as from the oil sands, is extracted in a very polluting manner. But much the same can be said for other countries – especially the emerging tigers of China and India that are huge polluters."

"So what got you involved with research grants to the three Americans on this Arctic research project? And what is this methane hydrate?"

"Methane hydrate is also called methane calthrate, sometimes methane ice, fire ice or natural gas hydrate. It's a solid calthrate compound, more specifically, a calthrate hydrate. It's pretty scary stuff – in quantity, that is. It's frozen methane. It's found in great quantities in permafrost and cold sea beds – mainly sedimentary areas. It's even found as ice cubes in shallow arctic waters – you can touch a lighted match to the cube and get a flame as the methane is released. And the by-product is water. It tends to burn far cleaner than most fossil fuels. Conservative estimates about quantity of the resource is over one hundred thousand trillion cubic feet – that has been discovered so far."

"You call it a resource?"

"Yes. Huge potential to replace most fossil fuels for centuries."

"You say 'scary stuff.' Why?"

"If released into the atmosphere in great quantities, it will increase global warming significantly. Thus, harvesting it has to be carefully controlled. It's tricky to transport and difficult to safely unlock the methane in commercial quantities."

"OK, and I suppose the Arctic research was all about this?"

"Safely capturing and harvesting it as well as identification of reserves and the pace of global warming. The Japanese have led in commercial harvest research and there was a breakthrough on the last Arctic trip. They have great support from their government and have funds to set up a pilot extraction plant offshore in the north near Sapporo."

"You say your institute is concerned with the environment. Is there a fear that global warming will naturally melt the permafrost and release methane to accelerate global warming?"

"You've got the idea! Permafrost is melting at a serious pace. A bit scary, isn't it?"

"Ouch!"

"In some ways, we're sitting on a global time bomb that's ticking away. We're not at the final hour yet but it's getting scientists very nervous."

"Can you describe this joint venture research project?"

"As you know, four countries – Japan, USA, Russia and Canada – have been involved. Really, there are many components in the project, from measuring composition and circulation of the Arctic Ocean on up to plotting methane hydrate concentrations, extraction technology and such."

"The findings are shared. It's been going on for the past ten years. The Arctic research is possible in the open water season and the scientists get together on an icebreaker research vessel for about six weeks, then return to their parent institutions but continue collaborating – sharing results – throughout the year. The Canadian government has acted as host by providing the vessel and the other countries share in financing the voyage. Japan pays for the fuel for the entire voyage. USA and Russia share the cost of provisions and Canada pays for the crew and their scientists. They rotate teams of scientists for various projects for the whole duration of the voyage. All share the cost of equipment, etc. The number of scientists from each country is proportionate to the value of the contribution. In this case, Japan provided half the team, as fuel is a significant portion of the cost of the voyage."

"How significant is the research?"

"Much of it seems pretty mundane stuff – such as ocean circulation and climate measurement."

"However?"

"However, the problem of effectively harnessing methane hydrate – methane calthrate, if you will – is significant. It has huge potential as the reserves are great. It also is a nuisance in oil drilling as it's found in ocean sediment wherever the bottom water temperature is two degrees Celsius or less and in permafrost – in polar regions – where the surface temperature is freezing or below. It may occur as part of the sedimentary deposit process over time or it can be induced by pressurizing oil and gas wells with fresh water in permafrost and along continental shelves worldwide.

"Hydrate is formed by water freezing – extracting pure water from salt water and trapping methane in the ice as it is formed. But then, it can also be formed in natural gas processing – by pressure reduction after liquid water is condensed in the presence of methane at high pressure. This often occurs in oil well drilling where the pressure is released and the methane hydrates flow up the well bore to the surface mixed in with drill mud, other liquids and drill cuttings. Unless there is a method for containment, the gas is flared off and that also contributes to global warming and pollution.

"Much of the devastating pollution comes from sulfur content in the cuttings burning impurely with the methane – often forming acid rain. This has been a great problem in the river delta of Nigeria, for example. As the fluid comes up from depth into lower pressures and warms, the gas expands, often violently. This can cause blowouts. It was a significant problem with that big oil spill in the Gulf of Mexico – a deep water well with lots of methane hydrate. It may have contributed to the blowout but it also slowed the harnessing of the well. Attempts at capturing the wild flow at the wellhead first failed because of the methane released pushing the control cap off."

"And the Arctic research on this?"

"It was a prototype method to safely extract methane from the hydrated state. They drilled into the permafrost and were able to control the pressure decrease to effectively extract the methane. Sounds simple, when put that way, but it is not. It's a major breakthrough!"

"OK, now the big question: who is behind this – if indeed it is not a string of coincidences?"

"Well, first off, I don't buy the string of coincidences idea. It's interesting that the Canadian government is backing away – yet the Japanese are heralding the discovery as the next best thing to sliced bread."

"And America and Russia, how do their governments view this discovery?"

"Good question. In scientific circles, we're excited. So too, I'm sure, is the Russian science community and that of the Canadians. However, as you know with the political mores of America, we can always find or buy two sides to an argument and there can be some huge vested interests that may not want to advance the discovery. I wouldn't be surprised if that was why the Canadian government withdrew the research funding – probably under pressure from vested interests who do not want to see commercialization. It could happen here too. Ditto in Russia but right now the Russian government seems to be flexing some muscles against the oil oligarchs – or that may be posturing for public consumption."

Returning to his office, Hector had a conference call with agents reporting from Alaska and Oregon. Each office had sent teams to interview the researchers. Stephanie Lees was interviewed in her lab at the University of Alaska on the Anchorage campus. She was aware of the deaths of her colleagues and had been starting to fret. She declined the offer of sequestering but accepted protective surveillance. A surveillance team would keep an eye on her condo, especially when she was in it, a security system would be installed, and a female agent would act as her driver and office assistant. She would not be alone when out of her condo.

Hayden Kincaid had been found in Newport Oregon, just settling in, checking his equipment, on a NOAA research vessel where he was about to depart on a three-month voyage working on a joint NOAA - U. of Oregon study in the Bering Sea. He was alarmed at the demise of his colleagues but felt he would be safer at sea on the research vessel than in his lab at the U. of Oregon. Together with Hayden Kincaid, the special agents met with the captain of the vessel, alerting him to the situation and leaving contact numbers in case anything unusual developed. As the vessel would be operating in or near Alaskan waters, the Anchorage office of the FBI was brought into the loop.

After clearing permission with his superiors, Hector then put a call in to Roger Pearson, the FBI's designated liaison at the Canadian Embassy in D.C. After making its way through the automated answering system, the phone was picked up on the second ring. "Hector, it's been a while! How are you?"

"Isn't caller ID great! I'm fine, thank you. I guess the last time we spoke was at the closure on the weapons smuggling issue."

"Yes. I understand the Chief is still working in Africa. Tanzania – last I checked."[1]

"Maybe. We've put that file on the shelf for now until he comes back this way."

"What can I do for the famous FBI?"

"I've been handed a problem that has seen an unusual string of deaths in Canada and the USA – all in different locations, different police jurisdictions, so difficult to see a linkage."

"But you've uncovered something that links them together and that makes the deaths look serial, as in possible linked murders?"

"You've got it. I'm into it because it looks as if this involves intellectual property – possibly significant industrial or strategic espionage or sabotage. Three research scientists, one American and two Canadians, have been killed and their colleagues from the same project may be in danger. One was killed in Winnipeg, one in Toronto and one in San Francisco. Also, a Japanese member of the team is in hospital in Japan from a hit and run. We were alerted to this by one of the team members, the team leader actually, who lives in Montreal. He contacted our consulate as he fears for his life and feels he's been ignored by the Canadian police. He also has a conspiracy theory involving the Canadian government."

"Give me the details and I'll get back to you as soon as I can."

Hector then placed calls to the liaisons in the Japan and Russian embassies, explaining the situation and asking to meet. Both set appointments for the next day, stating they needed a little time to check things out.

At four fifteen p.m. Hector took a call from Thelma Kenny, who, after formalities said, "I've discussed this with members of my Board of Directors, all of whom are now quite worried. I have someone you need to meet. Can you drop in soon, say, five-thirty?"

---

[1] See *NightHawk Crossing* by C. Edgar North ISBN 9781626756632 (e-Book)

At four forty-five p.m. Hector took a call from Roger Pearson and they set up a meeting for next day at two p.m. at the Canadian Embassy.

Chapter 5

To Ivan Kievekoff, it was a great feeling to be on holiday in Saint Petersburg after returning from his six weeks of research in the Canadian Arctic on the *Louis Riel*. The voyage had been delightful, as usual, and a lot of productive research was conducted. He had enjoyed his affair with the beautiful and sensuous Helen La Pointe, third officer of the icebreaker, and missed her greatly. However, they had both known the romance was not to be permanent, but casual and something both were looking forward to next time they met.

After spending three weeks back at his institute, the Murmansk State Technical Institute, he was looking forward to six weeks' holidays coming to him.

His flight arrived in Moscow where he transferred to a first class compartment on the overnight express train to Saint Petersburg. He found a great hotel near Saint Isaac's Cathedral and was going to spend most of his time as a tourist in the Hermitage, one of the world's largest museums. Rumor has it that one cannot begin to do justice to it in under ten days, even if only viewing the portions open to the public. The nights were something else. In the New Russia, Saint Petersburg was renowned for lots of nightlife to keep a fairly young bachelor scientist well entertained.

He managed to spend four full days at the Hermitage and half of the next. Accompanied by newfound friends he spent the afternoon of the fifth day viewing the Broken Circle Monument on the Road of Life, the Statue of Lenin, the Peter and Paul Fortress on Zayachy Island, Palace Square with the Alexander Column, the Winter Palace and Petergof and Nevsky Prospekt. Ivan and his friends, a group of ten, enjoyed each other's company and were well into the merriment of the evening at an excellent Russian cuisine restaurant on Vasileysky Island at the Petrograd Side of town. They had partied hard with many vodka toasts washed down with a great locally-brewed beer, whilst consuming a delicious seven-course meal. It was getting late when the party broke up. After settling the bill, Ivan and his friends staggered onto the sidewalk.

Most of his friends had hotels by the cruise ship terminal but Ivan and a few others would go in another direction to hotels near Saint Isaac's Cathedral. Ivan was walking with the traffic light in a marked crosswalk with three of his friends toward a taxi stand on the other side of the road, when he was struck from behind by a car. He was hurtled into the car's windshield, across the passenger's side, ending up in the roadside gutter. The car and driver attempted to drive off but the car was too badly damaged and swerved onto the sidewalk and stalled when it hit a newspaper kiosk. The driver attempted to flee but passersby, including two uniformed police officers, subdued him. Ivan was rushed to the nearest hospital where he was treated for a broken hip and severe concussion.

Three days later, Ivan was visited in the hospital by a plainclothes officer of the law whom Ivan thought to be a detective, probably with more questions. The fellow flashed his wallet credentials, and introduced himself. "Ivan Kievkoff, I am Rustum Pavel of the Federal Security Service. Your accident has attracted our attention due to your research – especially your last trip to the Canadian Arctic and your collaborators on the *Louis St. Real.*"

"That's the *Louis Riel.*"

"Ah, good! The doctor said you had a concussion, but it looks as if you are functioning well. Do you remember anything of the accident?"

"No, the last thing I remember was entering the crosswalk."

"In the past few days, did you notice anyone following you?"

"No. Why?"

"We are quite sure you were targeted. Fortunately for us, the driver of the hit and run vehicle was apprehended and we have been interrogating him."

"And?"

"He, unfortunately, died during interrogation but we were able to determine he was a hired assassin from Georgia. Paid to kill you. It was a contracted assassination attempt."

"Why me? I've done nothing! I don't think any of my ex-girlfriends would want to pay someone to kill me – we parted as good friends."

"No. Not that. It seems it is more for what you know – perhaps something to do with your capacity as a research scientist? We gathered some information before he died – enough of a trail to follow. We'll see where it leads."

"I'm sorry but I'm still a little slow. You mentioned my scientific colleagues on the *Louis Riel?*"

"Yes, Moscow has advised me that two Canadians, one Japanese and one American member of the team had similar accidents. You were lucky; three were killed."

"My God!"

"I have spoken with your superiors at Murmansk State Technical University and to my superiors in Moscow. Since we feel this has been a targeted attempt on your life we wish to initiate some personal security for your safety and to preserve the scientific knowledge gained in your Arctic studies. You will be relocated immediately to a secure location. I will arrange for your personal effects both here and in Murmansk to be delivered to your new location. Also, we will handle all your finances – banking, living quarters, and transportation – as you will be given a new identity. Regrettably, you cannot be in contact with anyone except those we clear until we resolve this issue. No internet, e-mail, Skype etc. without supervision."

"Oh!"

"The doctor has approved. You will be moved tonight. In the meantime, you will be well guarded."

Without having much input to his future all he could say was, "Where am I going?"

"Don't worry, it's a secure research facility. You'll enjoy it! It also has an excellent hospital, rehabilitation center and medical staff. I understand you will need at least ten weeks to recuperate."

Chapter 6

<u>St. John's Newfoundland</u>

The island of Newfoundland was in Jack Mahoney's genes. His family began its tenure on "the rock" in the late seventeenth century as early escapees from Ireland's potato famine. His ancestors were mainly shipwrights – a craft that was highly in demand at the time to supply mariners with vessels for the bountiful Atlantic great northern cod fishery. The Grand Banks, where cod were "so plentiful they would often jump into your boat," was just a short trip from Newfoundland's main port of St. John's. Founded in 1583 because of the cod fishery, St. John's was the first English-founded city in North America.

The Atlantic great northern cod fishery had served the Mahoneys well for generations – until its collapse. In 1992 the Canadian government declared a moratorium on the northern cod fishery and the Newfoundland economy was devastated. Fortunately, a decade later, since the offshore oil was discovered and developed in fields such as Hibernia, Terra Nova and White Rose, the Newfoundland economy was booming – and dependent on the oil industry.

Jack Mahoney managed to get a great education, leaving "the rock" for ten years to earn his PhD in Mechanical Engineering, and then jumping at the chance to return to his homeland as a professor at Memorial University of Newfoundland. He returned, promptly married a former high school sweetheart, settled down, helped raise five children – eventually savoring the joy of grandparenting – and became a renowned professor in his research field of fluid mechanics.

Jack lived with his spouse of thirty years in a sea-view house perched on a hillside in the Compton Bay suburb. It was a bit out of the city but an enjoyable drive to work if the weather was good. He had enjoyed his Arctic trip on the *Louis Riel* and now had settled into the rhythm of the fall term at the university. He left the house at his routine time of eight ten, plenty of time to get his usual third cup of coffee before his ten-thirty lecture to third-year engineering students.

Jack never made it. His SUV was found smashed on the rocks of the shoreline four hundred feet below the road. He was mutilated from the impact. The coroner and autopsy determined he was killed instantly on impact, even though all the airbags deployed. Police examined the scene where the SUV left the road and concluded Jack Mahoney tried to negotiate a tight curve at excessive speed and lost control. There was no sign of skid marks or other indications that he had applied his brakes. His SUV had punched through a protective barrier, indicating excessive speed. Later, when the SUV was recovered and examined, it was found to have excellent tires. However, the braking system had been tampered with and had not been functioning when the vehicle left the road.

Chapter 7

Iawama-san was woken by his cell phone. He reached for the phone and began to focus on the nightstand clock's large numbers. 03:35, he noted as he answered the phone. "Moshi-moshi?"

"Iawama-san, sumi ma sen."

"Hi!"

In Japanese, the caller identified himself as the University's security duty officer. He apologized for waking the honorable professor but there had been an explosion and fire at the research center behind the engineering building.

Professor Iawama said he'd be right over. He woke his wife and told her what had happened and that he was going to the lab.

When Professor Iawama arrived, he found the street behind the engineering building blocked by a campus police car with an officer keeping the curious back. Beyond the blockade a muddle of fire apparatus, lights flashing and trailing fire hoses to hydrants were taking up much of the road near the lab.

The professor approached the policeman manning the perimeter and was allowed through the line and directed to the officer in charge, Fire Captain Hiro Watanabe. After introductions, Captain Watanabe said, "We've got the fire out and are cleaning up now. No one was injured. There was no one in the lab at this hour. It is fortunate the building is solid concrete and that there were lots of windows allowing the explosion to vent itself through the windows. There is considerable equipment damage – both from the explosion and the fire."

"Have you determined what caused it?"

"At first, we assumed it was leaking methane gas that ignited when a spark occurred, such as a refrigerator turning on. We are sure it was started by leaking methane."

"But?"

"We found that some of the cryogenic vats you have been using to store methane calthrate had been tampered with. I am sure this is arson. We also discovered several CCTV security cameras had been painted over. Some of your computers in the lab were destroyed before the explosion. I've called in the police to investigate."

"Fortunately we back up all our computers both in "the cloud" and at a secure location. I am beginning to get the impression someone wants to slow us down. This work is strategic for Japan."

Later that morning, Professor Iawama and his dean, Professor Ibe, went before the University Management Committee. The committee, comprising thirty executives and department heads, was supplemented by a stranger whom the president introduced as Kiyoshi Seiku, a senior executive in the Japan Security Service. The president took the time to review the research done by Professor Iawama and his team and the process they were now engaged in involving technology transfer from their research to a practical production prototype.

He then introduced Mr. Kiyoshi Seiku from Japan Security Service who said, "As you all know, the Government of Japan deems this project to be of great importance for the security of our country. It is obvious, from the damage inflicted last night, from the attempted assassination of one of your colleagues, and from similar events with personnel in our partner countries of Canada, America and Russia, that there are people who do not want this work to proceed to fruition. We fear the members of the research team are in significant danger and that we must increase their security. That is underway as I speak. Our national security is at risk. This is war!"

Chapter 8

Norma was once again almost shouting into the phone to Robert Berubé. "No! Not again! Not Jack too! Oh, my God! How's Colleen taking it? Oh, my God, my God."

"Thankfully they have a large family. Colleen's in shock, but she's got lots of family support. She's a tough woman; she'll see this through."

"I'm terrified!"

"So am I. So is my wife – Marie is near panic. I also learned today that Iawama-san's lab was blown up. He feels it has set them back a month but it has resulted in him getting greatly increased security. For me, no one in Canada seems interested. I do not want to leave our condo. Marie does not go out alone. One of our daughters and a daughter-in law go with her when she has to go shopping or on other errands. It is like we are prisoners in our own home."

"It's the same with me. Carl insists on accompanying me everywhere. We're very careful crossing the street. We avoid empty alleys, seldom go out at night and we're always checking our surroundings. We've got all our neighbors keeping a watch for anything suspicious and we keep the yard well lit overnight."

"Did you talk to the police?"

"Yes, but I didn't seem to get anywhere. I haven't had anything suspicious happen to me, which makes them less than interested. They made a file on it and said they would alert the patrols in our area but they say that's all they can do."

"That sounds familiar; same with the police here. There doesn't seem to be much interest in trying to link the events as a series of murders and nothing untoward has befallen me yet – although it may be too late for me if it does. I did see the FBI person in the US Consulate in Montreal, a Pierre LeBois, and got a good reception, but so far, have had nothing back. He did say thast if I really felt my life was in danger, that Marie and I should seek political asylum at the consulate."

"Interesting. What about Peter Melville? Have you been able to contact him? There are only three Canadians remaining on the team. I've tried to contact him but he's not answering his phone or responding to e-mail."

"I've had no luck either. As you know, he lives in Edmonton and I've contacted the Edmonton police with our concern. They were reluctant to do much but they did send someone out to check. He lives in an apartment in a highrise – apparently none of his neighbors knew him. But, you know how impersonal apartment life can be; you may seldom know your neighbors. No one has seen him around. Apparently, he's still on sabbatical from the university until January and no one has seen him since he left for the Arctic. Also, he's a bachelor, he's not tied down and you remember, he was moaning about breaking up with his girlfriend when we were in the Arctic? He's not encumbered – he could be anywhere."

"I don't know what else we can do right now."

"Me either. I don't know. But let's keep in touch."

Chapter 9

Hector made it over to the Willard Institute by five-thirty and the receptionist escorted him to the conference room where he found Ms. Kenny and a gentleman, a familiar face. Thelma Kenny noted his surprised expression and said, "I understand you've met Sanford Crosley before in another capacity. I had a meeting with some members of my board of directors. One member is Ruth Dempsey, who as you know, is senior within the Secretary of State's office. She felt the situation is a significant threat to national security and involves nationals in other countries, and therefore warrants the attention of the CIA and others. The upshot of the meeting was that CIA has agreed to lend a hand, so to speak. Ruth said you and Sanford have worked well together in the past."

Sanford Crosley and Hector had worked together on a restricted covert weapons case where Ruth Dempsey had directed co-ordination between the various agencies involved.[2] Sanford, after twenty-five years in the Central Intelligence Agency, was a senior officer, one designated to work with the FBI on issues of national security. Sanford was impeccably dressed in a grey mohair suit, white shirt, navy blue tie and black oxfords. He had a medium build and greying brown hair cut short, parted on the left. At fifty-four, he was fluent in Russian and French, and a product of Cambridge University. He'd spent two years in the Peace Corps in Surinam after completing his M.A. in international economic history of the modern world.

"Hector," Sanford said, "our people have worked closely with you before with good success. As you well know, we are able to look at things, ah, differently and have resources to complement your investigation."

Hector, smiling, responded, "Sanford, it's good to see you again and I do appreciate your ability to, as you say, "complement" our resources. I take it this is a direct order from people on high in the State Department?"

---

[2] See *Nighthawk Crossing* by C. Edgar North ISBN 9781626756632 (e-Book)

"Yes. Ruth Dempsey had a pressing engagement and sends her regrets but will again oversee coordination between our agencies and others. She said she'll call you sometime early tomorrow but, in the meantime, she says: "Get the ball rolling or I'll kick some ass." Prime objective is to protect these researchers, to remove them from or minimize their danger, protect, advance and develop their knowledge."

"Does this go for the Canadian researchers as well? I've got a meeting arranged for tomorrow, two p.m., with my Canadian counterpart, Roger Pearson."

"If you'll give me their names and addresses, I'll have my people put them under protective surveillance – at least for now. We can re-evaluate that after we learn Canada's view and if they have surveillance established, but I understand the Canadian police, from local level to RCMP, did not seem interested. Maybe we can light a fire under them. I'll join you in that meeting with Roger Pearson, if you want. He'll probably have Martin LeRoy sitting in as well."

"I also have meetings arranged for tomorrow morning with the Japanese and Russian liaisons."

"I'll leave those to you for now."

Next day. Japanese Embassy

After screening, Hector had been led into a meeting room where the receptionist offered him strong, hot green tea and some miniature pastries. Shortly, two Japanese men entered the room and introduced themselves. The leader was Tadao Suzuki, of the Japanese Security Service, and the other was Seijo Abe', Second Secretary at the Embassy. Both were similarly dressed in blue suits, white shirts and blue ties. Tadao Suzuki was trim and fit, about forty years old. Seijo Abe was older, tall and husky. After business cards were exchanged, presented two-handed with deep bows by the Japanese, Mr. Abe' began the conversation. "We appreciate your concern and we greatly appreciate the fine collaboration between our researchers and yours in the methane hydrate energy project. Suzuki-san has been in contact with Tokyo and I will let him explain what we have learned."

Tadao Suzuki spoke. "As you know, our people have also been targeted. We have one team member recovering in a Sapporo hospital. He has been placed under tight protective security. Two nights ago, the methane calthrate research lab at the University of Sapporo was broken into, computers destroyed and the lab blown up. It was a professional job with little trace of the perpetrators. Since then, we have vastly increased security and are moving the researchers and their families to a remote and more secure location where they will continue their prototype and begin testing extraction. We are also investigating who may be behind the sabotage. But we do not have much information to go on."

Russian Embassy, D.C.
Hector left the meeting after both parties agreed to keep each other informed of progress and to provide assistance. He then went to his scheduled meeting at the Russian Embassy. After screening and being escorted to the meeting room, he was warmly greeted by Viktor Koss, Resident Liaison of the FSB, whom Hector met frequently concerning various aspects of his work. After some bantering about golf handicaps, Hector updated Viktor who said, "Our researcher, Ivan Kievkoff, was also targeted. He was on holiday in St. Petersburg, a hit and run. Thankfully, he was not killed but he did sustain a broken hip and a severe concussion. We have moved him to a very secure research site.

"We did have a break, though. The driver was apprehended and interrogated. He was a professional assassin from Georgia, paid quite well for the job."

"Any leads to who hired him?"

"A little that we are following up on. Nothing interesting yet. Regrettably, he died during interrogation."

Hector left after both agreed to exchange information and share the resources of their respective services.

Canadian Embassy 2 p.m.

After showing their credentials, checking their weapons, and individually passing through the body scanner into the secure area of the embassy on the other side of bullet-proof glass, Sanford and Hector were led by a receptionist to a windowless conference room on the second floor where Martin LeRoy and Roger Pearson were waiting. After greetings and being offered and accepting coffee and Nanaimo Bars (a uniquely Canadian rich chocolate delicacy), Martin started. "Well, it's not surprising to see you two working together again – especially when you sniff a potential problem with intellectual resources of a strategic nature and international scope."

Roger said, "Hector, I've reviewed what you gave me yesterday and made some enquiries. There certainly is a suspicious chain of events and the only common denominator seems to be they're all members of that Arctic research team. We've contacted all the police departments and spoken with the case officers."

Hector filled everyone in on what he had learned from his visits to the Japanese and Russian counterparts. "That's interesting," responded Martin LeRoy. There's certainly international outreach. I've spoken with the serial crimes coordination center of the RCMP. They were not aware of the linkage and are now, finally, going to investigate. Of course, I will inform them of what you learned from the Japanese and Russians – that may help trigger some interest."

Hector spoke, "That's a good start. What about protective surveillance or sequestering for the surviving Canadian researchers?"

Martin looked around the room. "There we have a problem. We'll have to get back to you. Hector, would you mind if we met in your office, say five-thirty?"

5:30 p.m. at a conference room in Hector's office area, FBI HQ

After settling down around the small conference table, Martin began. "It's better if we meet here than at our embassy – our walls have ears. I started to root around to determine how and why the research funding for our Canadian team members was terminated so abruptly. At first, I thought it could be a case of simple cost

48

cutting – you know, a peanut-brained bureaucrat seeking to make a name by cutting an obscure program assuming now that the process was discovered, there was no need for the government to assist in commercializing that form of energy."

"But?" said Hector.

"The cancellation order came directly from the PMO – the Prime Minister's Office – and not Science Canada, the department responsible for granting and administering the funds. This invoked my curiosity and I had some of our people in Ottawa, with utmost discretion, get to the bottom of the story. The funding was cancelled because of extreme political interference."

"As the cancellation came from the PMO, are you saying this was a decree by your Prime Minister – that it was his decision?"

"He signed the order in the presence of his Chief of Staff. But he did so at the request of three senior and very influential senators."

"And?"

"And they are very much entrenched with the oil industry. Two even serve on the Boards of Directors of some of the largest international oil giants. The other is one of the major fundraisers for the political party in power and has raised multi millions from the oil industry. They comprised a three-person committee that approached the Prime Minister to remove the funding."

"Ouch!"

"It gets worse. One of these sterling – permit me to translate from my native French – "pigs at the trough" is on the oversight committee for National Security Services and the RCMP. In other words, he is our master. He sees and approves what we do. If we were to initiate an action to protect these researchers, he would become aware of it."

"Double ouch!"

"You know, the Canadian federal civil service is very professional, but at times, our masters are pigs!"

"So, because of, let us say, the delicacy of the situation, your poor researchers are going to be left out in the cold? People have already been killed. They're all probably in immediate danger."

"Anything we did may get back to the big oil interests – these senators are just puppets on strings manipulated by vested interests. It is a shame. I know many senators who are very sincere and hardworking but we also have these opportunists."

"A problem. What about some outside help – if you were officially unaware of it? "

"Thank you. Our superiors in Ottawa cannot and must not go on record but I have been authorized to say we could help by providing some information but it will be on an informal basis."

Roger echoed Martin's comments. "Officially, the Parliamentary Oversight Committee of the Security Services has to be informed of investigations, wire taps and all that. In many instances, especially those with political overtones, they must approve in advance. That senator would become aware if we were investigating him and his associates."

Martin said, "I doubt if these senators have any knowledge or awareness of the deaths of the researchers nor would they be involved. Mind you, one is so self-centered and arrogant, he may not care."

Sanford spoke, "Do you think if they became aware of the deaths, they could be helpful?"

"Good thought!" said Hector. "But let's hold that thought for now. First priority is to protect our people. Let's review: for the Americans, we have Professor Stephanie Lees at U of Alaska under protective surveillance with a 24/7 keeper and we have Professor Hayden Kincaid bouncing around the Bering Sea on NOAA's research vessel the *Harvey North* where we assume he is safe. For the Canadians we have: Robert Berubé who has contacted the FBI liaison in Montreal; Norma Jensen in Victoria; Jack Mahoney in St. John's, Newfoundland; and Peter Melville in Edmonton."

They were interrupted by Roger's cell phone ringing. He motioned with his hand and said, "Excuse me, I'm being paged. This must be important as I left instructions not to disturb unless it was a matter pertaining to this meeting." He dialed, spoke to an assistant, listened and said, "Thank you." Closed his phone and turned back to the others. "Scratch Professor Mahoney. He was killed when his vehicle left the road on his way to work this morning. Local police found that the brakes were tampered with."

Sanford asked Roger and Martin, "Do you have these people under surveillance?"

"No."

"O.K. Well, since yesterday, our people located Berubé and Jensen and have been watching. But we were unable to locate Melville who seemed to have dropped out of sight. However, we found he's on a cruise ship on a twenty-three day repositioning voyage between Vancouver and Dalian, China and he signed up for a two-week tour of China upon arrival. Unfortunately, we did not have an asset in place in Newfoundland, so we didn't yet get to Mahoney."

"Assuming Melville's not in too much danger on the cruise ship, perhaps Berubé and Jensen can be moved to a safe location?"

"Yes. But let's look a few steps forward in this chess game. As Berubé began with approaching the FBI, let's assist him in seeking political asylum at the American Consulate in Montreal."

Both Martin and Roger said, "What?" Then Martin, after a brief reflection said, "Ah! You are building a poker hand, you want an 'ace in de 'ole.' Then this will not become public knowledge right away?"

"Right, but we can use it if we need to bring public attention to the situation."

Lapsing into his native French, Martin said, "Magnifique!"

"What about Jensen? Same thing?" asked Roger.

"No. I think it's better if she disappears. She can surface later claiming political asylum and backing up Berubé's claims if warranted. "

"How soon?"

"Time is of the essence. Tonight."

"You've been planning this."

"Since yesterday." He turned to Hector. "I suggest Pierre LeBois be the contact for Berubé, to bring him and his wife in."

"Done," said Hector. "How will we approach Jensen?"

"We're working on that."

Chapter 10

Pierre LeBois was on his cell phone speaking to Robert Berubé. The conversation was in French. "We are aware that Professor Mahoney died in a suspicious car accident. We feel your life is in danger. We don't think remaining in Canada right now is safe for you and Marie. We are prepared to give you safe haven."

"Marie? She is in danger too?"

"She is a way to get to you."

"I see. What do you suggest?"

"I am outside your home right now. I have people with me to protect you and I want to move you to safety in the American Consulate in Montreal."

"You mean, seek political asylum?"

"For now, yes. This will be done quietly – until you are safely out of the country and out of harm's way. You will be free to return home anytime, but for now we want you protected."

"OK, come to the front door."

"I'm coming. Don't open the door until you are certain it's me."

After speaking to Pierre from behind the locked door, Robert opened the door and let him in. Pierre spoke. "We will take you to the Consulate tonight. Now. Take only a few minutes to pack a small overnight bag each and bring your passports and other necessary papers. We will 'ave someone close up the house and bring other effects you want tomorrow. Do you 'ave any animals?"

Marie spoke, "Yes, a dog, Isabella, a miniature poodle."

"Does she have all her shots – rabies shot for crossing the border?"

"Yes."

"Bring Isabella and her food, some bedding and toys. I am sure she is like a child to you."

The hour and forty-minute drive to the US Consulate in Montreal was uneventful. Pierre, in the front passenger seat of their car, a large SUV with diplomatic plates and smoked dark windows, mentioned their vehicle was specially equipped and pointed out the other vehicles in their convoy – a maroon BMW in the lead, another SUV with diplomatic plates behind them and a large blue four-door sedan with Quebec plates which would occasionally come up beside them. Pierre took the opportunity of the drive to get Robert to phone Norma to explain what was happening and to be introduced. After Robert was through with his explanation, he handed the phone to Pierre who introduced himself. First, he told Norma to write down contact numbers for FBI Special Agent Hector Skog in Washington, D.C. He told her first to look up the general phone line for the FBI in DC to see if it matched the one he gave her. She was to call, ask for Special Agent Hector Skog and identify herself and she would be routed through to him 24/7. He also provided Hector's cell phone number. He then gave her his cell phone number and asked her to call as soon as she had spoken to Special Agent Skog. She called back fifteen minutes later and said, "Can you help us too?"

"It's still daylight in Victoria. A couple will come to your door in a few minutes. The man has brown eyes, a full head of curly black hair, is fairly handsome and is in good physical shape. He's dressed in blue slacks and grey tweed sports coat. The woman is wearing a navy blue pantsuit with white blouse, carrying a large brown purse. She's fairly tall at five foot ten and also of athletic build. They're both in their mid-thirties. The man is Bob LeMay and the woman is Wendy Friesen. Ask for their identification. The ID's will differ. They will get you to safety."

When he disconnected with Norma, Pierre called Hector and advised him that things were set for a visit in Victoria. Hector, sitting across from Sanford in the conference room, nodded and Sanford made a call and said, "Hi Bob. All set."

Norma, peeking out the front windows from between the curtains, saw a blue SUV pull up to the curb. She watched a man and woman get out and come to her front door and ring the bell. Carl went to the door, asked through it who it was. Bob said, "Bob LeMay and Wendy Friesen. We're friends of Robert Berubé." Carl opened the door but kept the chain on and asked for their IDs, which they flashed and Carl verified their names and noted their credentials. Wendy FBI and Bob CIA. Carl said, "CIA? And FBI?"

Wendy said, "Right. We work together in situations like this. Greater resources."

Carl let them in and shut the door behind them. After they were introduced to Norma, Carl spoke up. "OK, what do you have in mind?"

Wendy said, "Well, we expect you'll hear soon that Robert and Marie are safely inside the US Consulate in Montreal. They'll call. That may help give you some comfort. In the meantime, you need to pack an overnight bag each with casual clothes and shoes for outdoor hiking – something for stowage in an aircraft overhead bin, no larger. One laptop computer each. You'll need your passports and other important papers. I understand you have grown children here who can help gather other items and forward them on and look after your house?"

"Yes, a daughter and a son, both married."

"OK. You can call them tomorrow after you're settled. I understand you've had some of your neighbors looking out for you – sort of a neighborhood watch? You may call whoever you want tomorrow and tell them you have been moved to safety and will be away for a while until this settles down. Do you have any pets?"

"No, no pets."

Bob said, "Carl, I understand you fancy yourself a pretty good fly fisherman. You can bring a fly rod and a few favorite flies, if you wish."

"Is that a hint where we're going? What flies do you recommend?"

"Something for high alpine lakes this time of year, some black, some brown."

Norma said, "Hey, I get to bring a fly rod too!"

"OK."

After packing, while Norma was busy writing out a set of instructions for her daughter and Carl was selecting his favorite flies, the phone rang and Norma answered. It was Robert Berubé to say they were safely inside the US Consulate. Robert turned the phone over to Marie, who spent a few minutes telling Norma, in her own words, what had happened.

When the conversation ended Bob said, "OK, time to go. There's still lots of daylight. It's best to be visible. If one of your neighbors comes out to ask what's going on, you're free to tell them. First though, we need to do something about your tracking devices."

Carl said, "Our what? Our tracking devices?"

"Modern technology makes it easy to be tracked. You must turn off your cell phones and remove the batteries. Otherwise, the phones emit a signal and you can be tracked. No problem when we get where we're going though. Also, you have a credit card or cards such as a driver's license with the new RFID chip in them? You know, where you insert the card and punch in your PIN or wave it in front of a reader?"

"Yes, we both do."

"The RFID chip can be used for tracking you. We have to put them in an aluminum-foil- lined envelope or leave them behind. I have an envelope for each of you if you want." They each took an envelope and put their cards in.

After that, Bob said, "I guess we're ready." He pulled a two-way radio from his jacket pocket and spoke: "Exiting now." After Carl locked the door, they walked to Bob's car where Carl got in the front and Norma got in the back with Wendy. They drove off. One of their friendly neighbors saw it all, including the black SUV which came down the street half a block behind their car.

It was a short drive to the airport where an unmarked Challenger executive jet was waiting for them in the General Aviation section.

No one really took notice when the SUV drove right up to the aircraft's stairway and four people quickly boarded. The jet departed shortly thereafter, having filed a flight plan to Skagway, Alaska.

Chapter 11

Sanford and Hector were sitting around the coffee table in Hector's office discussing how to expose and trap the perpetrators. Hector was musing, "You know, the key may rest with those senators in Canada."

"Follow their patronage trail?"

"Sort of. Right now, there's every indication they can block an investigation."

"But there's also no indication they're aware of the deaths of the Canadian researchers."

"Let's try to keep it that way for now."

"It would be an idea to tap their communications, peek into their finances and travel, and put them under surveillance."

"Not legally, though."

"No, not the way the FBI would have to do it with a formal bilateral request. I'll get it done."

"You know, we'd have to build a case for the RCMP if we wanted to see anyone brought before justice in Canada."

"Right. Berubé has gone to them and been passed off. Either the issue has not registered or they've been told to ignore it."

"I doubt if they've been told to ignore it, but one senator is chair of the security committee – he could have flexed his muscle."

"Isn't one of the other senators involved with oversight of the RCMP?"

"Yes. But I'd like to assume the senators are not yet aware of the deaths and have not interfered with the RCMP."

"This may be the case. I think the series of deaths and their common link needs to be brought again to the attention of the RCMP. In a timely manner, so to speak. Above the basic level of a citizen's complaint. Let's discuss this with our Japanese and Russian friends and our Secretary of State people."

That afternoon, after receiving approval from Caroline Weston at Secretary of State, Hector sent an alert through the regular communication channels between FBI and the RCMP simply stating that the FBI was investigating a suspicious death of a professor who had been part of an international team conducting Arctic research and enquired if the RCMP could follow up to determine if any members of the Canadian contingent of the team (listed names, addresses) had encountered any life-threatening problems of a suspicious nature.

The next day, the Japanese government issued a formal alert to Canada, USA and Russia stating they feared the lives of the researchers on the team were in danger, citing a hit and run of one of their team members and the bombing of their principal research facility. This was relayed through the Interpol police liaison channel and copied to Japanese Embassies in Ottawa, Moscow and Washington for formal presentation to their host countries.

Similarly, the Russian government advised via Interpol and their embassy in Ottawa that their scientist who had been on the Arctic team had been hospitalized by a hit and run which they were treating as suspicious.

The next day, Sanford and Hector were sitting around a coffee table in Caroline Weston's office. Caroline said, "So, you've covered your asses by formally alerting the Canadians to the possible linkage of the deaths. Surely the RCMP can put two and two together and deduce the killings in Toronto, Winnipeg and St. John's are related and linked to the methane calthrate research? You have at least established for the record when the Canadians were hit over the head with this. Now what?"

Sanford said, "We listen. We watch. We track paper trails. We build a case that leads us to the source."

"Well, between you and the FBI, you're good at that. You may also glean some help from other departments, such as NSA, and I'll help you there. BUT, especially from you, Sanford, you and your CIA machinations, I do not want details – I may need plausible deniability. I don't want to be told what you're doing in Canada to keep tabs on whoever you want or how you're doing it. Understood?"

"Of course."

"What's next?"

"Let's put some pressure on the Senators."

"What do you have in mind?"

"It's time to publicly "out" Professor Berubé and sensationalize it."

Chapter 12

To Norma, the jet seemed to have been in the air for over an hour or so before it began its descent. It was dark now and few lights were visible on the ground. After about twenty minutes, the co-pilot's voice came over the intercom. "Ladies and gentlemen, we are on final approach to touch down shortly, please resume your seats and ensure your seat belts are securely fastened and your seat backs in the upright position."

The aircraft touched down and the pilots braked hard, then taxied over to an apron. Norma noticed the runway lights shut off as soon as they had slowed to taxi speed. Once the engines were throttled down, the co-pilot opened the hatch and deployed the stairs. Bob was first off and was approached by a man who came out of the shadows. "Bobby, it's great to see you again. Goin' to get in a little fly fishing?"

"You bet!" Bob responded enthusiastically as they shook hands. "I've brought along some experts." He turned around to where the others had come down the steps and were gathering around, motioning with his right arm, "Charlie, meet Norma, and Carl Jensen, and Wendy Friesen. Wendy's a fibbie. Carl and Norma are the clients. This is Charlie Rose, master of the lodge and all you survey."

They shook hands all round and Carl noted Charlie's very firm grip and calloused hands. Charlie was about sixty-five years old, tall at six feet and built strong. He had grey hair in a crew cut hidden by a badly beaten, sweat-stained Red Sox baseball cap. His face was tanned and wrinkled from extreme weather, and piercing blue eyes peered from under white bushy eyebrows in need of trimming. He was wearing a blue lumberjack shirt, open collar with tails tucked into loose-fitting jeans held up by a western belt with a large silver horseshoe buckle which also held his holstered 9 mm Glock pistol. He was wearing the type of RedWing oiled leather slip-on boots favored by woodsmen.

"Welcome to Area 3," he said. "It's a secret location out in the middle of nowhere. Actually, it's an old airfield – property left over from the cold war. It was a radar station and alternate airfield for military aircraft. Now, well…it's a large ranch. You'll see. There's a great lakefront lodge where I'm sure you'll be comfortable. My wife Heather's a great cook and has dinner just about ready. The fishing's been good – too bad you missed the sunset bite. It produced a seven-pound rainbow – hope you like fish for dinner. If you're beginning to feel the chill, I've got parkas in the SUV and there's better footwear up at the lodge."

As the SUV pulled away down a gravel road, the runway lights turned on and the jet wound up its engines for takeoff. Seconds later, it hurtled down the runway and was quickly airborne. The runway lights turned off and Norma noted she did not see the aircraft navigation lights. Norma remarked on this and Charlie said, "The use of the airfield, other than for emergency daylight VFR or visual landings, or use in daylight by rescue and firefighting craft, is not for public knowledge. We have an excellent instrument landing/takeoff system but that's secret. The runway is pretty good. It's six thousand feet long, in great condition, although some crack repairs have been painted into the surface to make it look worn. Officially, we have an emergency airfield. It even has fire/crash apparatus in a hangar as the strip is used for firefighting aircraft by the forestry service during fire season. We have a crew that mans the crash trucks when we get a plane coming in."

When Norma asked if the runway lights and the aircraft landing lights might attract attention, Charlie commented, "The planes only use their lights at the last part of descent and early takeoff. We're sandwiched in among mountains, out of sight and one hundred fifty miles from anyone not working for Area 3 and it's very sparsely populated for another hundred miles beyond that. We're also in a radar shadow and out of range of aircraft controllers. We're off the beaten track, well off normal flight paths. Officially, we don't exist."

The gravel road took them up, around and over a hill for what seemed like a few miles before they pulled up in front of steps to the formal entrance of a large two-story well-illuminated log building. Nora noted some outer buildings, a garage and work shed and three or four cabins. As they were getting out of the SUV and collecting their baggage, Charlie said, "It's best if we put you up in rooms in the main lodge. How about Norma and Carl in the middle suite facing the lake, Bob nearest the stairs and Wendy across the hall from Norma and Carl?"

Bob said, "You're an old hand at security. Sounds good with me." That was echoed by Wendy.

"Now, come on in and meet Heather. We'll get you all settled, then dinner. Drinks before dinner, by the fireplace in the big room. We have special telecommunications for internet, phone, etc, but I'll show you that later."

Heather turned out to be what one would expect of someone who loved the outdoors. She had no makeup and her long silver hair, complimenting her oval face and blue eyes, was tied in a ponytail. She wore blue jeans, comfort clogs, no socks and a checkered red jack shirt well open at the neck. She was five foot four, and amply endowed – a bright, lively and bubbly person. She and Charlie had been married thirty-five years, having met and wed while on a tour of duty at the radar installation. They had fallen in love with the countryside and had jumped at the chance to work in security at Area 3 when the offer presented itself. It was unclear what they had done during the gap between working at the radar installation and their return ten years ago.

A nicely chilled Pinot Blanc complemented the tastefully cooked trout, fresh greens and mini potatoes. Conversation centered on the local weather and fishing. The lake nearby was glacier fed, about two miles long and a half mile wide. Charlie commented that although they were into early fall, there could be cold snaps with snow but tomorrow looked to be good weather. The fishing had been excellent and the best flies for different conditions were reviewed. Charlie and Heather would show them some of the better fishing spots in the morning with Heather taking the ladies in one boat and Charlie the men. Charlie also mentioned that security was "heavy" for them, that there were 24/7 guards on various perimeters, as well as electronic monitoring. The guards were all local residents with their own homes scattered about on the property, all semi-retirees from the agency. He asked Norma and Carl not to wander off too far unescorted, except down to the dock and back. Charlie said, "I'll introduce you to the guards from time to time. We've got thirty on the three inner security perimeters taking turns 24/7. Also, all occupants in the area are security for you. This includes the ranchers dotted around for a radius of fifty miles – they're all semi-retirees from our agency on retainer and enjoying country living."

Looking at his watch, Carl said, "Well, it's been an exciting afternoon, and a very enjoyable evening with new friends and saviors. It's late, though. Time for bed. I want to be fresh for fishing tomorrow. The men have got to get the biggest fish the first day or I'm going to be embarrassed."

After Norma and Carl went upstairs to bed, Wendy and Bob helped clear the dishes off the table and load the dishwasher. Charlie asked, "Bob, what's your evaluation of the risk factor?"

"Well, from what we've seen so far, these people, whoever they are, have a long reach. They've targeted people in Russia, Japan, Canada and the USA. I'd say we have to really be on our toes – there could be a hunter out there. We'll keep our guns handy. I'd like to borrow a rifle from your armory tomorrow – just to keep it handy."

"Same here," Wendy echoed.

Bob and Wendy made their "good nights" and went upstairs as Charlie and Heather went to their master suite on the ground floor. On the way upstairs, Bob brushed Wendy's hand and she responded by pinching his bottom. As they reached the door to his room at the top of the stairs, she opened his door for him to enter and followed him in with her left finger by her lips in a "shushing" motion for silence. She closed the door quietly. They embraced and passionately kissed. Wendy groped his crotch and Bob responded with his hands on her breasts before she pulled his hand down to her crotch. They kissed deeply while he rubbed her crotch and she started to moan quietly. She pulled down the zipper on his fly and pulled out his stiff manhood. She felt it, squeezed it and murmured, "It'll do." They helped each other undress, and, while Wendy was standing, Bob licked his way from Wendy's left breast to her crotch. She spread her legs for him while holding his head in her hands and occasionally pushing his face further inward when he hit the right spot. She was very wet. After a few near orgasms, she sat back on the bed and pulled Bob's head toward hers and they French kissed while he slowly entered. She pushed him out and said,

"Condom time," which sent him scurrying for a rubber which she helped put on, then caressed with her tongue. Bob entered again and came too quickly but Wendy managed an orgasm. However, practice made perfect as both collided in strong orgasms on the second and third attempt.

Having a good cuddle later, Wendy quietly said, "You know, this could be a fun assignment. I'm single and you're single; let's enjoy it while we're here!"

Bob squeezed, cuddled and whispered, "Right on! Fun, lust, no commitments, and duty first. Right? Oh, and some good fishing!" That earned him a sharp elbow poke in the ribs.

Chapter 13

For Stephanie Lees, it had taken a while to get used to the idea of being guarded 24/7. Special Agent Joyce Fernandez, though, had turned out to be a pretty good companion with many similar interests, including love and lost histories with boyfriends and marriage and a good sense of humor. There was over a generation age difference with Joyce clocking in at thirty-seven and Stephanie in her late fifties. So far, they hadn't run out of conversation and they'd enjoyed each other's company. For Stephanie, a slave to her work in compensation for a bad marriage that had resulted in a not-so-friendly divorce three years ago, it was like having a good friend visit – and Joyce, ever considerate, had worked hard to develop that feeling.

Joyce was a career FBI agent with little current interest in men or marriage after being burned by a "handsome Texas dude" – as she called it – who was far less than monogamous during their short, one-year marriage. Stephanie and Joyce had ample opportunity to compare notes.

Joyce was a heavy-set Mexican-American who had earned a law degree in Texas and began her FBI career shortly after. She was five foot ten, one hundred eighty-five pounds, with mid-length black hair, brown eyes, and an oval face. She was a good shot, loved hunting and skiing and enjoyed the great Alaska outdoors.

Stephanie was diminutive at five foot two and a slim one hundred ten pounds. She could be very attractive when she chose to dress up, but she preferred jeans and jack shirt and no makeup, gray-brown hair in a ponytail. She spent most of her time in the lab on her research project and in her adjoining office working up her presentation for the Willard Institute.

Stephanie had the option of multiple security personnel rotating day, night and weekends, but had elected for just one 24/7. She had also been offered sequestering in a safe place but had refused as she was committed to her research and her students at the university.

Joyce occupied the spare bedroom in Stephanie's apartment and accompanied her everywhere – from lectures to lab and office to shopping mall, grocery store and auto repair shop. Two days ago, Hector Skog had requested beefed up security and the Anchorage office had added two people for external surveillance of the apartment overnight plus a "chase car" shadowing them when they were in transit.

The morning saw a light breakfast – orange juice, pop-up waffles, jam, peanut butter and coffee – with Joyce preparing it and Stephanie taking her turn to clean up, then off to the lab. When they reached the lab and adjoining office, it had become the custom for Joyce to enter first, as she did this morning. She entered the office with her hand on the gun in her purse as she scouted around to see if everything was clear, then turned and let Stephanie enter. She then went across the room to the door to the lab, opened it and began to enter – only to be blown across the office into Stephanie by the force of the explosion. The paramedics arrived quickly and worked hard, but she was pronounced dead on arrival at the hospital.

It was just after two p.m. when Hector got the news. The special agent in charge of the Alaska Division filled him in. "She was doing her job. She didn't have a chance. A bomb filled with shrapnel had been rigged to the door between the office and the lab and detonated when the door was near fully open. Thankfully she was directly between the bomb and Ms. Lees and took the full force of the explosion."

"And how is Ms. Lees?"

"She's relatively fine. Broken eardrums, bruising from being thrown against the wall and floor, a broken wrist and some cracked ribs from when Joyce landed on her. She's also totally pissed off that someone killed her new friend and ruined her lab. She had backup of her research data, so that's one good thing."

"How are you doing with forensics at the scene?"

"As you know, it's early yet, but we've recovered some good fragments from the bomb that may be revealing. Security cameras are being reviewed, etc. but nothing yet. We'll get back to you later with a progress report."

"It's time to move Ms. Lees to a secure location. Tell her she has to move – no ifs, ands or buts."

"We'll work on that. We've got a safe house – might be good for a few days."

"OK. That'll give us time to make other arrangements."

Chapter 14

Vladivostok, Russia

It had been a boring voyage so far. Peter Melville's dream of finding romance on the high seas fizzled quickly. There weren't very many single women aboard the *Northland Princess*. Any women in his age range were either couples of the same sex or unattractive buffet walruses. He knew he was in for boredom the first night at his dinner sitting when all at his assigned table were geriatrics as were most of the other passengers in the dining room. Fem hunting was no better at the bars, the casino, the floorshow or other venues. Although he had enjoyed the excursions off the ship in the various ports of call, life aboard ship was dull. The weather was consistently bad – overcast or rainy, with cold and bumpy seas. The only redeeming features were good food, cheerful and always helpful crew members and interesting pre-arrival lectures about the next port of call. Part of his problem was that he had chosen to really get away – away from modern electronic communications – to cut himself off. From work. From research. From friends and acquaintances. This was supposed to be a real "getaway and vegetate" trip. No worries – but hopefully, please, please, some good sex.

He had ended a difficult long-time affair just before he went to the Arctic. That affair had hurt and he needed time to mend. Time to think, to re-evaluate his love life and his career. At forty-two years old, he was in a mid-life crisis. He was beginning to feel a few aches and pains in his knees and shoulders from his days as a running back at university. His black hair was starting to speckle grey and recede and he now needed bi-focal glasses. Luckily, he was still athletic and maintained his six foot one, hundred eighty-pound frame. He wasn't too happy about the crow's feet around his dark brown eyes. It was time for a change. Although he was well respected in his field, he was tired of lecturing at the university and the institutionalization of it was grinding away at his soul. He was tired of his routine in Edmonton and in Canada. He wanted to change. This twenty-three-day repositioning voyage from Vancouver, Canada to Dalian, China with stops off the beaten path around the North Pacific on the *Northern Princess,* at least would introduce him to new sights – maybe generate some new ideas.

The *Northern Princess* was berthed in Vladivostok, Russia. Peter had taken the sightseeing tour which ended mid-afternoon. He had been impressed, star-struck, by the tour guide, Vanessa Kubic. Not only was she fluent in English with a West Coast American accent, she was a stunning beauty, five foot seven, long black hair in a ponytail, long legs, pink lips and matching fingernails, blue eyes, oval face, great ankles, small perfect ears, perfect white teeth. A casual discussion with her revealed she was thirty-three years old, single, and a Master of Science graduate in earth sciences from Vladivostok's Far Eastern University. She had a great sense of humor and seemed to single out Peter, joking with him as she narrated the tour. Peter was shocked and excited when, at the end of the tour while passengers were getting off the bus to return to the ship or go shopping, she pulled him aside and said, "Peter, the ship doesn't sail for six hours yet. Would you like a drink? There's a nice bar across the street."

The bar occupied the entire main floor of a historical four-story, ornate cutstone landmark dating to opulent Czarist times. A young couple seated at a table on the left side wall of the room hailed Vanessa and motioned her to join them. Vanessa introduced the couple as Serge Alexander and Sonja Minsk, grad students at the University. Vodka and beer flowed freely and Peter, for the first time on the trip, relaxed and enjoyed himself. After about two hours of drinking and innocent comradery, Peter passed out. He came to not functioning very well and was helped out of the bar by his new friends. He never saw the "date rape" pill slipped into the last beer. The ship sailed without him. The ship's purser's office notified the Vladivostok police and the local shipping agent. Peter disappeared.

Kodiak, Alaska

NOAA's *Harvey North* had a spacious helicopter landing pad. Tonight, it was illuminated for a nighttime landing as a Coast Guard Jayhawk helicopter made a final approach, hovering and settling down as deck crew sprang to secure it with tie-down straps. The ship was headed into the wind, and waves with twenty-foot seas made the flight deck a moving target for the skilled chopper pilots.

Red Smith, captain of the *Harvey North,* was standing beside Hayden Kincaid in the shelter of the aircraft hangar beside two crewmen dressed in fire gear who were part of the emergency crew "standing by" – ready in case of an accident. As the chopper cut its engines, and the rotor blades slowed, Red turned to Hayden and shook his hand, "Well, Hayden, it was great to have you aboard and I'm sorry I'm losing such a lousy poker player. Anyway, I wish you the best of luck. You must be into some heavy shit for them to send a chopper for you!"

"Thanks Red. You and your guys cleaned my clock. Maybe bridge next time? That, or I've got to take some lessons. Anyway, it'll be interesting to see what the fibbies and the Willard Institute people have in mind. My dean at the university said, in no uncertain terms, I might add, that I was to go along with this pick-up. So, I guess I've gotta go. Thanks again for a great voyage!" He dragged his kit bag across the deck and a crewman helped throw it into the passenger/cargo bay of the chopper. Then he climbed in, the door was closed and the pilots began to wind up the chopper. Tiedown straps were released at a signal from the pilot and the chopper was soon airborne, shuddering from the backdraft off the ship's bulkhead.

It was about an hour's flight to the Coast Guard base in Kodiak where Hayden was transferred to an unmarked Challenger Jet.

Chapter 15

Norma and Carl were up early the next morning and first stop was the kitchen where Heather pointed out the coffee and pastries and told them breakfast would be in two hours. She suggested they explore the grounds while waiting for Charlie and the others, then meet on the wharf for the first round of fishing. Carl and Norma took their coffees along with their fishing tackle and walked the path from the lodge to the pier, some three hundred yards away down a gently sloping wide path, passing six log cabins, each with porches holding a settee-swing for two and a couple of deck chairs. The cabins had stone chimneys and steep-pitched metal roofs designed to shed snow. The pier, up on pilings about six feet above the water, extended out into the lake about fifty feet, where it was linked by a ramp to a float about sixty feet long. There was an assortment of water craft – two canoes, two jet-ski seadoos sitting on the float and eight fourteen-foot aluminum open boats with twenty-horsepower outboard motors moored alongside. They walked to the end of the float, admiring the view of the pristine lake and mountains rising almost in a horseshoe around it. Looking back past the cabins, they could see the lodge on a promontory, affording it a grand vista of the lake and mountains. Norma wrapped an arm around Carl's waist and said, "Just like a holiday. We've got a gorgeous private lodge on a private lake! I hope the fishing is as good as promised."

Bob and Wendy, Charlie and Heather joined them a few minutes later. Charlie pulled life jackets and fishing tackle from a locker on the float and tossed the jackets into two boats while Bob and Wendy selected rods and flies. Charlie boarded one of the boats and started the motor, while Heather did the same with another boat. Wendy and Norma joined Heather in one boat and took off down the lake, with Charlie, Bob and Carl going in the opposite direction up the lake. Charlie shouted above the noise of the outboard, "We've each got our favorite spots on the lake."

After a few minutes Charlie slowed and cut the engine and everyone rigged their lines. Bob rigged a leech but was not as adept as Charlie who was first to be casting and caught a three-pound rainbow on the second cast, using a brown fly. Once it was safely netted, he said, "All right, gentlemen, I've led the way. I'll sit back and let you two go at it for a while."

In the space of an hour each man had their limit of two trout. Carl was smiling at his six-pound speckled trout, the biggest of all. Bob was happy with a four-pounder that put up a great fight. When they returned to the dock, the ladies had beaten them back and were busy cleaning their catch. Norma took the prize for the morning with a nine-pound rainbow, but Heather had a seven and a five and Wendy had managed a five and a three. The ladies had out-fished the men and were not going to let the men forget it.

While Heather was preparing breakfast, Charlie showed the others the state of the art communications room in the basement of the lodge. Its dedicated satellite relay was set up to avoid tracing. Anyone trying to trace the communications, Charlie explained, including cell phone and internet transmission, would find it originating from an office in Washington, DC. "You're free to use the internet and cell phones," he said, "but don't disclose the location in your correspondence. Also, everything will be monitored – just part of the security."

Charlie looked at the clock on the wall and said, "We can call Robert Berubé now, if you'd like?" Norma and Carl nodded, Charlie placed the call and, after a moment to set up the video, Robert Berubé was on a fifty-inch screen on one wall and Norma and Carl were seated in front of a TV camera. After greetings, Robert said, "Obviously, you are safe and sound. I understand you are in a private fishing resort? That must be nice!"

Norma said, "Robert, it's lovely. We've already had some great fishing among beautiful surroundings. It's magnificent! But where are you?"

"Apparently, I'm about two hours away by car from Washington DC, in what they call a safe house. It's a large horse farm with beautiful accommodations. We're happy here. The dog is quite cute trying to herd the horses."

Norma asked, "Any idea of what happens next? How long will we be here?"

"I met this morning with Mr. Sanford Crosley from the CIA and Mr. Hector Skog of the FBI. They've something planned. First priority is to rescue the others. Some will be brought to the fishing lodge. In the meantime, it is to be announced that I have asylum in America and why. Then I'll give interviews to the media via video conference.

"I also met with a Ms. Thelma Kenny of the Willard Institute. They've been funding the research grants of our American counterparts. The Willard Institute is very positive about the research and shocked that Canada chose to stop funding. She has offered to fund us and asked if we would prepare presentations outlining our progress and findings."

"What? Wonderful! That will give me something to do when I get bored with fishing and hiking."

"Not only funding, but she also offered a secure and very well-equipped facility in which we can work with other team members to complete the research and develop technology transfer. She has assured us that they will arrange protection. Once we have the others rescued, she will meet with us all to lay out her offer."

"That sounds great! Any idea where we will be located?"

"No. Not yet. Main thing now will be the announcement of my so-called "defection." I'll email you when the press conference will be held. They say it should make an uproar in the media. In the meantime, enjoy your vacation! Hopefully, I and others will be joining you soon."

After breakfast, while Carl and Norma were helping Heather with the cleanup and planning who was going to do what for cooking dinner, Charlie took Bob and Wendy to the armory in the basement. Bob selected a Knights AR25, a semi-automatic sniper with twenty-inch barrel, flash suppressor and twenty-shot clip of 7.62 x 51 mm NATO ammunition and a ten-power day/night scope, as he was a good hunter and wanted something for stalking. Charlie said, "The army's switching back to a bolt-action sniper rifle, supposedly for more trajectory as less power is lost to pushing a semi-automatic bolt." Bob justified the semi-automatic as good for closer distances and that he might need the quick fire capability.

Wendy opted for a semi-automatic Bushmaster AR 15 Patrolman's Carbine Cerakote (Police Special version) with a 16-inch barrel, an A2 flash suppressor, and double twenty-round magazine. She selected the NATO 5.56 mm instead of the domestic .223 caliber for greater punch. She also added a ten power day/night scope.

Charlie took them to an outdoor range about three miles away where they sighted in their guns. Charlie also gave them each a tracking device, like a large wristwatch, which not only sent out a GPS signal identifying them by name but also registered other "friendlies" within a one-mile radius. Charlie said, "The identifier system's a big help; we don't want you taking any pot shots at your security people or vice versa. All the guests will get one of these too."

When they returned to the lodge, Charlie had arranged for Wendy and Bob to do a familiarization tour of the ranch with Gerry McRae, one of the senior security personnel. That took all of the afternoon. Bob had seen it all before but it was new to Wendy. Charlie spent the afternoon with Carl and Norma in the communications center where they were kept busy notifying family and friends of their departure and safety, arranging for clothing to be packed and sent on, someone to pick up the mail, cancelling the paper and a myriad of other details.

After a sunset fishery that evening that yielded more large trout, Bob and Charlie went to the communications center while Wendy, Norma and Carl helped Heather with the meal preparation. Moose steaks, gravy, new potatoes, fresh beans were on the menu, along with a very reasonable red cabernet sauvignon followed by angel food cake and ice cream. At dinner Bob announced he had spoken with Sanford who advised him that they had located Peter Melville and that he was in safe hands. Stephanie Lees and Hayden Kincaid were also safe and would be joining them shortly. They planned a hike next day to the top of Crystal Mountain, the mountain skirting the east side of the lake. Charlie said the view from the top was breathtaking. He said the mountain was the second highest in the area, next to Barrack Mountain on the other side of the lake which was another two thousand feet higher. Barrack Mountain had the old early warning radar station on top. He mentioned it had recorded the lowest winter temperature in the region at -70 degrees. Carl asked if the radar station was still used and Charlie replied,

"The old station is full of asbestos and deactivated. However, they built a modern automated station nearby as part of an NSA linkage. We have maintenance people for it."

Chapter 16

"Dr. Melville, Dr. Melville…can you hear me?" Slowly, Peter was awakening. Very groggy. Headache. Fuzzy. He tried and managed to open his eyes to a squint. Mercifully, there was no sharp light to hurt. He could feel someone gently shaking his left shoulder and he slowly moved his head in that direction and started to bring his eyes into focus. He saw an older, balding man speaking to him. The man had dark stringy hair and steel rimmed glasses. A stethoscope hung around his neck, and he was wearing a white smock over white shirt and blue bowtie. "Ah, Dr. Melville, welcome back!" His nametag on his left breast pocket read: *Dr. P. Alexander*. Someone raised the head end of the bed to the half-way position, allowing Peter to slowly take in his surroundings. He concluded he was in some sort of a windowless hospital room and he noticed the beautiful Vanessa standing at the foot of the bed.

She came to the other side of the bed and squeezed his hand. "Welcome back, Peter. You're safe now." She handed him a small cup of water, which he took and readily drank.

"Where am I? Wha' happened?" His mouth was fuzzy. Vanessa gave him more water.

The doctor spoke in broken English. "I am Dr. Alexander. You're in a safe place. You will be all right now. Rest for a while and have some food. When you are a little stronger, then Vanessa will explain."

Peter turned to Vanessa. She squeezed his hand and said, "You were in great danger. But details later. Dr. Robert Berubé will explain later via video conference. I'll sit with you for a while." After a few minutes, Peter fell back to sleep.

He had no sense of time when he awoke again. Vanessa was curled up on a sofa at the end of the room. She awoke when she heard him stirring and came to the bedside. He said, "Gotta pee. Where's the bathroom?"

"Here, let me help you. The doctor said you may be a little unsteady. Sit first, then I'll help you take your first steps. You have a private bathroom over here."

After he had used the toilet and returned to the bed, she said, "Hungry? I'll get something brought in." He nodded and she used the phone on the bedstead to order breakfast for two – fried eggs, ham, coffee, toast. He was still groggy and nodded off again only to be awakened by Vanessa when the food arrived. He ate well and began to perk up. He started to think and soon said, "My clothes! I guess everything is on the ship except what I was wearing. I guess I missed the boat?"

"Yes, but not to worry, we've arranged for your things to be gathered up and sent on when the ship makes its next port. The clothes you were wearing have been washed and pressed and are in the closet beside your bed. We've advised the travel agent you had an emergency and will not be returning to the ship."

"What? Why?"

Vanessa put her right index finger on his lips. "Shhh. Get dressed. Then, let's call Dr. Berubé. He'll explain."

After he got dressed, they left the room, passing a few people in white smocks in the hallway and on the stairs (*Medical types*, thought Peter when he noticed the name tags and stethoscopes). Vanessa took him up a floor to an inside conference room which had a 50-inch flat-screen TV on one wall. She took a seat at the end of the table opposite the TV screen and fiddled with a small console imbedded in the table, finally turning on the TV and producing a dial tone. She dialed a number and told Peter to take a seat midway down the table in front of a small video camera and under a strong light. She dialed and soon the connection produced Dr. Robert Berubé on the screen. Vanessa introduced herself and asked, "Is your video reception and audio good?" to which he responded, "Yes, great, thank you Vanessa. Hello, Peter. How are you?"

"Hi, Robert! Good to see you! I'm fine, I think. Still a bit groggy. What the hell happened? What's going on? Where am I?"

"Peter, you were very hard to find. We were all worried about you – fearing for your safety. Much has developed that's pretty scary. Four of our members of the Arctic team, Jason Metcalfe, Victor Wong, Jack Mahoney and Marie Le Court have been killed. Another two were badly injured, nearly killed, run down by drivers in stolen vehicles. One was Ivan Kievkoff in St. Petersburg, the other was Kenji Ube in Sapporo. Two research labs have been blown up – Stephanie Lees' in Anchorage where one person was also killed and they just missed Stephanie, and Professor Iawama's lab in Sapporo. I'm in the US under protection from the FBI and the same for Norma, Hayden and Stephanie."

"Whoa, slow down a bit. Are you saying someone wants to, to kill me?"

"It's probable. Luckily, we found you before that."

"Unbelievable!"

"It looks as if the oil industry, or somebody, does not want our work to continue and will even kill to prevent it."

"It's bad enough the Canadian government shut down our funding and swore us to secrecy. Now, they want to kill us? OK … So, where am I and how did I get here?"

"I'm not sure exactly where you are. I've just been told you are at a secret Russian research facility where you were taken after you were rescued."

"Rescued? Somebody slipped me a "Mickey Finn" and I woke up here! That's a rescue? I was shanghaied! Russia? Who's responsible for it?"

"Apparently, the US and Japanese governments talked to the Russian government and made the arrangements. I've been told you are free to leave at any time, but we know your life is in danger and suggest you accept protective sequestering like we have – at least for now. Please?"

"For now. OK, but what next?"

"As you know, the Willard Institute has funded the Americans. Now that we Canadians have lost our government funding, the Willard Institute is offering to fund us. They will be making a proposal shortly and want you to attend the planning session. They will send a private jet for you."

"Interesting."

"Think it over. I'll get back to you in a day when all the arrangements can be finalized. I'll sign off for now. Thank you, Vanessa. Bye."

Peter sat for a few minutes. Thinking. Stunned. After a while, Vanessa sensed it was time to comment. "Peter, you're in good hands now. You're safe. Come, I want you to meet someone."

"Who?"

"An old friend. You'll see." She gently touched his hand and led him out of the room, down stairs again but down another hall to another hospital room. They entered. A man, with his back to them, was sitting in an armchair watching a game show from Moscow which was probably the most popular show in the country. Vanessa called to him. "Ivan, here's Peter."

Ivan turned and a huge smile lit up his face. "Peter! Great to see you!" He tried to stand up but failed and sat back down again with pain showing on his face. "Oh, oh, overdid it. Sorry. I'm still learning to walk again with a new hip and some ribs are still cracked. I'm also dizzy at times from the concussion. Please, don't make me laugh right now. But it is great, really great to see you!"

Peter said, "I heard you were mowed down by a car?"

"Yeah. Attempted murder by a hit man – can you believe it? They caught the guy and he talked."

"My God!"

"Anyway, my government sent me here for safety and to recover. The people here are great! I'm getting good therapy. You've got to meet my therapist. Tina. She's great! I've fallen in love with her.

They say I'll be able to get back to my research in a few months. They consider it part of my therapy."

Vanessa said, "I was about to show Peter around outside. It'll help him clear his head with some fresh air. Would you like to come?"

"Sure. I can walk with a cane for modest distances but let's take that wheelchair in the corner there. I get a little dizzy and my balance isn't too good. Let's go to the coffee shop across the square."

"OK." As they exited the hospital by the front door, with Ivan pushing his wheelchair using the support it provided as a walker, Peter stopped, looked at his surroundings, and did a double take. He couldn't believe it! He was facing a small square with a bandstand and a statue of a soldier on a horse leading a charge – an American soldier by the name of Teddy Roosevelt. The storefronts he could see across the park and to the right looked as if they had been transplanted from a mid-American small town with city hall, library, museum, police station, drug store, dollar store, coffee shop, hardware store, barber, beauty salon, chiropractor and others. To his left, covering a whole block, was a large five-story concrete building. The sidewalk was lined with large maple and oak shade trees. There were many pedestrians, men, women and children, on the sidewalks and in the town square. No automobiles were visible. Instead, some people were riding bicycles, all of the same design with white fenders and lime green frames and all had numbers down the back fender. There were some electric golfcart-type vehicles in various seating configurations, some parked and empty, some passing by with occupants, some carrying goods. "What the hell?" he said, bewildered.

Smiling, Vanessa said, "I thought this would be a surprise. We call it "Mayberry." The town goes back to the Cold War days and is one of a few the Soviets duplicated from America and used to train spies to penetrate America. Now, it's a high security zone for research and language immersion and witness protection. Everyone here is fluent in the American version of the English language. Our currency is American. Same for grocery brands and clothing. Everything. It's operated by a secret department of the FSB – directly under the Office of the President of Russia.

"The town is quite remote. We're in the southwest of Russia in the Jewish Autonomous Oblast – a state or province in your experience – where Stalin set aside territory for Jews to resettle. There aren't too many Jews left as most migrated to Israel when it formed but they left a legacy, such as the Jewish National University and schools teaching in Hebrew and Yiddish. For Russia, this is a mild four-season climate, but of course we still get a snowy winter. People enjoy life here. We're isolated, almost two hundred kilometers from the next town and surrounded by large farms, but the town has everything.

"A few years ago, the town went "green," banning most forms of internal combustion autos. There are the shuttles like a bus or taxi, plus the exchange bicycles you see – you pick them up at a corner bike stand and park them at a similar stand when you get to your destination and then they are available for someone else to use. You use a credit card with chip to pay for the rental – same for a shuttle ride. The shuttles are electric with long-life lithium-ion batteries but some are converted to hydrogen fuel cells. The Town Council is debating allowing electric scooters and that will probably come soon. All the shops and such are supplied by an underground tunnel system of roads. Vehicles using them – service vehicles, police, ambulance and fire vehicles – are all fueled by natural gas, hydrogen fuel cells or electricity.

"Let's wander through the park to the coffee shop," Ivan suggested.

As they began walking, Peter asked, "What's the big building on our left?"

"That's one of the research centers."

"What do you do for accommodations?"

"All American style. We have a three-star motel/hotel, a variety of restaurants from American fast food to specialty Italian, Indian, Japanese, Korean and Chinese. We have apartment blocks and condos and detached suburban housing. We'll move you out of the hospital today. You have a choice, either the hotel for a room of your own or you can share mine."

"Yours, please." The prospect of sharing a bed with Vanessa brightened him up. He was ecstatic.

The coffee shop seemed familiar, similar to a franchise found worldwide. After they got their coffees and settled in at a table, Peter and Ivan had some reminiscing about the last Arctic voyage, telling Vanessa about some of their highlights. Peter told Ivan about being asked to join the Willard Institute's team. "Yes, I've been asked to join too," Ivan replied, "but I need to recover more first. If I agree, my government will contribute my services and share in the benefits. They're even willing to provide a secure venue and facilities like this. It looks like a pretty good deal to me as I'll still get my regular salary here and also be paid by the Willard Institute. If Robert Berubé's the leader, it could be fun. He's great to work for and we had a great team on the voyage – albeit we have now sadly lost a few members."

"Interesting. So, a Russian and American partnership on this?"

"Looks that way. The Japanese too. Right now, the Japanese have the most to gain by freeing themselves from dependence on imported oil. There seems to be a race to get the technology developed and patented. They want to beat the oil people to it. If the oil people get it, they'll just bury it for a long, long time. The Japanese seem to be more interested in offshore extraction but I feel strongly about the potential to develop extraction from permafrost on land. That has great potential for Russia in the High North. You know, it would be the same for Canada. Can you imagine an Arctic city with everything running on local methane?"

"I agree. I'd love to be part of that."

"So would I!" said Vanessa.

Chapter 17

<u>10:00 a.m. US Consulate, Montreal</u>

After sowing hints through the social media, including Facebook and Twitter, with the national news desks of the big media in Canada and America, and through late night call-at-home-catch-them-in-bed personal invitations by the Consulate's Press Secretary to key members of the Montreal news media, the press conference was about to begin on the front steps of the Consulate. The news media were out in force, curious about the unusual situation of being called to the US Consulate. The street was lined with TV news trucks from all the major media with their satellite links up and operating. The front steps of the consulate bristled with microphones in front and beside the lectern that had been placed on the landing at the top of the steps. Pierre LeBois chose to remain behind the scenes, walking the perimeter of the front yard, eyeing the circus of reporters and camera people warming up, testing their equipment. Today Iris LaRue, US Consul of the Montreal office, would lead the charge.

Promptly at 10:00 a.m., the front door of the Consulate opened and Iris, a pretty, middle-aged African American from Louisiana, walked out to the lectern and tapped the microphone of the consulate's speaker system. It worked. She spoke into the mike in French, "Raise your hands back there if you can hear me." And someone at the back, a cameraman, shouted, "Loud and clear."

She placed her prepared speech in front of her and began to read in French, "Ladies and gentlemen of the press, thank you for coming. It is a most rare occasion for us to call a press conference like this but something unusual has happened." She repeated this in English.

"We have given refuge to a Canadian national and spouse who have sought political asylum as they are fearing for their lives." This solicited a rumbling of comments from the gathered members of the new media. She paused, repeated this in English, and continued to do this throughout her speech, after every few sentences.

"Upon reviewing the case, we felt there is sufficient cause to grant asylum and so have granted it. There certainly has been a chain of events that seems to justify their fearing for their lives – especially if they remained in Canada. We have prepared a statement which we shortly will hand out to you explaining the circumstances and providing some background."

"At their request, the couple, Professor Robert Berubé and his wife, Marie, of Trois Rivieres, Quebec, have been removed to a safe haven in the United States. We also have a statement from Professor Berubé which we also will shortly hand out."

"Professor Berubé has been engaged on a multi-national research study into the development of methane hydrate, also known as methane calthrate, as an energy source. Methane hydrate has been found in significant quantities in the Arctic permafrost both on land and offshore in areas such as Alaska, Haida Gwaii, the Beaufort Sea and northern Japan. Since returning from research in the Arctic last summer, three Canadian members of the team died in separate accidents under what we deem mysterious circumstances – one in St. John's Newfoundland, one in Toronto, and one in Winnipeg. Two more Canadian members of the research team have disappeared." Pause. Loud rumblings from the press members, as she repeated this in English.

"As well, one of the American researchers has died under mysterious circumstances, and an FBI agent was killed in Alaska by a bomb while protecting another American member of the team. That team member has since been removed to a safe location." She paused, then translated.

"Japanese and Russian members of the team have not been spared. Two have suffered serious injuries from suspicious hit and runs and a research lab in northern Japan was blown up."

"Professor Berubé sought asylum with us only after he had gone to the Canadian authorities – that is the Quebec Provincial Police and the RCMP. He feels he was ignored – considered a "paranoid" person. Indeed, he was passed off on the argument that nothing had befallen him – yet. He feels there was no interest in linking the series of deaths and near deaths, nor does he feel there is a mechanism in Canada's system of policing to link the tragic events."

"Professor and Madam Berubé will be available tomorrow via video conference. You may confer with our press secretary to arrange times. I will now accept questions, if you please."

In French, a very bright reporter from the premier French language newspaper asked, "You say an FBI agent was killed while guarding one of the American members of the team. Why was your person given security and why does Canada not provide it to our members of the team?"

In French, Iris said, "I cannot speak for the Canadians. However I can say that when the American authorities learned of the possible linkage, they quickly provided security. I understand the Japanese and Russians did so as well for their people."

In English, a TV reporter from a major cable news network that was beaming the press conference live throughout North America and beyond, asked, "How did you determine there was a problem? Why are these researchers being targeted?"

"I am not at liberty to say when American authorities became aware of the problem. However, I can tell you that the research they were engaged in recently had a significant breakthrough toward commercialization of a methane hydrate extraction process. As the proven reserves of methane hydrate are significant, for example North American deposits could fuel all of North American for more than one hundred years, the governments of Japan, America and Russia consider the discovery of strategic national importance and will do everything to protect these researchers, our intellectual resources." She translated into French.

In the bilingual press kit that was handed out, the reporters found: a copy of Iris's speech; a statement from Professor Berubé stating he had sought protection from the Canadian authorities but it had not been forthcoming; a statement from Marie Berubé echoing her husband's comments and that she was leaving Canada under her own free will; and a paper describing methane hydrate and its potential as a clean energy resource. There was no mention that Canada had decided to end participation in the project.

Within twenty minutes of the first TV broadcast, which had been live from the press gathering at the US Consulate, the US Embassy in Ottawa, Canada's capital, received an urgent request for the Ambassador to meet with Canada's Minister of Foreign Affairs to explain.

Canada's Minister of Foreign Affairs and the Prime Minister were livid with indignation that they had been snubbed – "Blindsided by the bastards," as Prime Minister Eugene Rogers was heard to have raged after viewing the broadcast. "Insulting and calculated" were other words heard as the PM raged on that the "f-ing" Americans chose their Montreal Consulate as the venue for the press conference, rather than from the US Embassy in Ottawa where protocol expected the Minister of Foreign Affairs should be apprised in advance of the tenor of the press conference. Eventually, a clerk in the Department of Foreign Affairs produced an e-mail, advising of the press conference. It had been received in the routine way and logged two hours before the press conference began. As the DFA Minister was holding his weekly staff meeting that morning, the advice came to his attention in his IN basket after the fact.

The office assistant of Alistair Jacobs, America's Ambassador to Canada, booked the Ambassador for a meeting with the Minister at Foreign Affairs Canada for four p.m.

4:00 p.m. Ministry of Foreign Affairs, Ottawa

Ambassador Jacobs, age sixty, a former Mayor of Chicago, former college all-star football linebacker and proud African American, was an imposing figure. At a ramrod straight six feet four, two hundred sixty pounds, and wearing a crisply tailored navy blue suit, he made a point of giving a firm, almost crushing handshake when Canada's Minister of Foreign Affairs, Wayne Harrison, greeted him. Harrison tried to return the firmness of the grip but failed while smiling and gritting his teeth. They were in Harrison's opulent office, each accompanied by an assistant. Wayne Harrison was a corporate lawyer by profession and into his third term as an elected Member of Parliament representing a riding in oil-rich Alberta and into his third year as Minister of Foreign Affairs. Harrison motioned for them to sit around a coffee table, offered coffee or tea which was politely declined, then began, "Alistair, your people hit us with quite a surprise with that press conference in Montreal. I don't know what to make of it."

87

"Well Wayne, the press conference just brought out the facts. As Professor Berubé sought refuge in our Montreal Consulate, we felt it best to make the announcement from there."

"But you did not inform our office in advance."

"No. We did inform your ministry in advance."

"You have caused us great embarrassment."

"We did only that which Canada chose not to do. We are protecting Professor and Mrs. Berubé. Our FBI people alerted their security counterparts in your Embassy in DC and your RCMP liaison here in Ottawa to the suspected danger and you have not acted upon it. Professor Berubé sought us out for sanctuary only as a last resort. Owing to the targeting of other members of the Arctic team in Russia, Japan and America, our people feel Professor Berubé is in great danger – yet you chose not to protect him. May I ask why?"

"I have no idea but I can assure you, I will look into it."

Chapter 18

"Looks as if we're going to be busy tomorrow," Charlie announced at lunch, "There'll be two flights coming in with VIPs."

"Yes," Norma replied. "Robert and Marie Berubé are coming in with Sanford Fleming, Hector Skog and Thelma Kenny on one flight. Peter Melville, Hayden Kincade, and Stephanie Lees, plus three others providing security for them, will be on the other. Apparently Ivan Kievkoff is still unfit for travel."

Heather spoke up, "How long will they be here? I've got to plan the menus and call in some help."

Charlie looked at her and said, "Weather providing, they'll all be here for four to five days. We'll need to ready nine or ten more bedrooms. We'll use some of the cottages as well as the remaining bedrooms in the lodge. The Berubés are bringing their dog, a little guy, apparently. May be best to give them the cabin closest to the lodge."

Next day

The executive jet had picked up Peter and Vanessa in "Mayberry," Russia, then flew to the Coast Guard Base in Kodiak, Alaska where Hayden Kincaid and Stephanie Lees joined the flight. Hayden had been flown in by helicopter from the research vessel and Stephanie had been sequestered in a safe house on the base since her lab was destroyed and special agent Joyce Fernandez killed. Stephanie was escorted by Special Agent June Williams.

June was a fifteen-year veteran of the FBI who had seen assignments in Fargo, Salt Lake City and Anchorage, having joined the service directly from graduating law school in Seattle. She was single, never married and preferred women.

Hayden only met his security escort when he stepped off the Coast Guard helicopter at the Kodiak base. He introduced himself as Special Agent Fred Tobias. Fred was African American of stocky build, his muscular six foot two frame honed by cross-country

89

jogging and weight lifting. He had a great sense of humor and came across as a sincerely empathetic listener who strove to put his "clients" at ease. He was a great interrogator. Fred joined the FBI after eight years in the army, which he had entered directly from earning a degree in Criminal Justice at a college in Baltimore. He left the army with the rank of a Captain in the Military Police. Now forty-one years old, single divorced, no children, he had seen assignments in Boise, Idaho and Washington, DC. Fred had been on the aircraft all the way from its point of origin in Seattle, flying to Russia and picking up Peter and Vanessa, returning to Kodiak for Hayden and Stephanie where they refueled and changed pilots, then onward to Area 3. He was fatigued but still cheerful and alert, having managed to snatch a good sleep during the flight.

Hayden and Fred made an odd pair. Hayden was five foot three, of average build. His Scottish heritage was reflected in flaming red hair which he wore long to his shoulders and parted in the middle, and in his blue eyes in a ruggedly handsome angular face. He was thirty-five years old, divorced, no children.

They were welcomed by Charlie and two of the security men as they came off the aircraft. Piling into three large crew cab 4x4 pick-ups, the guests were driven up to the lodge, where they were greeted by Norma and Carl and introduced to the others. They were assigned their rooms and, after a bite to eat, given time to rest, explore the grounds and settle in before the others arrived at noon. Peter and Vanessa opted for the greater privacy of one of the cottages.

At noon, Charlie, Bob and Wendy were at the airfield to greet Thelma, Sanford, Hector and the Berubés. After a pause for Isabella, the Berubé's miniature poodle, to relieve itself at the side of the road, they loaded the baggage and passengers into the three crew-cab pick-up vehicles and drove up to the lodge. Charlie, a dog lover, took to Isabella right away. "Isabella has the free run of the lodge and your cabin," he assured the Berubés, "but I think you had better keep a close eye on her when she's outside. She could make an easy meal for some of the wild animals here. We have raccoons, mountain lions, eagles, grizzly bears and coyotes who would be tempted. The coyotes are the ones to really watch out for as they will lure the dog away, then kill it. The raccoons could be a problem too, as they're pretty big. We've got a female husky, Nikki, who's real friendly and can keep Isabella company and provide some protection but I still think you might want to keep a close eye on Isabella when she's outside."

At the lodge after introductions and reunion time, Heather called everyone to lunch. She had set up a buffet along one wall by the kitchen and put together a long table to seat everyone. Toward the end of the meal, Thelma called everyone's attention by rapping a knife on a water glass and said, "Ladies and gentlemen, I guess you can say that I called this meeting."

Laughter. "But let's get on to business, at least, the plans for discussions today. Let's finish up our lunch, a very fine lunch thanks to Heather and her people."

A round of applause. "I'd like to start the meeting in half an hour from now. Heather suggests we use the living room. For now, relax and explore the grounds, if you haven't already done so."

Norma spoke up. "Thelma, may our spouses sit in on the meeting?"

"Of course, Marie and Carl are welcome. They have a say in your decision making. Vanessa and Sanford will be sitting in and I will explain that later."

Charlie spoke up. "While you all are busy, Bob, Wendy and I will give Fred and June and Hector some orientation."

"You're going to get a head start on the fishing?"

"No, but I suggest you plan to break for the evening fishery at, say four p.m.? I understand Heather promised to show you her favorite spot. We're planning seven-thirty for dinner."

"Agreed. Four p.m. will give us plenty of time for the meeting."

Thelma opened the meeting. "Hayden, Stephanie, you're familiar with the Willard Institute, as we've been funding your methane hydrate research for the past ten years. But, permit me to explain to the others and you can jump in with clarification whenever and please feel free to discuss everything with anyone after the meeting.

"The Willard Institute has funded Hayden, Stephanie and Victor Wong – may he rest in peace – with an annual fund of seven hundred thousand dollars each for their research expenses plus we have covered their entire salaries at their respective institutions."

Norma, Robert and Peter looked at each other with jaw-dropping expressions of amazement as the funding was well beyond anything ever heard of in Canada.

"Each parent institution provided lab, office and computing facilities in consideration that each researcher also provide some teaching and mentoring and share credit for the fruits of their labors. Each institution and researcher has a share of the financial benefits of any technology transfer – that is in the form of patent and processing licensing revenues."

Peter said, "Similar to my arrangement with my university. But what are the percentages?"

Norma stated, "Any sharing is better than my situation. I was just a part-time contractor to the research center that sub-contracted to the federal government."

Frowning, Robert Berubé said, "I don't even get that. The research is just part of my job. I'm expected to publish my research but there is no way for me to financially benefit and now, the Canadian government has shut us down."

Hayden said, "The Willard Institute contracts for a 75/25 split. They take seventy-five percent and the remaining twenty-five percent is split equally between the professor and the institution. The Willard Institute may even buy the patent outright for a lump sum – depending."

Thelma stepped in. "Correct. First of all, let me say that the Willard Institute has been closely following all of your research and we are familiar with your contributions to the goal to harness methane hydrate. We feel you all are integral to our goal of a rapid development of the necessary technologies. We want you to join our team and not only complete your research but push it through to practical application – to be part of the technology transfer process. We offer you patent and royalty sharing on a team share basis, plus generous salary, accommodations, lab facilities and, of course, protection."

Peter said, "But I have some loyalty for my university. They've been very good to me."

"We will look after your institution. We will propose to fund an endowment for an academic/research chair in your discipline. In consideration the university will reserve the seat for you, on one year's notice. Same for Stephanie and Hayden."

Robert spoke up, "And for me?"

"Yes, if you wish it."

Peter said, "What do you mean by the words "team share basis"? And what do we have to do or sacrifice for this?"

"We want to direct all effort toward developing safe and effective extraction and distribution systems for tapping into the vast reserves of methane hydrate both in permafrost and subsea. We want to apply for patents in everything possible and we don't want delays by personal competition. We are in a race against "Big Oil" interests who want to stifle the development. They're doing their own research and plan to beat us and others to patenting and then delay use until they feel it is profitable to them. Time is of the essence for us. We want sharing of ideas, close collaboration. The revenues from all patents and processes would be shared equally across the team.

"As for sacrifice – good word in a way. You would have to devote all your time and maximum effort, say for the next three years or so. Plus, for your safety and secrecy, you will be placed in a very comfortable but isolated location, with unlimited lab and personnel resources, including mechanical engineering and software development support."

Robert spoke up, "What about the Japanese? They've been fundamental collaborators."

"Good point. As we speak, we have a team of patent attorneys working with them filing for world-wide patent protection on the extraction method they tested last summer in the Arctic. The filing took place today at patent offices throughout the world. We are fifteen percent partners with them in their patent application in consideration of the rights for exclusive use in the Americas and shared rights for many other parts of the world. Russia is also a partner in the application in consideration for exclusive use in Russia and shared use in some other regions. We will collaborate very closely."

Stephanie said, "This will upset the oil people."

"Indeed. It already has, as you can see. We, with the help of the governments of Japan, Russia and the USA, will strive for your full protection."

Carl said, "Who is the Russian partner?"

"The president and prime minister of Russia and the Russian FSB."

"Ah!"

"That's why Sanford is here. He brokered the deal through his CIA contacts with their FSB."

"Very interesting!" Robert said.

"Senior elements in the Russian government want to hold something over the so-called "oil oligarchs" as they feel they have grabbed too much of the country's resources," explained Sanford.

"This is also why Vanessa is present today. She's a scientist with experience in cryogenics and mechanical engineering but also is in the FSB and is representing their interests. Ivan was not yet fit to travel but he has agreed to be part of the team and will join us when he is able. Vanessa has studied all his research and feels confident she can make a contribution."

Norma said, "Isolation can be pretty hard on our spouses. Is there a way to involve Carl and perhaps, Marie, if she's interested?"

"Yes. Carl, you took early retirement from a production management position, I understand?"

"Yes."

"If you like, you could take on the role of office manager for the project. We can whip up TORs – Terms of Reference – later, but it would cover budgeting, ordering, scheduling and liaison with the patent attorneys. This will relieve Robert to get closer to the work, to work with my office on planning and scheduling, as well as deal with our Japanese associates. We'll work out your salary after this meeting. If you feel you need help, we'll get you some."

Robert spoke up, "Marie and I met at university. She was a lab assistant for me."

Marie chimed in, "I'd love to work in a lab again! Would it be possible?"

"Of course. That or in the office or both. Again, we'll work that out and your salary after the meeting."

Stephanie said, "Where's the lab? I understand it's isolated?"

"Yes. We have the choice of a few locations. If you join us, you can have a part in the selection process."

That invoked a comment from Peter. "What about 'Mayberry'?" To which the response from Thelma was, "There are a number of 'Mayberries'."

"Is this more directed or applied research now that the first patent is applied for?" Hayden asked. "I gather you want to file for as many patents as possible? Such as what Thomas Edison did when he developed the light bulb? He developed everything from transformers to fuses, even the screw base. Same for Bell and the telephone. He invented the switchboard system, power sources, everything."

"Yes," replied Thelma. "Plus improvements to the process. Everything focusing on taming methane hydrate extraction and use that hasn't been invented or perfected yet."

Hayden frowned. "You know, we made great friends with virtually all of the Japanese on the Arctic team. Does this mean we're going to be competing with them?"

"Not at all. We are still partners. They're taking the lead on undersea extraction but we will assist on separation of methane hydrate from oil wells and removing impurities. We are to take the lead on extraction from permafrost. They have invited you to share their secure facilities on the Island of Hokkaido. Right now, they need some help on developing adequate backflow valves to keep the methane in check, and also on recapturing impurities for commercial use. They've got excellent engineering support and a fully equipped prototype machine shop."

"Great!" said Peter, looking at Vanessa. "Ivan, Vanessa and I'd love to set up a whole Arctic town running on methane hydrate!" Vanessa nodded and smiled broadly in agreement.

Robert looked serious. "I love that idea too. But we've lost some of our key members. How do we handle that?"

"We'll replace them, somehow."

Hayden said, "I guess Peter and I could contribute to developing the backflow valves and impurity separation. Does that mean we might get to go to Japan?"

"Me too," said Vanessa. "I would love to assist in the valve and safety engineering."

"Yes. But, your knowledge is precious. We're not going to put everyone in the same place at once, nor will you all travel on the same aircraft. Right now, we're thinking it may be best to accept the Russian president's offer of "Mayberry" for half the team and the other half would go to Japan. Actually, the two locations are not too far apart, a few hours by jet, so there can be visits as well as electronic linkage."

This evoked various comments and side discussions around the room. Eventually, Stephanie said, "The Willard Institute has treated me well for the past ten years. I'll be delighted to join the team."

This was echoed by Hayden who said, "That goes for me too. This could be a lot of hard work but also a lot of fun."

Peter spoke up, "Well, I was looking for a change in life. You know, time to explore new things and set new goals. I think I've found it! I'm interested – provided salary and benefits are good." All the others agreed. "You know though, deep down I'm a research scientist who enjoys pure research but I accept that it has to be funded, and that means transferring the technology from pure research into applied. We've done a lot of research on global warming and the delicate Arctic environment. I wish we could push this more as well."

"I understand. The Willard institute will arrange for the team to present a paper to the United Nations in two years' time on your global warming issues and discoveries, if that will help. We will supplement some ongoing assistance for you to carry on your global warming research but commercialization must be the priority.

Norma said, "I'm sure we would all look forward to that."

"Thank you, all of you. We'll spend the next three or four days in planning. I'll meet individually with Marie and Carl to settle remuneration packages. But for the researchers, you will all get the same salary, revenue sharing and benefits package so we may as well go over that. I'd like to get you all to sign off on your contracts before the end of this session." She opened her briefcase and handed out a contract copy to each of the researchers, including Vanessa, then said, "While you are reading and discussing that, let me meet with Carl and Marie to get them started refining TORs and thinking of salaries."

By the end of the day, Thelma had recruited her team. Signed, sealed and committed.

She ended the session by saying, "Great! We've accomplished a lot today. Welcome aboard! The race is on! In the next few days, we'll develop a plan. Let's teach Big Oil a lesson!"

Charlie poked his head into the room. "Time for the evening fishery!" he declared. "Who's gonna catch the biggest one? How about a prize pot, fifty dollars each?"

Chapter 19

True to Sanford's prediction, it didn't take long for members of the Canadian news media to dig into the facts behind the Canadian government's cancellation of the methane hydrate research project. Like terriers with a rat, he thought, they won't let go. The story unfolded, verifying that the Canadian government cancelled the funding abruptly after the new technology proved successful. Questions were asked. Why did the Japanese consider the breakthrough so valuable and why did the Canadian government not? Yet the deaths of the researchers suggested much more intrigue.

This was headline news in the national media for a few days and the political opposition parties of the federal government were drawn into the fray, homing in on the opportunity to embarrass the politicians in power by raising the issue in Question Period in the House of Commons. Sanford considered this Phase One. The Prime Minister (PM) and his Unity Party were beginning to be publicly embarrassed.

The PM tried to pass over the issue in Question Period, stating, "We have an abundance of natural gas and see no need to further invest in methane hydrate research." And, "We see no connection in the deaths of the scientists." This was met with uproar both in the House and in the media.

The structure of the Canadian government corresponds closely to the British system, with members elected from electoral ridings by public vote for the Parliament of the House of Commons. A Prime Minister is chosen from the elected Members of Parliament (MPs) by the political party in power – currently the Unity Party led by Eugene Rogers. Similarly, there is an "upper body of sober thought" in the form of a Senate, which parallels the British House of Lords and the American Senate but is unique as senators are appointed by the political party in power when vacancies arise. Once members of the House of Commons pass a bill, it is reviewed by the Senate who may either endorse the bill or return it to the House of Commons for more debate. At that point, the Bill may be reworked and passed back to the Senate for approval or simply approved by the House. Often, standing committees consist of a mix of senators and elected Members of Parliament.

In the Canadian system, senators may remain in office until the compulsory retirement age of seventy-five (unless convicted of a serious criminal offense). The senators are from a mixture of political parties stemming from whichever party was in power when a vacancy opened. In theory, the senators are representatives of the individual provinces and territories based on a long-established quota of seats. To be appointed for a representative seat, a candidate must be a resident of that province or territory in which there is a vacancy. Most senators earned the appointment either as a reward for their proven ability in and dedication to advancing the public good in their province or territory, or for their significant contribution to advancing the political party or ability to blackmail the leadership. As it is the political party currently in power that appoints the senator, it is most likely that the candidate will be loyal to that party. Most are hardworking, taking the role of the Senate seriously, but some are in it only for themselves, viewing their appointment as a reward for services rendered and an opportunity for enrichment.

Similar to the British parliamentary system, when in session, the House of Commons holds a daily question period in which members of the opposition question the actions of the party in power and the affairs of government. The game tends to be "ask embarrassing questions and get it on the record." This may make headlines and draw public attention to the faults of the government and leadership by the party in power with a view to changing the government during the next election. Or it may actually point out inequities and push for remedies in governance. The impression of the first-time visitor to the gallery of the House during Question Period is often of bad-mannered petty children. Regardless of the childlike behavior, the Question Period has benefits – especially in highlighting a problem and demanding action.

Phase Two of Sanford's plan was to expose the senators who convinced the Prime Minister to cancel the research funding. Over the space of a couple of days in Question Period where the Prime Minister obtusely answered or sidestepped most questions concerning the importance of the research and the deaths, the opposition started to prod deeper, showing proof that the cancellation originated in the PMO and from an action by the Prime Minister. It scored national news headline points with the question, "Would the Prime Minister please explain why he acceded to the request by Senators John Marshall, Christine Lamont and Manfried Rule to immediately cancel the methane hydrate research funding by direct order from the Office of the Prime Minister, signed by the Prime Minister, and to demand surrender of all research papers, demand their silence and forbid further research stemming from the findings of the researchers?"

The PM reiterated that there was an abundance of oil and gas, thus no need for the methane hydrate research to continue.

Somehow, the opposition member who asked that question had obtained irrefutable proof, later released to the media, of the senators requesting the order. The next question caused further uproar. "Is the Prime Minister not aware that Senator Marshall serves as a member of the board of directors of Double A Oil Company, one of the largest in the world, and is paid a director's fee by Double A Oil Company of over one point three million dollars a year? Is not Double A Oil Company a large corporate donor to your political party and even to your own political campaign? Is this not a blatant conflict of interest and an attempt to favor the interests of the oil industry by cancelling the research?"

After the PM spent a few moments sidestepping with a nonsense answer, another opposition member rose, waiving a piece of paper and asked, "Is not Senator Lamont a former lobbyist for the oil industry and has she not delivered more than fifty million dollars in donations from the oil industry to your party in the past year? Does she not also sit on the board of directors of one or more oil companies for which she is receiving over a million dollars a year? Is this not a blatant conflict of interest?"

After much repetition of the question and the presentation of documentation, the PM had to admit this was correct, that Senator Lamont had been a lobbyist for the oil industry before being appointed to the Senate but that he had no information at hand on party donations although he did concede that she was actively sought out as a speaker at fund-raising events for the Unity party. He ignored the point about conflict of interest.

101

Another opposition member jumped up and said, "Cause and effect suggest that the oil industry and, in turn, Senators Marshall, Lamont and Rule need to be investigated not only for complicity to end the research funding but also in the deaths of some of the researchers. Will the Prime Minister initiate this action?"

The PM stated he felt there was just a string of coincidence in the deaths and that it was highly improper to infer involvement by the honorable senators or the oil industry, but after much further badgering was forced to concede that the deaths should be investigated by the RCMP and that they would be ordered to do so. This prompted another member of the opposition to stand and ask, "If you are involving the RCMP, it must be noted that Senator Rule, one of the three who approached you to stop the research funding, is on the oversight committee for the RCMP. The good Senator is also on the Board of Directors of ZA Oil, Pan European Oil and Asian Oil, earning in total over five million dollars a year for his directorships. Is this not a conflict of interest? And, what will the PM do about it?"

The PM stated that he felt the senator was very honorable and would step down from the oversight committee if requested but that he did not see the need. The PM was then badgered by further demands that he require the honorable senator to step down from the oversight committee. He refused. The opposition requested the PM strike an unbiased committee to review the perceived conflicts of interest. This was refused. The media had a field day.

A few days later, Sanford Crosley and Hector Skog met in Hector's office. After greetings and some small talk, Hector said, "I see the Prime Minister is still on the hot seat. Looks as if you choreographed things very well."

"We really didn't have to do much – just point some very eager reporters with close ties to the opposition parties in the right directions. It certainly is an uproar. The opposition is trying to pull the government down. Canadian public opinion of their government is at its lowest point in decades. There's beginning to be serious questioning as to why senators are allowed to have conflicts of interest like serving on a board of directors of a large corporation while they're in the senate. And why the public has no say in the appointment of senators."

"Do you think it may lead to one or all of the senators resigning?"

"Hard to say. Right now, they're all calling in personal markers and fighting back. Each has met with the Unity Party leadership, including the Prime Minister and his Chief of Staff and the head of the Unity Party Association. The deaths came as quite a shock to all. They all readily admit to dealing with the oil industry lobbyists and thought the cancellation of the research was a simple favor for a big donor, but they didn't suspect anyone would die as well. One is very afraid of the power of big oil as evidenced by the deaths of the researchers. One is mad at being compromised and the other is attacking by threatening to reveal some party secrets that could hurt in the next election."

"Interesting summation. How did you learn all this?"

"Off the record. I'll just say the walls in Ottawa have ears and we have a lot of friends. Plus, we have some interesting phone taps."

"Phone taps? Of course!"

"Yes. We've unearthed a connection to the Global Association of Refiners and Petroleum Producers. Looks as if the association paid the senators quite well for delivering the cancellation of the research project. Senator Christine Lamont is thoroughly afraid of them right now but she did accept an additional sum of US$100,000 to one of her offshore personal bank accounts as payment to keep quiet. We've found the bank transfer and had a good peek into her finances worldwide. Senator Manfried Rule also was in contact with the association and accepted a donation of US$100,000 to one of his offshore personal bank accounts to keep quiet. We've also had a peek into his finances – very interesting. Senator John Marshall was offered a similar deal, and his finances are very interesting, but he's much more aggressive. He's threatening the PM and the Unity Party leadership to reveal some incriminating stuff if they don't protect him. They've already approached him to resign from the Senate but he's asking for five million dollars, an ambassadorship to a major location and a pension in consideration.

He's also gone back to the oil producers association demanding more – currently ten million dollars – because of the murders."

Sanford pulled out his iPad. "Here's a portion of what we overheard between Marshall and a group on a speaker phone at the Association of Oil Producers headquarters in Curacao."

Marshall was speaking loudly. *"Listen closely, you assholes. I did your bidding and got the research cancelled and buried the findings – at least from the Canadian side – as requested. You have complicated the issue with murder and attempted murder of the researchers – three killed in Canada and one so clumsily done it was instantly recognized as not an accident. I didn't bargain for that. It's going to cost you more than the paltry hundred grand. I expect to see you add ten million US dollars to my Grand Cayman account within the next ninety-six hours if you want my continued goodwill. If not, you're going to see some hellish problems related to future drilling rights, environmental assessments, aboriginal agreements and oil transportation in Canada. No ifs, ands or buts. Good-bye."*

Hector said, "No remorse with that guy! His phone conversation was right out in the open? No scrambler?"

"Nope! He acts as if he's untouchable. You should hear him talking back to the Prime Minister and the Chief of Staff." He pulled up another conversation on the iPad and played it. *"Don't talk to me about conflict of interest! There's nothing in the rules saying I can't receive money as a member of a Board of Directors while serving as a Senator. I'll not resign from the Senate. It'll take a scandal to do that and I'll pull you all down with me if it comes to that."*

"How much cash would you want if the party paid you to resign?"

"At least five million plus the usual senate pension... And an ambassadorship to London."

"That's too rich."

"And don't give me this shit about signing the order to rescind the research funding. The party got a five million dollar donation and you two split a million that was sent to your offshore accounts in

Mauritius. That's just good business. It's obvious "big oil" got a little carried away trying to eradicate the researchers. That's not our fault. Mind you, we could make a few dollars by putting a cap on the murder investigations."

The PM's voice: *"That's going a bit far, screwing with the judiciary. You've attracted a lot of attention. We've got to do something about the perceived conflict of interest."*

"I'll resign from my directorships, if that'll satisfy you. But then that should be applied to all Senators then."

"Right, we can bury a study toward that end in a committee for at least a year. That's a way to shelve it for now. In the meantime, we've got damage control to worry about."

Hector said, "Wow! At least we know who's behind all this."

"Right. The Global Association of Refiners and Petroleum Producers is headquartered in Curacao. It has a branch office in Calgary. One also in Galveston, of course. We've taken an interest in telecommunications in and out of their Curacao, Galveston and Calgary offices but it's a bit early."

"The problem will be in proving that the Global Association of Refiners and Petroleum Producers commissioned murder and sabotage."

"Not easy. Especially when we're dealing with multiple countries, police forces etc. Our Japanese friends may be able to build a case eventually. We're not close to it in Canada or the USA. We can move things along a bit, though. I'd like to see the pressure on the PMO continue. Perhaps some investigative journalism types could be encouraged."

"Please don't tell me how you'll do that."

Chapter 20

The expertise of Peter, Vanessa and Hayden had been requested by Professor Iawama. The Japanese team was well along in their ramp-up to a full-scale test of their extraction technology but had encountered some difficulties. The rest of the team flew directly to Russia's "Mayberry." All were to rendezvous eventually in Mayberry to complete a prototype of a system to fuel an entire Arctic village and to produce a joint paper for presentation to the United Nations Conference on Global Warming planned for two years hence. Once the development work was completed, they would move north to a remote northern village to test the prototype.

In the late afternoon, the unmarked Challenger jet landed at Sapporo's Chitose air base and was guided into a large hangar in a remote part of the airfield. When Peter, Vanessa and Hayden deplaned, they were greeted by Professor Fred Iawama and a small welcoming committee of a few of the Japanese team members and a lovely young lady. After bows, hugs and handshakes, Professor Iawama introduced the young lady. "Peter, Hayden and Vanessa, permit me to introduce Ms. Ikumi Watanabe."

Ikumi was dressed in a white short-sleeved blouse, pearl necklace, tight navy blue skirt and matching shoes which complemented her slim athletic figure on a five foot five inch, one hundred twenty pound frame. Her long hair was in a ponytail. She took a step forward and made a deep bow. "It is a great pleasure to be chosen to work with you. Iawama-san has told me a great deal about you."

Iawama-san went on. "As I have had the privilege of studying and working in North America, I appreciate the difference in our cultures and the potential for culture shock if you are new to Japan. In working with others from North America who have come to Japan, I have found it is beneficial to have someone to guide you in the differences so that you may recognize and enjoy the new experiences you will encounter. I hope you don't mind, but I have lumped both Canada and the USA together as generally one culture – but I am well aware of the difference between them and of local nuances such as between French and English and East and West in Canada and North and South and East and West in America. After all, I earned a degree in Texas and another in New York State – talk about contrast!"

Peter spoke up. "Add in Russian culture for Vanessa. Mind you, she has become immersed in American culture."

"Yes, I know. One thing I've learned about first-time visitors to Japan: one can study the culture at a distance in preparation but the differences still hit you hard upon arrival. We have learned that orientation is best upon the first weeks of arrival. That is where Ms. Watanabe comes in. She is expert in cross-cultural nuances and has studied in America and Canada. She is our cross-cultural guru, you can say. She will be working with you and is also assigned to work with your Japanese counterparts and others you will encounter so that we may better bond as a team. She is also a full professor at our university. We have seconded her for this project with the permission of the Prime Minister. You see, one of her specialties is American slang and she is on retainer by the PMO to be a special interpreter to the PM and ministers when serious negotiations or meetings take place with North Americans. She helps to properly explain the true meaning of some slang comments. You know, like what does "nerd" or "awesome" mean?"

Hayden, noting that there was no wedding band visible, also took in her beauty and swimmer's broad shoulders, and tried to figure out her approximate age. Looking directly into her eyes, he said, "We are truly honored to have such assistance." This was met by a bow and a blush from Ikumi.

Peter and Vanessa exchanged knowing glances, silently conveying their opinion that Hayden was awestruck. Iawama-san put his hand to his lips trying to hide a tight smile. Except for Iawama-san and Ikumi, the rest of the welcoming committee took their leave. Fred Iawama noted that the full team would be meeting tomorrow at the lab and would have dinner together the next evening. When they got in the van that would take them to their new accommodations, a nonverbal conspiracy among Peter, Vanessa and Fred ensured that Hayden and Ikumi sat beside each other. Hayden, looking out, noticed a police motorcycle escort and two more vans with blacked-out windows, one in front and one behind them.

In the van, Ikumi pulled some paperback books out of her briefcase and handed one each to Peter, Vanessa and Hayden. Hayden noted the cover: *Cultural Differences Japan – A Guide for Visitors by I. Watanabe.* "Is this homework?" he asked.

Ikumi bowed slightly. "Hi! Oh, sorry, yes. That is for our meeting tomorrow morning. It would be nice if you read the first few chapters. However, I must review or introduce you to a few things now, before we arrive at the accommodation and during this evening." She handed each a business card bearing her name and phone numbers and handed each a cell phone and charger. "First, you can reach me any time on that cell number. Second, there are few of us Japanese who speak English, so it will help if you learn and use some everyday Japanese phrases and learn to recognize some signage. We have a high state of security on this project and many of the upper level security personnel are fluent in English. All of your bodyguards are, but few others are fluent. We Japanese admire someone attempting our language."

Peter said. "Bodyguards?"

"Yes. They will accompany you everywhere. One will be with each of you but there will also be others helping. You are being housed in the university's VIP cottage and it will be well secured. Now, I must explain a bit about the cultural differences for life in the cottage and in case you get a chance to visit a Japanese home. First of all, you will each have a bedroom to yourselves, if you wish. Perhaps Peter and Vanessa wish to share a room?"

A nod from Peter and Vanessa.

"The VIP cottage is partly in Japanese Traditional Style. The bedrooms are Tatami rooms, meaning you sleep on soft comforters on tatami reed mats on the floor and the rooms double as living rooms when the sleeping mats are put away. Bathrooms are communal – that is, not ensuite – so you will have to walk a short distance down the hall to separate rooms for the bath and the toilet and vanity. There are two of each and I will show them to you when we arrive. As the bedroom walls are also made of woven reed, noise travels and you are expected to keep your voices down. We never wear shoes in the house but switch to slippers. We tend also to leave our slippers in front of the bedroom door and enter the tatami room barefoot. That also shows others the room is occupied. That goes for the toilet as well. You will find a pair of "happy face" or "hello kitty" slippers in front of the closed door of a toilet. This means it is not occupied. You switch slippers, leaving yours in front of the door showing others the toilet is occupied. Each toilet is Modern Japan – with electronic dials for seat heat, douche, warm air and flushes. You will find instructions in English, Japanese and other languages in a magazine rack behind the door. You keep the toilet door closed when it is not in use. There are nightlights in the halls and in your rooms.

"The bath is another story. First, we expect everyone to bathe daily. We fill the bath once an evening with very hot water that is not to be diluted, as others may use the same water."

"What?" Peter frowned. Vanessa looked puzzled.

"Yes. The bath is not to be polluted with soap either. We sit on the stool in a corner of the bathroom and wash thoroughly with a shower and soap, then rinse off before entering the tub. There is a drain in the middle of the floor to take the water. When we are clean we may enter the bath for a hot soak. We do this nightly as the heat helps us sleep. In a Japanese household, the most senior person gets first bath and we take turns by seniority. Our guests go first."

Peter looked at Vanessa and smiled. "This will be fun! Does it matter how many are in the bathroom?" Peter teased.

"As many as you like. We are not modest about nudity indoors. In fact, there are many public bathhouses in Japan. Ah, we're arriving! I'll show and explain more when we're inside."

Hayden, looking deep into Ikumi's eyes said, "Will you guide us through all this?"

Blushing slightly and bowing her head but smiling with a twinkle in her eyes, Ikumi responded, "Yes, I'll ensure you are comfortable."

When they got out of the van, Hayden took Iawama-san aside. "Fred, she's gorgeous. What's her status? Is she married? Tied to anyone?"

Smiling, Fred Iawama turned to Hayden. "Ah, I thought she would catch your attention! No, she's divorced from a failed marriage while she was in grad school at Syracuse, New York getting her PhD. She's thirty-four, no children. She's heterosexual and no current love interests. You owe me one, bro!"

"I'll say!"

"As a good friend, I should warn you. We have a saying that a good Japanese woman is steel wrapped in silk. They take classes in high school on how to manage the man but let him think he's the boss."

"This should be fun!"

That evening, Ikumi led the group through a traditional Japanese dinner of miso soup, sushi and sashimi, and teriyaki pork with noodles and snow peas, accompanied with hot saké, beer and green tea. She continued her orientation lessons on the finer side of Japanese culture. Saké should only be poured for someone else, never for yourself. All were expected to be skilled with chopsticks. One should never ask what they are eating. It was a complement to slurp your soup.

Dinner ended around ten o'clock with a green-tea-flavored sherbet dessert and a twenty- year-old Suntori sipping whisky. Upon pouring the whisky into small shot cups, Ikumi said, "We tend to end our more formal dinners with a hard liquor for the men. At the end of your main course, there should always be some food left on your plate or your host will fear they haven't fed you enough. For drinks, ladies tend more to seek warm saké or a robust green tea. Men tend to favor beer, whisky or saké. But wines have become increasingly popular. In fact, Japanese investors have more acreage in wine grapes growing in China than grape production in all France. This twenty-year-old whisky is our imitation of Scotch. I'm sure you'll find it smooth." All agreed it was.

"Now, it is time for the evening bath ritual. You'll find kimonos and bath towels in your rooms. The bathroom is off from the main living room in this house so we can gather there first, once you have changed. There's always hot tea in the kitchen or dining room for those waiting their turn in the bathroom." They all adjourned to their rooms and returned in kimonos. Hayden was surprised that Ikumi had also changed into a kimono.

"The tub is filled with very hot water. Please don't add water to cool it. You'll just have to get used to the hot temperature. The wash station is immediately to your right inside the door – you'll see the plastic stool by the flexible shower with the taps at knee level. Soap is on a ledge beside the taps. Remember to wash off the soap well before entering the bath. Peter and Vanessa, you can go first."

After about twenty minutes, Peter and Vanessa emerged, kimono-clad. Pointing to his exposed calves, Peter exclaimed, "Look at me! I'm a lobster! Boy, that bath's hot!" A smiling Vanessa said, "But it was fun!" They said goodnight and went off to their room, leaving Ikumi with Hayden. Half bowing but looking him in the eyes, she gave him a coy look. "Are you ready?"

"I'm very nervous."

"I'll help you if you'll scrub my back." Hayden was in lust-filled shock and could hardly speak. She took him by the hand and led him into the bathroom.

She also led him back to his tatami room and spent the night with him, shocking Hayden with her gentleness and skill. After their first go-round, Ikumi snuggled into Hayden and said, "Ah, thank you. Thank you. It's been a long, long time. Thank you for the pleasure." Hayden hugged her tight and said, "The pleasure was all mine!"

Between testing their sexual compatibility and pillow talk about their histories and interests, they didn't get much sleep. Hayden learned that Ikumi had been an athlete in her youth, entering university on a competitive swimming scholarship, and that she had been considered a tomboy by Japanese standards – too liberated for most Japanese men who tended toward chauvinism. They found mutual interests in jazz, gourmet cooking, hiking and outdoor sports such as fishing, sailing, skiing and scuba diving.

"Hayden, in the Japanese society, marriages are often arranged and we marry fairly young. It's difficult for a divorced woman to meet eligible men. I'm labeled what is translated as "a high-miss" –

single and older and probably set in her ways. It's hard for a single woman my age to get sexual satisfaction – not like the men who can go alone to massage parlors. Oh, that's a sign recognition lesson for you, by the way. The massage parlors that provide sexual services have a sign showing a purple heart with an arrow through it."

"I hope I never have need for that."

By breakfast, lust had been overcome by enchantment and Hayden was swearing that he would never let her go.

Mayberry

Another Challenger jet transported Stephanie, Norma and Carl, Marie and Robert and Isabella the puppy to "Mayberry" where they were met on the tarmac of the airport by Ivan, now walking with a cane, and a woman he introduced as Una Yakodev, the mayor, who was accompanied by her Chief of Security, Uri Sawatsky. Ivan said he had been recovering well and that his doctor felt he could return to work on a limited schedule.

In the van on the way into town, after some small talk about the climate, Uri said. "You'll find our village very secure. It won't be obvious, but you'll have round-the-clock protection."

"Yes," said Una. "You'll also find we strive to duplicate all aspects of a typical American small town, say a university town, so you should find all the comforts of home. We have all the activities and foods you can expect in America. Marie and Robert, you'll also find a pet store, pet groomer, a vet and pet-friendly places. You're welcome to meet and socialize with your neighbors but we ask you not to talk about your project or your backgrounds or pry into theirs.

"Now, you have a choice of accommodations. I understand Robert and Marie, you lived in a condo in Quebec and that Carl and Norma had a house in a suburb of Victoria. Do you want a condo or would you like a more suburban detached or semi-detached house? We'll drive by some available properties and you can decide. Stephanie, you're free also to choose what you want. I gather you had an apartment before but you may want to try a condo or house?"

"You know, I'd like to try a house. I'd love to start a flower garden, maybe even grow some veggies. Maybe get a cat for company."

After an hour, they had selected and moved their luggage into adjoining 1970s rancher-style bungalows, fully furnished, with manicured lawns and shrubbery, each with fenced back yards and situated in a cul-de-sac which Una said was a ten-minute walk to the Center for Development campus where they would have office and lab facilities. Ivan said it was about a fifteen-minute walk to his apartment.

Una took Marie, Stephanie and Norma to the supermarket where they stocked up on groceries while Ivan took Isabella for a walk and played fetch with her. Uri gave the men an orientation to the houses and reviewed a directory of social activities, local emergency services numbers, garbage collection days, newspaper and magazine subscriptions, lawn care and building maintenance service, and how to get around town by bus, bike and golf cart. Credit and debit cards were provided and bank accounts opened with a draft that the Willard Institute had provided for the purpose. When evening descended, Ivan's friend Tina joined them after she got off work. They agreed dinner would be at Norma and Carl's place and Uri ordered in pizza.

At dinner, a few toasts were made with red wine from Georgia, beer and Pepsi. Uri noted that toasts in quantity were more a Russian tradition than American, but were acceptable in Mayberry among good company. After the toasts, Una asked an open question: "You've been here ever so briefly, but what do you think of our village so far?"

Robert, slipping a piece of pizza crust under the table as a treat for Isabella and holding a glass of red wine in the other hand said, "For me, I'm most truly impressed! We could be in one of many places in North America, both in Canada or the USA. This is very comfortable. I'm looking forward to discovering our work environment and meeting our neighbors."

"So am I!" said Norma. Stephanie, Carl and Marie nodded agreement.

Stephanie said, "I'm a single woman. I hope there'll be opportunity here to meet single men and women my age?"

Uri said, "I don't think you'll have any problem. In addition to the campus, with a large population, there's a great community center with dance club, tennis club, theatre club, swim pool and sauna, gym and fitness club, just to name a few – lots of social activities. There's a great bridge club and I understand you play bridge. I'd be pleased to introduce you and be your first partner. And you've got to meet the neighbors. They're all very sociable."

Ivan said, "Tomorrow's soon enough for that. I've helped set up the lab and have all the computers up and running. In fact, I've started some of our new assistants building computer simulations for extracting permafrost-embedded methane hydrate, based on my research and the materials you forwarded. I'm excited that we have this opportunity to capture methane hydrate to support habitation in the Arctic."

"Right now though, it's getting late and you need some rest," Una commented. "Uri will pick you up in the morning, say, eight o clock?" All nodded. "Ivan, I can see you're fading. It's time for Tina to get you home to bed."

Chapter 21

Paddy took the call in his office on the penthouse floor of the Calgary business tower housing the headquarters of Extraction Inc. Chairman Van der Zalm was terse. "Be down here for a meeting at nine a.m. Tuesday." It was barely two days away, but Paddy agreed. He had been half expecting a call like that. He called in his administrative assistant and ordered her to make the travel arrangements. Next day, he was on his way business class to Curacao.

Curacao
When Paddy arrived on the executive floor of the oil industry association's headquarters, a receptionist immediately escorted him into the boardroom where ten men were seated. Conversation stopped when he entered. Chairman Van der Zalm did not stand up from his seat at the head of the table or offer to shake his hand, but spoke in clipped tones. "Gentlemen, most of you know Mr. West of Extraction Inc." He motioned to Paddy to take an empty seat at the other end of the table. Paddy recognized most of the men as CEOs or presidents of some of the largest oil and gas companies in the world – all customers of Extraction Inc.

After Paddy was seated, Chairman Van der Zalm continued. "The political situation in Canada is getting a little tense for our best interests. Regrettably, it was caused by our agreed policy to suppress the methane hydrate technological advancement. We were successful in getting the Canadian government to drop their funding and curtail further research. This has not been possible in Russia, Japan or the USA, although our lobbyists have successfully prevented direct funding by the American government. The Japanese government fully endorses the technology development as a way to gain energy independence, so we have no influence there. Russia is questionable and we are still working on that but, as you know, there is friction between the political leadership and the oil oligarchs. Reasoning that a more expedient route may be to remove the knowledge base, we contracted for a special effort by Extraction Inc. to remove or set back the knowledge base but that has been less than satisfactory."

115

"Less than satisfactory indeed!" roared the CEO of Mega Oil, a Dutch-Anglo company. "Very sloppy! You could get away with that in India, Indonesia, Venezuela or Nigeria but not in North America or Japan – nor even the new Russia. You were very sloppy in Newfoundland."

"What do you have to say for yourself, Mr. West?"

"Gentlemen. I offer my most profuse apologies for the Newfoundland incident. We expedited the contract through a local contractor who turned out to be not very experienced. Murder and attempted murder is very uncommon there – the lowest by far in all of Canada. We contracted a local, as an outsider would have stood out and time was of the essence. Unfortunately, the police crime investigation team were very capable and identified that brakes were tampered with. This was inexcusable. I'm sorry."

"You killed an FBI agent in Anchorage," commented the president of an oil company with extensive drilling in Alaska.

"But succeeded in destroying the lab and research notes and injuring the scientist, which has probably bought a year's delay."

"Not good enough. She can duplicate her research."

"You asked for a significant delay, and you got it. Same for Japan. We contracted with their mafia, the Yakusa out of Ikebukeru Ward of Tokyo, who were effective in destroying the lab at the University of Sapporo and immobilizing one of the key researchers. Same for Russia. Their researcher will be out of operation for at least six to eight months. The four most important to the advancement of the technology are dead except for those on the Japanese side. It will take many months, maybe a couple of years, to catch up and advance their technology transfer if they had the funding to do so – and you've cut off many of the potential funding avenues. Next, we're planning to delay the Japanese by sabotaging the test production platform they're building."

Chairman Van der Zalm spoke up. "May I remind all of you we wanted the delay for three reasons: one, to continue our profitability with the status quo as long as possible; two, to be the first to tie up the technology either with our own patents or purchasing; and three, to control all that develops as well as to secure significant fields of methane hydrate. We are nearing a breakthrough on our own research – specifically for controlling methane hydrate encountered in drilling and extraction, and we may be able to beat the Japanese to the patent registry. Gentlemen, although, as you say, it is "messy," we are still heading in the right direction."

Nods from all around the table.

"Let's not attract any more attention, if you please," said the CEO of Mega Oil. "No more messiness."

The chairman spoke. "Let's return to the Canadian situation. It looks as if Senator John Marshall has become a liability. He's threatening the Prime Minister and his party and us. Currently, he's demanding a ransom of some ten million dollars from us."

"What's the downside if we discontinue his services?" asked the CEO from a large oil company dominating much of the west of America.

"The other two senators we have on our payroll are still compliant. Although Marshall often took the lead on things, they are still good resources and, I am confident we can recruit others."

"I presume removing Senator Marshall may be met with some relief by the Prime Minister and his people?"

"Undoubtedly. He has become too arrogant for all – and a liability."

"Are we in agreement to dispense with the services of Senator John Marshall?" There was a unanimous show of hands from the members.

The meeting ended for a lunch break with the chairman holding back Paddy. They pulled two chairs together at the table and the chairman said: "You won't be needed in the meetings after lunch and you will not be joining us for lunch. They're on to some economic reviews and planning. You can head on home. I have to agree with everyone, Paddy. Your approach to the scientists has been a bit sloppy and you've got to do better."

"Yes, sir."

"Maybe you can prove your capability with Senator Marshall."

"Is this a sanction?"

"Yes. But it must be very clean. No traces."

"Let's discuss my fee."

Chapter 22

Senator John Marshall was a weasel. Or, at least, that's what his three ex-wives thought of him. He almost looked the part. He stood five foot three, a thin, one hundred thirty pounds, with small hands and stubby fingers. He proudly sported a Hitler-like moustache on a narrow angular face, had sunken cheeks, a pock-marked face, and brown penetrating eyes which were too close together. His teeth had been perfected by one of the best orthodontists, and his straight brown hair was parted on the left side, tinted at the best salon in Ottawa, and impeccably cut and trimmed weekly on Thursdays, at a one p.m. standing appointment paid if he showed or not. His nails were manicured at the same salon. He completed his image with custom-tailored suits and shirts, silk socks, Gucci black loafer shoes, always a blue tie and lapel handkerchief with his political party's Unity monogram. He was seventy years old and alone, with no children. All his siblings had predeceased him. He hated pets. In fact, he hated everybody, it seemed. One acquaintance in the party's executive said of him, "Better to have him working for you or the conniving bastard will get you good."

He lived by the motto: *Knowledge is Power.* From his early childhood he was a tattletale and an eavesdropper, finding great delight in telling his parents of the misdeeds of his siblings or holding a sibling to ransom for promising not to tell. He had always been bright and excelled in school, getting a law degree and entering the corporate litigation realm. He would do anything to win and had absolutely no conscience. As he matured, he perfected the arts of information mining, manipulation and blackmail. He became an excellent public speaker renowned for his ability to feed off and entertain an audience, especially a politically partisan one, playing back to them what they wanted to hear and sharing just a bit of innocuous "insider information."

Ottawa, 11 p.m.

John Marshall was savvy enough not to drink and drive. The thousand-dollar-a-plate fundraising dinner across the river in Hull, Quebec had been a routine affair, coddling some of Canada's industrial elite and raising significant funding for the party. John

119

was the keynote speaker and he had delivered a crowd-pleasing speech. Proof of that was the speaker's fee, ten thousand dollars cash in an envelope in the left breast pocket of his suit which would soon be deposited in his wall safe and not declared to Canada Revenue. He had stayed after the dinner to network and had downed a good number of gin and tonics.

The taxi delivered him to his three-story townhouse in a luxurious suburb of Ottawa. Although feeling the alcohol, he easily navigated the keypad for the door entrance, disarmed the alarm system and climbed the first flight of stairs inside the front door to the main floor which consisted of an open layout living/dining room, kitchen, and two-piece bathroom. He went to the bar in the dining room area and poured a generous gin and tonic into a large cut-crystal glass, then went to the fridge and added some ice cubes from the automatic dispenser on the fridge door. He swirled the cubes in the drink for a few seconds then took a large gulp, devouring half the contents of the glass. He went back to the bar and added more gin, then swirled the glass and took a sip. He smiled and reflected to himself that it had indeed been a good evening, as the crowd enjoyed his speech and he had picked up some gossip while networking that he could soon use to his advantage. Glass in hand, he proceeded up his second flight of stairs to the next floor and went into his office, where he lifted a picture off the wall, an oil painting by a famous artist of people skating on the Gatineau River in winter. He opened the wall safe thus exposed, removed the envelope of cash from his breast pocket, opened it, thumbed the cash, and was just about to place it in the safe when it was snatched out of his hand as the intruder said, "Thank you!"

Stunned, John Marshall didn't move but said, "What the? Who're you?" As he spoke, he began to turn slowly to get a view of his adversary and came face to face with a large, youthful, tall man dressed in black slacks, brown polo shirt and black leather jacket. He saw the man had large hands encased in latex gloves (not a good sign, he thought), a large round face, bright blue eyes and sandy brownish crew-cut hair.

The man smiled as he pocketed the envelope and said, "I've cleaned out the rest of your money in the safe, photographed all your documents in there and copied your computer files. Thanks for the cash, looks like over three hundred thousand. But then, you won't be needing it."

"What do you mean?"

"Well sir, looks as if you've pushed some buttons and annoyed some very powerful people. You're out of here." As he was saying that, Paddy grabbed Marshall's head in his two large hands and quickly snapped Marshall's neck by a right twist and held him until he died. He picked up Marshall so that his feet were off the ground, walked with him over to the stairs and threw him down. The body tumbled against the wall and the bare wood stair treads to the landing. Paddy followed him down and repositioned the body to correctly place Marshall's neck between the stair tread and the wall, ensuring it was plausible that the neck had been broken in the fall. He then retraced his steps to the den, closing the safe and returning the covering picture, picking up a briefcase and Marshall's drink. He descended the stairs, dumping the drink in the sink, and depositing the glass in the dishwasher. After resetting the alarm system, he left the way he had entered, through the side door in the garage, casually strolling four blocks to his car.

After he reviewed the contents of Marshall's computer drives and the documents photographed from the safe and selecting to copy that which might be insurance for him, he would courier everything to Curaçao. He was pleased with his little bonus of the cash from the safe.

The body of Senator John Marshall was discovered by his housekeeper at eight a.m. the next day. Toxicology testing revealed that the Senator had been intoxicated well past twice the legal limit of impairment at the time of his accident. There was no sign of forced entry and the alarm had been set about the time of death. Investigators assumed the Senator had had the presence of mind to set his alarm before retiring and, as the injuries were similar to those sustainable in a fall down stairs and, as the investigators found no trace of foreign objects or residues not likely to be in the home, the forensic analysis team concluded that Senator John Marshall fell down his stairs.

Prime Minister Eugene Rogers was with John Roberts, his Chief of Staff, when he learned about Senator Marshall's demise. The PM put down the phone, gave John a summary and commented privately, "That's a relief. Although he was a great fundraiser for the party, he was quite dysfunctional recently. That methane hydrate thing brought us a lot of bad press. At least we don't have to force his resignation from the Senate."

That sense of relief lasted only a few seconds until a frowning John Roberts said, "That S.O.B. will have covered his ass with all his secrets. I bet he has stuff stashed away in various spots to be revealed upon his demise. I think we'd better prepare for a load of scandals."

"No question about that. He got appointed to the Senate through threatening to expose kickbacks to the party and us on the replacement ice breakers contract. He showed us a copy of the documents he had in his possession. He threatened to use that and more if we tried to force him out of the Senate without a payoff. Yeah, we've got to track this down and get it before others unearth something and start using it."

"That's easier said than done! We have no idea how many secrets he has, who he coerced and how many people he left material with to be used in case of his demise."

"But we've got to try."

"It'll have to be turned over to the Unity Party leadership caucus. They'll have to commission someone."

"I'll pass it on."

"Time will tell. The police will have access to his computer and files – even his safe. What will they do if they come across some controversial stuff?"

"Generally, I think they know how to be discreet. That is, unless they have solid proof of a criminal act or acts. Something may surface to set them off on a blood hunt. However, we do control the RCMP by the oversight committee. Maybe we can claim the papers under the Government Secrets Act?"

"Yeah, but the City of Ottawa is under the Ottawa Police Service and above that is the OPP, the Ontario Provincial Police, before you get to the level of the RCMP. It's messy. The local Ottawa police have the case and, thankfully, they consider it a home accident."

"Best to let sleeping dogs lie for now."

"Agreed. If someone feels certain the death was not an accident, that may trigger the release of some deep shit."

Chapter 23

As usual on a weekday, Jack Haskell had been at his desk since seven a.m. He was a very fit, sixty-three-year-old on a firm six foot, one hundred ninety pound frame, who managed a forty-five minute workout routine at a nearby gym before work. Piercing blue eyes accentuated his handsome angular face and full head of silver hair. He was a "Westerner," having been born in Winnipeg, Manitoba, but had gone to law school in Toronto. He had worked his way up in Marshall, Garneau, Haskell, LeMonde, Saganaw and Jones to senior partner. His law specialty was corporate litigation – a craft he had successfully polished under the tutorship of John Marshall. He was happily married, a second marriage, to Jeanette, ten years younger, who had produced twin girls, now in university.

As the administrative partner of the law firm which partially bore his name, he welcomed the "quiet" time before his administrative assistant and legal secretary clocked in at nine. It gave him time to review the client log, plan his day, prioritize correspondence, prepare for meetings, and prepare the workload of chores and correspondence that he could hand off to his assistants. And, if time was left, he could plan how to bring in more business for the firm. He was well into his fourth cup of coffee at eight forty-five when Margaret (Peggy) LeMonde, another senior partner, barged into his office without knocking. "Jack, I just got a news tweet that Senator John Marshall was found dead in his condo!"

"What? I just saw him last night at the party fundraiser over in Hull. He was his normal self. What happened? Do you know?"

"Not much." Her cell phone chimed and she looked at the display as she fiddled with it. "Oh, here's a text from Marc Rouel. He's at the courthouse and the death was confirmed by a police lieutenant he knows well. Apparently John Marshall may have fallen down a flight of stairs in his condo. That's all they know right now."

"He was drinking pretty heavily last night, but that's normal for him. Maybe it was an accident."

"And if it wasn't an accident?"

"Yeah… Ah, let's not go there right now. Didn't we do his Last Will and Testament and aren't we executors for his estate?"

"Yes, I'm his executor. It's a pretty simple will as far as beneficiaries go, BUT with a twist. He left some envelopes of documents in trust with us not to be viewed until his death."

"I have a good hunch they're potentially explosive. I guess you get to open Pandora's Box. We also have the problem that he was a senior partner in this law firm and did bring in a lot of business. I'll call a meeting of the senior partners for five-thirty if that'll give you time to review the documents. Then you can bring us up to speed and we can strategize."

"OK, that should work. I'll be well clear of my last meeting by then." Peggy went to her office assistant and legal secretary, Donna Tremblay, who had a workspace guarding Peggy's office door, and asked her to retrieve John Marshall's Last Will and Testament and the box of John Marshall's documents that were in the main safe. Peggy was a career lawyer who, some said, was married to her job. She was tough and sharp and loved corporate litigation and mergers and acquisitions. At forty-five years old, she had been a senior partner for seven years and was considered one of John Marshall's protégés. She was currently carefully exploring a relationship with a girlfriend whom she had known since high school, but was still reeling from a failed partnership which she had left three years ago.

When Donna returned with the documents, Peggy noted she had a good hour before her first appointment and asked Donna to ensure there were no interruptions until then. She reviewed the will, noting it was straightforward with token amounts for the ex-wives and his housekeeper and the residue to go to the law school of his alma mater university in Vancouver. She then moved on to the file box of documents, noting there were over forty large and thick 9 x 12 manila envelopes numbered in sequence with the first bearing a label, *For my executor, Peggy LeMonde, and the senior partners of the firm. In the event of my death, this envelope must be opened first. John Marshall.* It also bore his signature beside his name. She noted he had sealed each envelope with a red legal seal upon which his signature crossed the seals, overlapping onto the paper of the envelopes. The rest of the envelopes were not only numbered but

125

had also been dated and bore single-word descriptions, such as *#3 1987-95 Aircraft.*

Peggy called Donna into her office and said, "I need you as a witness while I open some of these documents." Donna was a notary and could attest to Peggy's handling of the documents. Peggy picked up envelope #1. "Examine this to note the seal has not yet been broken. When I open it, note on the envelope when the seal was broken and that you were witness." After Donna carefully looked at the seal, Peggy opened the envelope, extracted the papers and keys it contained and read the letter, then said, "Oh, shit!"

Donna said: "Problems?"

"Could be." She then moved to the pile of envelopes, reading the labels and selected one. "I'm going to sample one of these envelopes. Here, note the seal and witness when it was broken." After Donna did that and handed the envelope back, Peggy opened it, read the contents and said, "Oh, double shit!"

"What is it?"

"Best you don't know – at least for now. Put all of this in my wall safe. But first let's put a new seal on this last envelope. I'll take the letter to the partner's meeting as it has instructions. Then, we've got to do the usual notifications to seal bank accounts, secure property, and such."

The senior partners assembled in the main boardroom promptly at five-thirty and Jack Haskell was quick to bring the meeting to order. "We all know the purpose of this meeting. John Marshall was found dead in his condo this morning. Not only was he a senior partner of this firm for many years, and we have to address restructuring of the partnership, but we, Peggy in particular, are executors and trustees of his estate. The restructuring of the firm is relatively straightforward as John was not active in the everyday clientele of the firm since he became a senator. We can leave the appointment of a replacement and/or additional partners to a later date and after due deliberation. The estate matter of John Marshall and his legacy must be addressed first. Peggy, can you elaborate on that side please?"

"Thanks Jack. As we all know, John Marshall was a firm believer in the motto: *Knowledge is Power.* We all know he gathered knowledge and used it to his advantage. We can't deny our firm benefited from this."

This was met by snickers, nods and muttered comments from the partners.

After a brief pause, Peggy continued. "As part of his will, John left us a legacy of over forty envelopes of documents. I have only opened one, envelope #38 which was currently dated and bore the label *Methane.* It contains detailed and substantiated proof that the Prime Minister's Office accepted a large amount of money from the oil industry to cancel methane hydrate research. John orchestrated the deal and kept all documentation on it. Apparently, there is also a stash of phone and meeting conversation recordings in a safety deposit box to which we have the key. In fact, there are many keys, presumably for stashes of more materials."

There was a murmur of comments from around the room ranging from "Oh shit!" to "That would be John!" to "Dyne-o-mite!"

One of the partners, Pierre Saganaw, spoke up. "Peggy, how far do these envelopes go back in dating?"

"The earliest one seems to be nineteen eighty-seven and is labeled *Aircraft.*"

"I presume it may have to do with the government at the time contracting to purchase aircraft?"

Randolph Jones, the most senior partner by age spoke up. "Most likely. I can remember some controversy over government aircraft purchases back then. I presume the envelopes will reveal dirt on all the governments elected since – probably something also on the parties in opposition, if I know how John Marshall operated."

"I told Peggy this morning that we were probably opening Pandora's Box with this. Looks as if it's true," commented Jack Haskell. "Next question, ladies and gentlemen, what do we do with this? Peggy, what else have you got?"

"Well, the Will seems pretty straightforward and airtight. The ex-wives and housekeeper get token consideration and the rest goes to his alma mater law school in Vancouver. From the executor and trustee point of view, we've arranged to secure his condo here in Ottawa and his principal residence, a penthouse apartment in Kamloops, B.C. which he seldom visited. Technically, he was appointed to the Senate to represent part of British Columbia and he had to have a quote "principal residence" there. We don't yet know what is to be found there but I've requested people in our affiliate law firm in Kamloops to secure the premises. They have added new security monitoring and have a reputable private security firm staking it out. I've done the same for the condo here. I've learned he had a safety deposit box and accounts at a bank in Kamloops and have notified them to freeze those. I've done the same for all other accounts and safety deposit boxes in Canada and USA and three offshore accounts – Antigua, Mauritius and the Channel Islands. Luckily, he gave us a list."

Marie Garneau said, "Sounds good."

"We have a problem. He left a note with instructions. Let me read it. The envelope has a label which says: *In the event of my death, this envelope must be opened first. John Marshall.*" She began to read.

Dear Peggy and Senior Partners of our firm:

You are reading this upon my death. First, I thank you all for the excellent comradeship that helped build such a successful law practice. For a great many years, the firm has been a significant part of my life. It is my hope that my death may provide a legacy for the firm as I have no next of kin – save for my ex-wives, and they deserve nothing.

As you know, I have spent my life trading in secrets, manipulating people to my advantage. I have done it well. I have made many enemies and there is no doubt many people will be happy with my death. Therein lies the possibility that my death may not be natural or accidental.

I am providing you with files of my "dirty secrets." They are not to be destroyed but entrusted to the senior administrative partner of

128

the firm to use for the good of the firm. If the firm disbands, they are to be placed in trust with a major trust company, not to be opened for fifty years, then placed in the archives of the law library of my alma mater.

In case my death proves not to be natural or accidental, I expect you to wreak havoc on the people responsible – that is if they are the subject of one of my files, as you will have sufficient ammunition to destroy them. In case of accidental or natural death, you may use the files discretely to benefit the firm.

May peace and prosperity be with you.

John Marshall

There was silence for a few moments, as everyone was lost in thought. Then Jack Haskell spoke. "I guess we've got to read some files. Peggy and I could do that and then prepare a summary of what we have."

"Agreed," said Randolph Jones. "The pressing questions: 1) Was John murdered and if so, who did it? and 2) If he was not murdered, should we use the material?"

"Let's learn the secrets first. Then decide. Perhaps they may lead to business opportunities?" mused Pierre Saganaw. "In the meantime, we must keep quiet about the papers, and recordings etc. And we must keep them secured. Maybe we should make backup copies? There may be others after these secrets. I wonder if John had duplicates?"

Jack Haskell frowned. "I'll bet he did. OK, we'll make backup copies to be secured off our premises. We'll try to trace any other materials and duplicates and we'll be very careful about security for his file, his premises, etc."

That weekend, Peggy and Jack met in one of the office conference rooms and began their task. They felt it best if they read the files together, making careful notation of when a document was unsealed, read and then resealed. They had elected to begin with the newest documents, working their way backward chronologically. Peggy picked up envelope #35 *China* and opened it while Jack noted the time in the log. Jack was preoccupied reading another file when Peggy said, "Holy shit! Jack, you're not going to believe this!"

"What's that, Peg? You find a big bomb?"

"Oh, yeah! And with well-documented transcripts too. There's also reference to more supporting files and tapes in one of the safety deposit boxes. This could involve billions of dollars. Shit, it's almost unbelievable!"

"You're keeping me in suspense."

"Here, you read it." She handed Jack the first ten pages she had read and continued her reading.

Halfway through the first ten pages, Jack said, "Whoa! Oh my God! Unbelievable! Did they follow through?"

"Looks as if they're still negotiating. But some dollar figures are being bantered about. First offer was one hundred billion US and that was countered with three trillion."

"Trillion?"

"Yeah. Trillion. The next offer was five hundred billion which was countered with one trillion." She continued reading for a few minutes. "That seems to be as far as we have documentation. It seems to be serious, as there's been mention of how much commission goes to the party coffers and how much goes to the PM and the boys in the PMO and what John Marshall's finder's fee would be. There's also some argument that the island wouldn't even be missed. And how to justify the sale to the Canadian people by making the government deficit-free for years, providing funds for infrastructure and social services improvement."

"Dynamite! You know, I'd say there's some money to be made with this knowledge – especially if it develops a little further or the PMO tries to screw us."

"Agree. But let's keep it in reserve. "

"I guess we'd better bone up on sovereignty law. We may be able to get a crack at some of the legal work."

"It will be interesting to see if our political leadership can sell the idea to the public."

"You know, the rake-off to those making the deal happen will be huge. Let's say ten percent of whatever they settle on will be under the table – my God, we're talking billions!"

Chapter 24

Professor Iawama, his team members and his dean were gathered in the university's board room. Also present were Keisi Fujimoto, university chancellor, and three people from the Japan Oil, Gas and National Metals Corporation, Mr. Sei Matsumoto, president, and Messers Uchi Watanabe and Kenjo Iebe, both directors. Professor Iawama was leading a PowerPoint presentation updating the executives on progress and next steps. A series of slides on the screen illustrated the professor's talk, showing the new lab and equipment that was being installed on an ocean drill rig.

"We are most grateful for the new secure facilities and for your generous financing of the prototype extraction process. We have been able to take the results of the Arctic research forward to a full-scale test, thanks to the success last summer at the Mallik Methane Hydrate site in Canada's Mackenzie Delta. There, we were able to test our prototype extraction method. The extraction of methane gas from a solid calthrate form is very tricky but our process was highly successful. Previously, the first technique we attempted failed: that of heating the methane hydrate layers to release the gas. However, other tests that reduced the pressure in the layers did work. That led us to a full-scale test whereby we drilled into a deep layer rich in methane hydrates, then pumped water out to lower the pressure. This resulted in the methane crystals disintegrating and releasing the methane. It is also highly cost-effective.

"Since that success, our follow-up analysis of the data and technical and environmental aspects of production has resulted in the design of larger-scale equipment and the development of an infrastructure for our local offshore conditions. We have been fortunate to have the Willard Institute researchers, who have assisted us greatly in designing the safety equipment, especially the backflow valves to prevent escape of gas in case of pipe rupture. We have three of their personnel currently stationed with us and we are in close collaboration with their research facility in eastern Russia where they are making great progress in up-scaling equipment for removing and capturing the impurities often present in the methane hydrate deposits. I am pleased to say we are making excellent progress and are on schedule for the full-scale test of a production platform. This will be off the eastern coast of Hokkaido in two months."

Mr. Watanabe, ever pragmatic, said, "In your test in the Arctic, you produced twelve hundred cubic meters of gas in a twenty-four-hour period. What expectations do you hold for this scaled-up test?"

"We expect about one hundred thousand cubic meters in the same time span."

"That is significant."

"Yes, we will be able to thoroughly analyze the new equipment we designed. After that, I visualize full-scale commercial production within five years."

"We will finance your technology transfer with the goal of shortening that time."

"You are most generous."

Mr. Matsumoto asked, "Is your security adequate?"

"It seems so. Tokyo has sent two hundred Special Security Police to guard the facilities and housing. They are well armed and trained. They have been supplemented by fifty special Ko-an Keisatu personnel from the Secret Service who have infiltrated the district to gather intelligence. Electronic monitoring is very intense – they call it "in-depth monitoring." The offshore rig is equipped with underwater side-scanning sonar and high definition radar. We are concerned about the potential of an assault on the rig and underwater pipeline and the navy is partnered with the Ko-an Keisatu for that security. They have assigned a Special Forces team to protect it. I understand they even have surface-to-surface and surface-to-air missiles. As well, the Chitose airbase in Hokkaido – it's the closest – has fighter jets on standby 24/7. The airbase has been drilled on a coordinated response supporting the Special Forces team in case of a potential threat."

Mr. Iebe said, "My contact in the Secret Service, the Ko-an Keisatu, informs me that they have tracked down those responsible for the destruction of the lab at the university. A foreign interest hired

Yakusa criminals in Ikebukeru Prefecture, Tokyo. This lead is being followed up. The Yakusa members responsible have been dealt with. Senior leadership of Yakusa have apologized – as you know, they are loyal Japanese and were shocked to learn that the destruction was related to national security. They will ensure none of their members participate in similar work again. They have also agreed to alert the Ko-an Keisatu if they are approached again."

Mr. Watanabe asked, "Do we want to know what the Ko-an Keisatu person meant when he said those responsible were dealt with?"

"Apparently, once they told all they knew, they were disciplined by the Yakusa executive in the traditional way. Apparently, the widows were provided good life insurance coverage."

"Let's hope we do not have to fend off an assault. But the oil companies can be rough and determined."

"One way to thwart them will be to win the race to patent the process. When can we file something that will cover the successful process?"

"It would be good to wait for the large-scale test."

"I do not want the delay. We are in a race with the oil industry. Can we move now?"

"For the basic process, yes. We are confident the large-scale test will be successful. Supplementary applications for the safety machinery and applications to separate the methane from oil and other impurities can follow."

"Do it. Now. As you know, the Willard Institute and the Russians have an interest in our success. They are willing to help expedite the patent application worldwide. We must take advantage of this."

"I concur," said Mr. Watanabe. "However, security will have to be vigilant as the patent filing will aggravate the oil industry. It will be like, what the Americans say, "waving a red flag in front of a bull." But again, the security of the country is at stake. We have the opportunity to get away from the dependency on imported oil. We are at war!""

Chapter 25

Senators Christine Lamont and Manfried "Manny" Rule were sharing a table over lunch in a remote corner of the parliamentary cafeteria. Both were upset, nervous, taking sideways glances and speaking in whispers to ensure that they were not overheard. "Manny, I'm scared," said Christine. "I don't think John's death was accidental."

"I don't think so either. Mind you, this came up in the RCMP Oversight Committee meeting this morning and the RCMP, the Ontario Provincial Police and the Ottawa Police have no reason to think otherwise."

"But so far they don't know what we know."

"True, and I'm not saying anything to anybody."

"Me neither. But I'm scared. We've gotten into bed with "Big Oil" and they're playing rough. John was holding them to ransom. He was bragging to us about it. He wanted more and set a deadline. They got him. I'm sure of it."

"Ergo, the moral of the story is: Don't hold them to ransom. Just keep quiet. Do their bidding and take their pay. You've been sitting on the board of Western Oil, earning, what, a million and a half a year for making things happen for them in Ottawa?"

"Plus two others. Yeah. And how many boards of directors are you sitting on? "

"Right. You get the point. I can see a lot of shit hitting the fan if some of John's secret papers come to light. Good thing we always kept our distance."

"I think it is a matter of WHEN they surface, not IF."

"Yeah. That issue came up in the Oversight Committee this morning. Any sensitive stuff the police find in John's safe, filing cabinets, safety deposit boxes and computer files is to be surrendered to the PMO. The argument being as the good senator's papers are considered state secret and, as the police deemed the death entirely accidental, all papers are to be turned over to the executor of his estate or the Senate Archives after review by the PMO – if they're not deemed sensitive, that is. We should be able to bury much of it unless it's too blatant."

"Invoke the *Official Secrets Act*?"

"Something like that. It's nice to control the RCMP budget."

"I wouldn't be the least bit surprised if that rat had documents in trust with one or some of the law firms to be released to the press in case of his untimely demise."

"Yeah, well, despite three marriages, he didn't have any children – at least none that he would admit to bearing – and his ex-wives all hated him, so I doubt if he left anything with them. All his siblings are dead. It will be interesting to see if anything surfaces and who does it."

"Maybe we should be covering our asses with incriminating documents secreted away."

"You mean, you haven't done so yet? You've got to have some CYA files squirreled away – just in case. This can be a rough business and a little leverage goes a long away. The party has little loyalty to us if we're perceived to be liabilities. You need to have some dirt on the party and/or the PMO to trade your silence for a payoff."

"Yeah…yeah…Facts of Life 101."

Chapter 26

What used to be a bomb shelter under the road back in W.W. II and through the nuclear fears of the 1950s was now a favorite restaurant for the Yakusa, Japan's premier organized crime syndicate. Rumor had it they owned it too. Paddy always enjoyed the ride down the small elevator one entered at street level on a very crowded side street in Ikebukuro Central. It was always busy. Crowded. Intense. A giant building covering a few square blocks housed a vast terminal for the subway and rail system. It was topped off with a massive six-story department store and five upper floors of small restaurants.

Once the elevator stopped its subterranean descent, first-time passengers were always awed as the doors opened onto a vast cavern holding a Bavarian-themed restaurant for over two thousand people, complete with German-style picnic tables and Bavarian-dressed servers negotiating the room with huge trays of beer slopping from overflowing mugs for the hundreds of patrons, seemingly diminutive under the arched dome of the huge cave. It was noisy from the cacophony of voices bouncing off the concrete walls and ceiling and especially noisy when the band of Japanese musicians, dressed in Lederhosen, white shirts, white knee-high socks and green Tyrolean hats, tore into favored German drinking songs. It was also smoky from the hundreds of patrons who had yet to give up cigarettes, stretching the limits of the ventilation system.

Paddy was met at the elevator by a young hostess whose Bavarian costume – a short olive green skirt, black lace pantyhose and white, low-cut, short-sleeved blouse – accentuated her beauty. She escorted him to the table of the person he sought. The band was playing the "chicken" song and many patrons were standing up, some standing on the tables, singing along, flapping their arms like wings. Two Japanese men sat at the table, both smoking and sipping from monogrammed beer steins. Paddy bowed to one he knew to be the boss and said, "Konichi-wa Ohori-san," then bowed slightly to the other, whom he knew to be Miazuki, Kenzo Ohori's bodyguard. Kenzo Ohori did not get up or bow but motioned with his left hand for Paddy to take a seat. Paddy took note of the missing distal and intermediate digits on Ohori's left hand pinky and ring fingers. He pointed to them and said, "Is that new since we last met?"

"You know that cutting off part of a finger is a way of discipline in Yakusa." He raised his hand and pointed to the stumps. "You have caused me this embarrassment."

For a few moments, Paddy thought of nothing to say. Both men stared at each other and Paddy could see intense anger in Kenzo's eyes. Eventually, Paddy took a sip of beer and said, "What happened?"

"I gave you a reference and I introduced you to the people you hired to do your dirty work in Sapporo. They did the job well and you paid them well as agreed. That is not a problem. However, you did not tell them, or me, that the sabotage was connected to our national security. For us in Yakusa, that crossed a red line. Let's say, we co-exist with our many layers of government. They tend to leave us alone up to a point. In World War Two and the Great Manchurian Expansion, we helped the government and have always been seen as loyal to the best interests of Japan. My indiscretion resulted in a mild discipline to me." He held up his left hand again. "I am fortunate. The associates you hired were terminated as our gesture of apology to the Secret Service."

Paddy apologized profusely and took his leave. Kenzo would not shake his offered hand and his eyes still seethed. Paddy bowed low to show he understood and respected Kenzo, and quickly walked across the room to the elevator, making sure to join a happy couple for the ride up to street level. Keeping an eye on store windows to see if he was being followed, a difficult thing where the crowds overflowed the sidewalks and took over the streets, he made his way across the busy road to the first subway station entrance and ran down the stairs, instead of taking the escalator.

Regrettably, once he got down to the level of the subway line that would take him back to his hotel in Akasaka district, he had just missed the train and the platform was empty.

This helped him spot the three heavy-set muscular men coming up behind him. He started running for the next exit but was blind-sided by others who had come down from the next set of stairs. He managed a good fight, blinding one when he came within range, cold-cocking another with a crushing blow that took him out of the play. His head butted into another and broke his nose. But he was sapped on the back of the head at the top vertebrae, stunned and tossed onto the tracks.

He managed to miss the electrified third rail, lying stunned on the track bed for a few seconds and gradually becoming aware that the aggressors, for some reason, were not going to jump down to finish him off. By the rumbling of the rail bed he began to comprehend that a train was fast approaching. He could see the headlights and hear the wheels screeching on the tracks. It was close. Coming fast. He had only seconds before he would be splattered and trampled under the wheels. From a crouch, he dove over the third rail through a gap of a couple of feet between the third rail and the protruding floor of the platform that jutted out to meet the side of the train. He landed hard in a space about two feet wide and three feet high, with a concrete wall on one side and the third rail on the other.

He lay still for half an hour, tolerating the rats who came up and sniffed his face and scampered across his body. Then he began crawling, following the rail, eventually finding a gap where the station platform ended and the tunnel began. He stood up on a maintenance path beside the track, out of sight of people on the platform. The tunnel was dark but periodically lighted and he could make good time walking along the path but ducking for cover every time a train passed.

He was filthy dirty when he emerged into the next station and climbed a short ladder onto the platform. He managed, without attracting too much attention, to ascend the escalator to a promenade beneath the road that had numerous convenience stores. Paying cash, he bought a new polo shirt and pair of slacks from a discount vendor, went into a restroom, cleaned himself up as much as he could, changed and threw his tattered clothes in a garbage can. Checking for a tail and not seeing any, he surfaced at street level, caught a taxi and made his way back to his luxury hotel. Once in his room, he called the concierge and had him rebook his flight to the soonest North American-bound one he could make. Then he showered, cleaned up, changed and checked out, taking a hotel VIP limousine to the airport, where he immediately went through security and nestled into the comfort and safety of the airline's first-class lounge. He concluded the Yakusa were not too serious about killing him, but just wanted to give him a lesson or he would have been hunted down and dead by now.

The assault on the offshore test rig would be a little delayed until Paddy developed Plan B.

Chapter 27

Hector and Sanford were meeting in a conference room in Hector's office. Hector said, "You said over the phone that you had picked up some leads?"

"Yeah. From both Russia and Japan. The Japanese tracked down the people responsible for the destruction of the lab at the University of Sapporo. Turns out they were a couple of men from one of the Yakusa crime families, one of the ones in Tokyo. Anyway, the Yakusa leadership gave them up when they learned the crime was related to a national security issue. The Yakusa are criminals, sure, but very loyal Japanese and have helped out in national security issues dating back to before World War Two.

"The Japanese Secret Service, with the help of the Yakusa bosses, did a thorough interrogation and the men spilled everything they knew. They were hired by one Paddy West of Extraction Inc. It's based in Calgary, Canada. Apparently, he was known to a mid-level boss who vouched for him and helped set up the deal."

"That fits. What are they doing about it?"

"They traced the money flow back to an account of Extraction Inc. in Antigua and shared that info with us. The mid-level boss was disciplined in front of a council of crime families. The Yakusa leadership reaffirmed their loyalty to Japan by decapitating the two who did it in front of senior representatives of Japan's Secret Service."

"That's severe."

"It's steeped in history. Apparently that's the way they have been doing things for centuries."

"I presume they want to track down Paddy West?"

"Yeah. Funny thing, he recently visited Japan. He managed to slip in and out of the country before an APB was posted. Apparently he contacted the mid-level boss for something but they don't know what. That boss was too steamed to discuss business and had him roughed up on his way back to his hotel."

"Maybe he was planning another attack in Japan?"

"Likely. The Japanese researchers are well ahead, building their full-scale offshore test. The Japanese expect an attempt on the offshore rig and are prepared for it. They're really pissed."

"Do they want him apprehended in Canada and extradited?

"They have yet to put out an international warrant for Mr. West. They're holding back but it may come to that. Right now, the matter is being managed by their Secret Service and they don't want any publicity or formal police protocol. They want to build the case to really nail him hard.

"That's your department. You said something had developed with the Russians as well?"

"Some. Not too much that we don't already know or presume. Their assassin was an Islamist from a rebel gang based in Chechnya. The gang is more into criminal activities than terrorism. Looks as if someone higher up in the gang got the contract and assigned the task to him. The Russians monitored some e-mail and phone traffic pertaining to it and traced it back to our friend Paddy West of Extractions Inc. They're tracing the money trail now."

"I guess we've got to keep a close watch on Mr. Paddy West and Extraction Inc."

"Right on!"

"How about our Canadian friends?"

"They're closely watching the dynamics of the death of Senator John Marshall. He had no next of kin and his law school alma mater got the majority of the estate. One of his law firm partners is executor/trustee of the estate. They expect some dirt may surface. It's likely the good senator stashed away lots of incriminating files and duplicates. His condo yielded some files. Same, apparently, for his apartment in Kamloops. Also, there were a number of safety deposit boxes that the trustee accessed and we assume they may have yielded interesting documents. Regrettably, the PMO has claimed all the material in his senate office as state secrets. And the argument is holding for now."

"The good senator has a significant amount of money stashed in offshore accounts."

"But we knew that and the trails are being traced. We'll also work on the interesting documents angle. The senator's law firm and the PMO now have some flies on the wall that may tell us more."

"Don't give me the details of how. On the other hand, our FBI liaison with the RCMP has been informed that the RCMP is now taking an active interest in the Methane Hydrate Murders – as they call them. They're on the trail of something and have asked for some records from the PMO, including access to Senator John Marshall's materials, but they've been stonewalled by the PMO refusing to surrender any documents. They haven't picked up on Paddy West or Extraction Inc. involvement – yet. Roger and Martin have some tidbits they are prepared to get into RCMP hands when they feel the timing is right but they have to keep below the radar of the oversight committee."

"When the time is right, I'm sure the official channels of the FBI will help build a case for their RCMP counterparts."

"Of course. We've been making some progress. In addition to what we know Paddy did in Japan, we've placed Paddy West in San Francisco, Winnipeg, Anchorage, and Toronto coincident with the murders. We've got our people working on that lead in San Francisco and Alaska and have turned over what we've discovered in Canada to the RCMP and they're following through with the Toronto and Winnipeg police. So far, there's no correlation to the Newfoundland murder. Paddy was in Nigeria then."

"I can help you there. Our NSA liaison this morning sent over phone records gleaned from Extraction Inc. There are some unusual phone calls to a person in Newfoundland from an oil platform in Nigeria that may be helpful.

"Unusual?"

143

"Yeah, not to anyone connected with the oil industry there. More to an underworld fellow. So, we got curious. There are also offshore money transfers, one before and one after the murder, that look as if he was paid for services rendered."

"Let me guess. When Paddy was over there in the River Delta, he placed calls to this guy in Newfoundland. With the money trail, is there enough to help the locals build a case?"

"Should be. The guy's not too swift. He's already brought a good chunk of the money into Newfoundland and is spending it hard. I'll give you the details. Although we can't reveal the source or depth of our knowledge, you can point the RCMP and the local Newfoundland constabulary in the right direction – at least finger the guy and let them build a case. If they bog down, we can always give them something more to work with."

"Good!"

Chapter 28

John Roberts and Jack Haskell were meeting over lunch in the Poplar Lounge at the Beaver Club, a members only exclusive club with a membership roster filled with old and new money, politicians, lawyers and senior bureaucrats. It was in a venerable but refurbished building dating to the 1860s located only a couple of blocks from the Parliament Buildings in downtown Ottawa. John and Jack were in a quiet booth in the private area, well away from other diners. After being served the entrée which had been preceded with light conversation about hockey, John broached the subject. "You invited me here to talk about John Marshall?"

"I hope you don't mind. I thought it best to be away from both of our offices."

"No problem. But, as you called the meeting, your firm is covering the meal chit."

"Right. There's no easy way to begin… What did you think of our late Senator John Marshall?"

"He served the party well as a fund raiser. He was a great public speaker. We, that's me speaking for the party and the Prime Minister, were sorry to see him go."

"So much for the official party line. You and I both knew him well."

"He was giving us some problems just before he died. His death was timely for us."

"He entrusted his Last Will and Testament to the senior partners of our law firm. We're acting as his executor and trustee."

"And?"

"Let's say, we've become aware of the substance of the difficulties you were recently having with him."

"He left behind some interesting documentation?"

"That is so."

"Does this also go to the rationale for his appointment to the Senate?"

"Indeed."

"How much material and how current?"

"There's a lot of material covering many issues. Some very current and other stuff going back as far as the early 1980s. All with corroborative chains of documentation from diverse participants and even some recorded conversations. "

A sigh. John put down his fork and rubbed his right temple. "And what is your position?"

"As trustees, we are required to keep the information safe and secure. There is an interesting covenant that we are only to reveal the contents to the press and police if his death was murder."

John looked over his shoulder around the room, seeing no one, then leaned closer to Jack's face and whispered, "Yes, he was a thorn in our side. BUT we did nothing, I say NOTHING, to hasten his demise. From what we have been told, everyone has concluded he had an accident. He's known as a heavy drinker. He had more than enough alcohol in him to explain stumbling down the stairs."

Sitting back, smiling and gesturing expansively with both hands, Jack said, "Then we have nothing to worry about. Do we?"

"What if someone else has duplicate info? Marshall was too much of a rat not to have covered his ass with duplicates."

"That's true. We've been looking but have turned up nothing so far. I agree, it's probably out there somewhere. The only hope is others have the same instructions not to do anything unless it is a case of murder. You're not to worry about our firm; we're loyal to the party. We've had some good business from you and would appreciate more, of course."

"Yes, and I'll make sure you get it. Government department business. There's a tender coming up for legal services for Aboriginal Affairs you should bid on. It's a pretty large tender and you may have to add staff for it. You well know that department as a bottomless pit with mistreatment lawsuits, contracting and treaty negotiations. We both know the game. What scares me is what other stuff did he leave behind other than the two things you have alluded to? I know that rat also had stuff on the opposition parties, some of which he made available for our use in the past. We'd always welcome some help that way, you know."

"As trustee, our firm cannot reveal any of the information in our possession, unless to honor the covenant in case his death was not natural or accidental."

"OK, I'll buy that. But, if we also hire your firm to help solve some problems of a political nature, I assume you may be able to steer us in the right direction when searching for certain information?"

"That's possible. By the way, we've got some expertise in the area of sovereignty law."

"Excuse me?"

"We're growing. We've even added four lawyers fluent in Mandarin and are considering opening a partnership in Beijing."

"I don't like veiled threats."

"We're on your side. Relax."

"I'll pass it on. Thanks for lunch."

Chapter 29

It was a rusty bucket but, in a way, the little freighter fit right in to its surroundings. It would pass as a coastal tramp freighter of the type very commonly plying runs between Korea and Japan and up and down the Chinese, Japanese, Russian and Korean coasts. Paddy, using a dummy company registered in Liberia, had purchased it from a disreputable shipbroker in Keelung, Taiwan. The ship, if you could call it that, had seen better days. It was forty years old, two hundred ninety-two feet long, rigged for mixed cargo and might make eighteen knots if the hull was clean and the engine held out. It was ready for the scrapyard and Paddy got it dirt cheap. It met their specification as it had a freezer hold.

It had taken five weeks to get the ship operational again to the point where a marine inspector certified it seaworthy – and that took a large bribe. However, close attention was paid to the rigging, and to ensuring the cargo cranes and lifeboats were in excellent condition and fully operational. Shake-down sea trials went as expected with the engine room crew muttering about the crap they had to work with, but finally admitting after many setbacks and repairs that they could keep the engines running for the length of the mission, as long as they weren't pushed hard.

Paddy changed the name and registry, insuring it for its new persona as a fishing fleet provisioning vessel, a tramp to intercept vessels fishing in international waters, purchase their catch and provision them, then deliver the catch to the highest bidder in Taiwan, China, Korea or Japan. Appropriate for their cover, they renamed the ship *Bountiful Sea* and painted it on the bow and stern in both English and Korean.

His contacts with the Taipei underworld supplied the C4 explosive and sufficient weapons, stolen from an armory of the National Guard. Under the command of Captain Park, the ship sailed on the evening high tide and set a course for the port of Busan, South Korea to pick up their passengers.

Captain Kim "Johnny" Park had been with Paddy many times on seaborne operations in the Nigerian River Delta. He was South

Korean, ex-navy with a soldier's stocky build, too restless at age forty-five to settle down. Fluent in Korean, English, Mandarin and Japanese, and a long-time friend of Paddy's from military days when they first met on a joint exercise, he had proven to be reliable in tight spots.

Captain Park was running the ship with an eight-man skeleton crew, four for the engines, two for the deck operations, galley cook/deckhand and a first mate, all trusted ex-Korean navy men who had been with him and Paddy in Nigeria and on other operations.

They stopped in Busan just long enough to take on fuel and fresh vegetables and their passengers under cover of darkness. They sailed again at midnight with the high tide, heading north and east up the Sea of Japan, following one of the normal shipping lanes midway between Korea and Japan.

Paddy had not come aboard with the passengers. Using an encrypted phone, he had told Johnny that he thought he might be under surveillance and that it would be best for him to be somewhere else, far away, when things went down. Instead, he had sent Rob, "Robbie" Roberts, an Irishman from Belfast and one of his Nigerian team, to handle the assault side of the operation. Robbie had another valuable skill: he was fluent in Arabic.

Robbie joined Johnny in the wheelhouse as soon as he came aboard and after old friend greetings, Johnny said, "Get your guys and the guests settled in and fed. The cook will show you to your bunks. I'll see you all in the galley in about an hour after I get this tub out of port. What do you think of our guests?"

"Pretty intense. Very young. Be prepared when you meet them to tell them which way to face toward Mecca when they pray."

After clearing the harbor approaches and getting the ship settled on its heading, Johnny Park turned the helm over to First Mate Victor Lee, and went to the galley to meet his passengers. In addition to Robbie, five more made up the assault team: Guy LeBois, Stan Thomas, Abe Northrup, Ed LaBelle, and Stu Clancy. All were part of Paddy's team stationed in Nigeria's River Delta and well-known to Johnny.

Speaking Arabic, Robbie introduced Mohammed and Hasan to the others. Mohammed Abdul and Hasan Salat were unknowns. Both were young – Johnny guessed maybe late teens or early twenties – thin and wiry, of average height and weight, with very dark complexions and Arabic features. They were also clean shaven, with fresh haircuts and well-dressed in slacks, polo shirts, sweaters and windbreakers at Paddy's request; he'd wanted them to attract as little attention as possible from authorities when travelling. Paddy had obtained their services from a Pakistani Al Qaeda leadership council who accepted Paddy's plan after it had been endorsed by a Saudi prince, Sheik Mustafa Bin Rizal, who was a board member of the Global Association of Refiners Petroleum and Producers and also ensconced in Saudi's oil ministry.

They were Jihadist zealots, two urchin orphaned boys who had been picked up off the slum streets of Sana'a, Yemen. For the security of shelter and one spartan meal a day, they'd spent their childhood years at a Madrassah, a Muslim school funded by a grant from Saudi Arabic wealth and devoted solely to memorizing a biased, hateful version of the Koran. There, they'd learned that their role in life was Jihad martyrdom. Once they reached the age of fifteen, they had been sent to a militant training camp in the South Waziristan region of Pakistan and graduated to test their new skills in Afghanistan and Yemen. They were young, resolute, hardened zealots who had been promised the opportunity for martyrdom by this operation. Perfect for Paddy's plan.

Johnny clapped his hands and called for attention. "Right! Great to see you all. We've got a full two days of travel before you get busy. In the meantime, get some rest. The galley is always open for coffee and tea and something to snack on but meals will be served at six, noon, and six." He turned to Robbie. "Robbie?"

"Thanks Johnny." He spoke in Arabic, interpreting for Mohammed and Hasan, then said in English, "We'll go over plans and check equipment after dinner tomorrow."

150

Chapter 30

"The moment of truth has come," said Hayden as he, Vanessa and Peter stood with Professor Iawama and some of their Japanese team members a few steps away from an instrument panel in the control room of *Ichiban,* the deep ocean drill rig. Another of the Japanese team members sat on a chair in front of the panel with his right hand on a control knob that he was slowly turning counter-clockwise while all were watching a gauge monitoring pressure at the wellhead, encased in a concrete "collar" on the ocean floor some three thousand three hundred feet (one kilometer) beneath them.

A moment later, someone said, "Valve fully open."

Pressure dropped as the methane began to flow. They watched as a second gauge registered increasing flow rate and volume of the gas passing down the pipeline. A third set of gauges registered ambient temperature at various points down the drill pipe from the valve. Part of the new technology was to control temperature and pressure in the line, and possibly induce water, to help "free" the methane gas from a solid state. The flow would be controlled to help the conversion into gas. A major problem was the danger of the well and pumps clogging with sand but new technology had been developed to overcome that.

"OK, so far, so good!" burbled Hayden. "The pipeline is filling. Up-line at the storage tanks, they're bleeding off the water left in the line during laydown. If we're lucky, we shouldn't see the pressure build up too much until they finish the bleed-off and the tanks are filled with the gas. Our current worry is frozen methane or sand building up in the pipes and choking off the flow."

Professor Iawama turned to Peter and Vanessa. "After this, we will test the backflow valve system you invented. It worked very well in the lab and on simulator; now for the real thing. We followed your recommendation to place backflow valves periodically along the entire length of the pipeline and to build redundancy into the seabed wellhead."

They were willing to conclude that the extraction process was working as planned. As they looked at the flow rate, Peter said,

"That's pretty good flow and it's steady. I guess we could open it up full but let's let it run at two-thirds for a while more. Anyone willing to wager what the daily flow rate will be under these conditions? I'm betting we'll pass one hundred thousand cubic meters a day."

Professor Iawama said, "It's early yet. We've got a lot more testing before we can safely conclude anything but I'm sure you're pretty close. No bet."

A week of testing proved up the system. Methane was flowing to land-based storage facilities. Professor Iawama then approached Hayden, Peter and Vanessa while they were finishing breakfast in the mess hall. "Everything has been working well here on the rig. We are, however, encountering a few problems at the storage and cleaning end and I feel your close review of our storage system may be beneficial. I think we need to improve some compressors and pressure valves. Would you mind joining me? We can fly out on the supply chopper this morning. I'll leave some of my team here and begin rotating them on a weekly basis. On shore, we have much more to do in the technology transfer lab and there's the paperwork on the patent applications."

Hayden beamed. "Fine with me! I'll give Ikumi a call and tell her I'm coming."

Chapter 31

Prime Minister Eugene Rogers and his Chief of Staff John Roberts were meeting in the opulent Prime Minister's Suite overlooking Rideau Canal, in the building that housed the large staff and many sub-departments of the PMO – the Prime Minister's Office. The PM was sitting at his desk when John relayed the conversation he had with Jack Haskell. The PM pounded his desk and threw some papers toward the nearest wall shouting, "F---ing blackmailing bastards! They're sitting on a powder keg that could bring our whole government down."

"The question is, what should we do about them?"

"You say they claim they're loyal to our party. Have you ever had cause not to believe it?"

"No. Then again, these guys are all disciples of John Marshall and masters of the art of manipulation and blackmail. They're all a bunch of poisonous snakes. They'll change loyalty pretty quick if there's more money in it for them."

"Right! For now, best to play their game and give them some more business. It really bothers me that they know about the China deal."

"Remember, John Marshall was brokering it."

"Yeah. We could put it on ice – sorry for the pun – for now until things calm down."

"Shame though, ten percent of multi billions is hard to ignore. And we've already got a ten million dollar deposit in our offshore bank accounts."

"You're right, we'll have to move on it. But I want you to deal directly with the Chinese. No more intermediaries and stray paper trails."

"OK. We've got to begin our plan to sway the Canadian public into supporting the idea."

"Yeah. We've got to slowly and carefully build up the idea. It's got to look as if we're just responding to favorable public opinion and that it will really benefit Canada in the long run."

"I'm working on it."

Chapter 32

After a good night's sleep, Robbie and his men spent much of the day with Hasan and Mohammed and two of the deckhands breaking out, readying and testing their equipment. They assembled and tested two large and seaworthy semi-inflatable Zodiac boats equipped with huge twin outboard motors. Rigging them on bridles attached each to a deck crane, one on each side of the ship, they practiced hoisting them over the side. They split their quantity of C4 explosive equally between the Zodiacs, just in case one was lost approaching their quarry. They rewound their grappling ropes in the German loop style for easy unraveling and no tangling, tested their grapples, cleaned and loaded their weapons and checked their two-way radios.

Right after dinner, the plan was reviewed over navigation charts laid on one of the galley tables. The plan itself was simple: They would hijack a freighter, preferably an oil tanker, throw off the crew and drive it into the methane test well drilling platform. The ship would be rigged with explosives to be detonated on collision. The two jihadists would remain on board to ensure the ship reached its target and they would achieve their martyrdom. Mohammed and Hasan had been given some training before leaving for the mission to familiarize them with steering, setting and disengaging auto pilots and throttling the power. Johnny took the time to have them demonstrate their skills in the *Bountiful Sea's* wheelhouse and felt comfortable with their basics of International Rules of the Road, steering and maneuvering the ship and recognition of their target. First Mate Victor Lee would transfer to the prize and set them up, ensuring auto pilot was locked on to the rig and they could handle the equipment in the pilothouse.

Mohammed and Hasan insisted on taking their prayer rugs with them and that was agreed to.

Next day, they drilled and drilled and checked and cleaned their firearms and tested all equipment. Then they waited. Rested.

At dinner that evening, Johnny announced, "OK, guys, we're within range. We'll take a ship tonight and have a fireball by early dawn. Get ready. We're in a busy shipping lane so we should find something acceptable within an hour or so." Robbie translated for Mohammed and Hasan, who were all smiles.

A short time later, Johnny, Robbie and Victor were gathered around the color radar which was set on a fifty-mile sweep. It was showing not only the blips of vessels but also their names, course settings and speeds. Robbie asked Victor, "Does this mean we're also sending out full identification like that?"

"Oh, yes. We're a registered vessel, just minding our business and passing through."

Johnny had a laptop computer running on a nearby desk and was typing in the names of some of the vessels. He was working in a website that furnished a full description of each vessel. After a few vessels, he settled on one that looked suitable. "Here's a reasonable one: The *New Kobe Maru*. She's twenty-two miles away and heading with us on a course that will have her overtaking about six miles off our portside. She's a twenty thousand ton tanker."

Victor said, "She's doing eighteen knots."

"Good," remarked Robbie. "We've done assaults up to twenty-five knots. A Japanese tanker will have a minimum crew all housed in the stern superstructure. That'll make it easier to round them up." Johnny used the mouse to bring up the ship's profile which showed a modern vessel with a stern superstructure. "Let's go for it!"

"OK, we're doing ten knots so they're closing on us at six, that's close to three hours before they pass us. They'll be abeam the drill rig three hours after that. There's plenty of time to ram the rig in darkness. If you launch the boats now to fall back to intercept the ship and by the time you've secured it, your ride back to us will be a lot shorter."

"Sounds good!" Robbie turned to Victor, "Let's go."

They had the boats and men hoisted over the side and slipped away within fifteen minutes. All the men were dressed the same in black rubber-soled boots, trousers, gloves and sweaters. Only Hasan and Mohammed did not wear full knit hoods covering their faces.

Johnny, closely watching the radar monitor which he had set for high definition short range, could not see any tell-tale sign of the rubber assault craft. The fast boats would make a wide arc, circling behind the target vessel and approaching from the stern, coordinating their approach. The starboard boat would pick a grapple point on the starboard (right) side and the port boat would come up on the port side and pick a grapple point. That would bring two assault teams aboard, one on each side of the superstructure.

The assault went like clockwork as the sea wasn't very rough. Both boat crews managed to get muffled grapples over the lowest railings on each side near the stern. They were close to the self-righting lifeboat, which was stored almost vertically on a pair of rails, allowing it to be launched off the stern by the flip of a lever once the crew were inside and strapped in. With the first man on each side on the deck vigilant for wandering ship's crew members, others soon clambered up the ropes and assembled on the deck, taking shelter behind the lifeboat by one of the access doors to the superstructure. Once all were up, the coxswains of the rubber boats eased their craft away from the ship and took up following positions in the ship's wake out of sight but close enough to be out of the ship's radar signature. Those on deck knew their tasks and split up into pairs to secure the crew.

Mohammed and Hassan ascended an external ladder to the wheelhouse, barged in and surprised the two people on watch, a mate and a deckhand. The officer of the watch, the first mate, lunged toward the engine throttle and was shot dead by Mohammed who used his MP5 silenced automatic to stitch a half dozen slugs into the back of the luckless mate. The deckhand stood still and raised his hands over his head. Meanwhile, Victor and another pair had accessed staterooms on the deck below the wheelhouse and captured the ship's captain and the second mate, both asleep in their bunks, and had determined the remaining two staterooms were empty. Similarly, the third team assaulted the third deck, commonly considered the territory of the engine and deck crew, and captured six, the chief and second engineers, two oilers and two deckhands. Subsequently, the cook and his helper were taken on the mess deck (the 4th deck below the wheelhouse) and one more, an engineer on his watch in the office of the engine room. All were handcuffed with plastic cable ties, their cell phones confiscated and smashed, then they were taken to the galley. A quick look by Victor into the ship's log revealed a list and names of the crew. After a quick count, Robbie concluded they had rounded up all. He motioned for Ed and Stan to follow him out of the galley while Stu and Guy kept guard of their prisoners. In the passageway, he whispered, "OK guys, go set your charges."

Victor was in the wheelhouse with Mohammed and Hasan. The deckhand who had been in the wheelhouse had been taken down to the galley. Robbie joined them and said, "All secure." Ten minutes later, Stu and Guy entered the wheelhouse and Guy announced: "Charges all set. Here's the remote detonator." He handed it to Robbie.

Victor altered the course settings on the autopilot and said, "All set here. This heading will take the ship right into the drill rig in an hour and ten minutes. It's an autocorrecting pilot with GPS. It'll correct for wind and tide." Robbie translated.

Robbie turned to Victor. "OK, next task is for you to disable the emergency beacon and navigation lights in the lifeboat and get rid of any emergency signaling devices, then load the crew in it. Take Stu and Guy with you. You've got seven minutes. We'll call in our boats and leave the ship to Mohammed and Hasan as soon as the lifeboat launches."

Hasan had taken the time to unroll a prayer rug and had positioned it toward the rear bulkhead of the wheelhouse, roughly facing Mecca. Robbie said to Mohammed, "Looks as if you're all set, but stay off the bridge unless you feel the steering disengage. The bridge will be a target. Better to hole up on the bow so you can drop anchor and drag it when you're just about on the rig." He handed a small electronic gizmo to Hasan. "Here's the remote detonator. The charges have been set. The ship's riding high in the water which shows its tanks are mostly empty. The petroleum fumes in the tanks will make a better explosion than a full tank of oil. It doesn't look as if they were flooding the empty tanks with nitrogen to prevent explosion, so it looks as if things will blow nicely."

Mohammed said, "One of us will be at the bow anchor winch and one of us will stay on the stern well below the bridge just in case we need to get to the wheel house to steer manually. We have the walkie-talkie radios. We can stay in touch."

158

"Excellent. You have been well trained."

A few moments later, Victor called on Robbie's radio, "All set, last crewman is boarding the lifeboat. Time to go."

Robbie turned to Mohamed and Hasan, hugged each, then stepped back and saluted them saying, "May Allah see you quickly to Paradise!" He ran down the interior staircase to the mess deck and joined his team on the port side just in time to see the lifeboat break away from its quick-release shackle, slide down the rails and plunge bow first into the ship's wake. It corkscrewed as its bow dove deep then bounced back like a cork and righted itself. It was soon lost in the dark. Quickly, both assault boats came alongside and the team members slid down the grapple ropes into their boats. The manoeuver had gone like clockwork and the coxswains soon were running full out toward the *Bountiful Sea,* now only ten miles away, where they were quickly brought aboard.

Captain Johnnie greeted Robbie when he made his way into the wheelhouse. "Well Robbie, successful?"

"It went well."

"Fine. We just maintain speed and course to clear the northern tip of Hokkaido into Russian waters on a shipping lane course for Vanino, Russia where we'll buy some seafood. We'll turn around in a day and head back to Korea to sell our cargo and drop you guys off. After that, I return this tub to the scrapyard in Taiwan. We should be getting quite a light show behind us in a little while."

"OK. We'll throw the weapons overboard and sink the assault boats while it's still dark. No sense having any trace of our activities left aboard. Shame to throw away those beautiful outboards, but they've paid for themselves."

Chapter 33

Hector and Sanford were meeting with Roger Pearson and Martin LeRoy in Hector's office. After exchanging pleasantries and settling down with self-serve coffee and donuts from the credenza at one end of the room, Roger began. "You know, the uproar you guys seeded over the methane hydrate research cancellation went very well. The PMO took quite a hit. The PM was embarrassed to the point that his popularity ratings dropped over twenty points. There's some rumbling in the Unity Party's inner circle that he should be replaced but I doubt if it'll go too far – especially if the issue fades away."

Sanford asked, "Do you want the issue to fade away?"

Martin frowned. "Not really. There are a lot of senior bureaucrats who are of the opinion that the current government has gone too far in some areas."

"We still have the problem of a senator we want investigated sitting on our oversight committees," Roger added.

"Let's take each of these as separate issues," said Sanford. "Martin, what do you mean senior bureaucrats are concerned?"

"I'll give one example that follows along with the cancellation of the methane hydrate research. It's raised concerns not only within the department of Fisheries and Oceans but very much so within the military. Shortly after the PM cancelled the methane hydrate research, he also issued orders to gag all hydrographic data at Fisheries and Oceans. No one is allowed to access their data bases. They've been shut down. Hard copy libraries are also shut down and much is being shredded. Many jobs are being terminated."

"What?" asked Hector. "How can this be explained?"

"Well, the latest hydrographic survey work has been in the Arctic, plotting the sea floor. It was associated with the plotting of methane hydrate deposits and shipping channels. Understandably, this has also upset the Navy as that knowledge is important for northern defense plans."

"And have you pinpointed who is responsible for this?" asked Sanford.

"We know the directive originated with the PMO."

"The big oil interests again? Is there a money trail back to them?"

"Not sure."

"I wonder if it's a bit bigger than that," mused Sanford.

"What do you mean?" asked Martin.

"Let's look at it from this perspective: Russia is doing the opposite to Canada. They've given the Arctic a very high priority – partly due to global warming and the prospect of shortened shipping lanes in the ice-free season and partly due to the riches that abound in the high Arctic. They're advancing their territorial claim to go deeper into the high Arctic and probably have a fair case for the territory which is on their continental shelf. They've created two new full-strength Arctic defense battalions, increased their Arctic naval patrols – both subs and surface ships, and are establishing at least a dozen new towns along their Arctic coastline and rebuilding and populating existing ones. Hell, they're even building a dozen nuclear-powered electricity plants and putting them on barges to supply energy for the new towns. On top of that, they've tripled their oceanographic research. They're really going at it.

"Right now, they're paranoid that China is awakening and is thinking of making a claim for part of the Arctic. I don't know how China can do that unless they lay claim to some land that is lightly guarded and sovereignty could be disputed."

"Merde!" said Martin. "If anyone has lightly guarded land in the high Arctic, it's Canada! The PM has given lip service to encouraging local militia – the Rangers – up there but they are few and poorly equipped. There is now a move to establish a deep water port on Baffin Island but little has come of that – in fact, the funding has been cut."

Roger chimed in, "And you guys along with Japan and others haven't helped by making the argument to the UN that some of the shipping lanes in the North East Arctic passing between Canadian islands are in international waters and do not belong to Canada."

"Don't forget, Denmark has been trying to make a case with the United Nations to take Hans Island away from Canada and that's considered just the thin edge of the wedge in the door for prying loose more Arctic land that Canada has been ignoring."

"Do you think China may be involved?"

"Interesting. Not unrealistic. Hell! I can even see a small country like Denmark selling off its Arctic claims to China if the price was right," said Martin. "We do know there's a hell of a lot of methane hydrate and minerals up there. Maybe others are taking aim at claiming it."

"Yeah. BUT your PM and the Unity Party – let's call it "the party in power" – are they selling out to another country?" asked Sanford.

"It would be interesting to try to find out. Maybe some intelligence agencies could broaden their intelligence nets to research that issue. CSIS and our other agencies have some ability but would welcome some assistance. Our problem is the Security Oversight Committee. They can squash what we turn up," said Martin.

"We'll have to run this past our State Department," said Sanford. "I'll get back to you for another meeting. In the meantime, we could follow some money trails of the PM and those close to him."

"What about your other problem? That one of the corrupt senators is sitting on your oversight committee?" asked Hector. "I gather the PM has been slow to get around to removing him even though there's been a lot of pressure from the opposition."

"Right!" said Roger. "I'm afraid he's waiting for the uproar to be history and then he'll just leave him there. Problem is that Senator Manfried Rule sits on both the RCMP and National Security oversight committees. He's been influential in getting the death of Senator John Marshall ruled accidental and burying the good senator's papers under the National Security Act. We feel he was following directions from the PMO for that."

"So, you need him off those committees before you can assist the RCMP to build cases against both Senators Rule and Lamont."

"Yes. Maybe even targeting the PMO. It would be nice to peek into the late Senator Marshall's secrets."

Sanford, scratching his chin, said, "We've seen some of the money trail while digging into Marshall's affairs and those of Senators Rule and Lamont. We'll take a close look at the source or sources and see if they also lead to the PMO and others. Well then, time to develop public awareness that the two senators are liabilities to the Unity Party."

Martin frowned. "Perhaps one at a time. Manfried Rule seems close to the PMO and Senator Lamont currently seems to be the one closest to the oil interests. Maybe keep her in reserve just in case we need to use her to get to the ones pulling her strings."

"Good point! Let's focus on Senator Rule."

Roger spoke up. "We may be able to help you there. Ah, we have a tame investigative journalist on one of Canada's most influential newspapers. She's well known and most influential. Perhaps you could help feed her some information?"

"Tame?" Asked Hector.

"Well, she's the widow of one of our people, actually. I'll be the go-between if you wish."

"Great!"

Martin said, "Did you know that Senator Rule sat on the committee that recommended the reductions at Fisheries and Oceans?"

"Ah! We've got lots of ammunition for embarrassment. No doubt many bureaucrats would welcome the PMO being taken to task for the cutbacks. Wonder if we can link Senator Rule to a Chinese connection?"

Hector asked Sanford to stay behind after the Canadians left the office. Over another cup of coffee, Hector said, "Why do I get this impression you're feeding the Canadians some tidbits? What's up?"

"That's above my pay grade. It's time we had a meeting with Caroline at Sec. of State. You need to be in the loop." He pulled out his cell phone and placed a call, then said, "She has time for us if we can get there in the next half hour."

"Let's go, then."

Caroline Weston greeted them at her office and motioned for them to take seats at the small circular table she used for mini-conferences. "Well Hector, you're perceptive. I told Sanford to let me know when he felt you should be clued in on the Chinese connection. Of course, you know this is highly classified."

"So, what's going on?"

"Sanford, I gather you dropped the hint of the "Chinese Connection" on our Canadian friends?"

"Yes. But I didn't get any feedback that they were already aware of it. I suspect there are those within their intelligence agencies who may be aware but it would be compartmentalized."

"Likely. Anyway, Hector, we are well aware that certain elements in the Canadian PMO have been approached by Chinese government representatives to see if they could purchase one of Canada's largest Arctic islands: Ellesmere Island. It's at the far northern extent of Canada and adjacent to Greenland. It's rich in minerals and abundant in methane hydrate, perhaps also oil and gas, but it's sparsely populated. Canada established a token base there, called Alert, as an attempt to prove ownership. I call it token as it has only five people there over the winter. Their government has declared plans to establish a deep water port at one end of the island but that has not materialized.

"In a way, we, the United States, contributed to the issue by declaring that shipping lanes in the Arctic that run between Ellesmere Island and southern Arctic islands are, or should be considered, in international waters. There's an opportunity for a large country like China to take Ellesmere Island by force as Canada could not defend it. But it looks as if the Chinese think the simplest way would be to purchase it from Canada. "

Hector mused. "Not without precedence either."

"Right! After all, we bought Alaska from Russia and Louisiana Territory from France. Money talks and the current party in power in Canada seems willing to listen."

"OK. So what's our point of view on this?" asked Hector.

"Needless to say, we don't want it to happen."

"So, what are we going to do about it?"

"We try to nip it in the bud by building Canadian public opinion against such an idea."

"And the PMO will be trying to do the opposite, right?"

"Right! But we have the advantage. They don't know we're aware of their negotiations – including the financial consideration demanded for the PM and his cronies in the PMO and the Unity Party leadership."

"How do we begin?"

"We already have by bringing public opinion of the PM and the party down to its lowest ebb. We can grind that a bit more with issues like the Fisheries and Oceans cutbacks, then raise some sovereignty flags."

Chapter 34

<u>02:17 hrs aboard the drill rig *Ichiban*</u>

The drill rig *Ichiban*, which means "the First" in Japanese, was anchored in a kilometer (3300 feet) of water, over a bed of methane hydrate in the Sea of Japan, thirty miles east of Cape Kamui, on Hokkaido's eastern coastline. Drilling had been completed and a "collar" of over one hundred tons of cement embedding the wellhead had been installed on the sea floor. After initial tests where the gas was "flared off" at the drill rig and a problem with sand clogging the well had been overcome, the wellhead had been connected to a pipeline running to shore and gas had been flowing to storage tanks on shore for the past week. The rig was a large platform floating on four partially submerged legs secured over the well with multiple anchors. It had a drill tower on one side of the lowest or drill deck standing about forty feet above the waves. The other side comprised six stories of superstructure, housing machinery, command center, lab and living quarters and a large helicopter landing deck hanging out over the water on the top deck. The rig had two Escape Pods – fifty-person self-righting lifeboats sitting on a lower deck that slid down rails at a forty-five degree angle into the water when launched.

The drilling crew remained aboard, along with two of the researchers, monitoring the flow of gas from the well and preparing to sink another hole. There was also a contingent of two Special Forces officers and eight men from Japan's Naval Force who manned a missile defense battery consisting of six surface-to-surface missiles and six air defense missiles. The rig defense personnel monitored high definition marine surface and air radar and a sonar array of eight sonar buoys surrounding the rig on the sea floor. In addition to missiles, the Special Forces team also had grenades and grenade launchers to lob grenades into the water if there was an underwater assault.

The *New Kobe Maru* first appeared on the drill rig's radar when it was fifty miles out. Sojo Ucchi, the Navy Ensign monitoring the set, noted it was headed in a northerly direction in the nearby shipping lane. He followed it for an hour along with the many other vessels plying past in the shipping lanes. He took a brief smoke break in the washroom from his boring duty and returned ten minutes later. After once again focusing on the screen, he noted the *New Kobe Maru* had altered course and now was on a heading directly for the rig. He punched the emergency alarm button and toggled the intercom to summon his superior officer, Lieutenant Chouda, who tumbled out of his bunk amid the clamor of the Special Forces team turning out of their bunks and running to their defensive positions. He ran across the heliport deck to the communications room. "What is it?"

"Sir, I have a ship, identifying as the *New Kobe Maru,* that has altered to a collision course with us. Judging by the speed it is making, estimate collision is about fifty minutes."

"Well done. Alert Chitose Air Base and ask them to scramble the stand-by fighters, then advise our headquarters and keep communication with them open. Then get back to Chitose Air Base and keep a direct line of communications open with their command center. I want to know what the jets are doing and I want them to be kept advised of what we're doing." He then picked up the PA microphone and announced, "This is NOT a drill! This is NOT a drill! We have a large ship that has changed course and is heading directly toward us. Break out the weapons. Prepare for an attack. It will intercept in less than an hour."

He turned to the marine radio and called on the international standby frequency. "*New Kobe Maru, New Kobe Maru, New Kobe Maru,* this is the drill rig *Ichiban,* this is the drill rig *Ichiban,* this is the drill rig *Ichiban,* change course, change course. You are heading directly toward us. Change course." He waited a moment and repeated it in Japanese. No response. He tried again. Switched to English. No response. He switched frequencies to Coast Guard Emergency and called. "Pan-pan, pan-pan, pan-pan, Coast Guard Radio, Coast Guard Radio, this is the drill rig *Ichiban* stationary at (he gave the coordinates), we have a vessel, the *New Kobe Maru,* bearing down on us and unresponsive. Over."

"*Ichiban, Ichiban, Ichiban.* This is Coast Guard Radio, Coast Guard Radio. We read you 5x5. Are you declaring an emergency? Over."

167

"Coast Guard Radio, this is the *Ichiban.* Affirmative, affirmative. We have a threat status and have advised Chitose Air Base. Over."

"*Ichiban*, Coast Guard Radio. We copy. We have a Coast Guard vessel on patrol approximately seventy miles from you and will deploy it to you. We are in contact with Chitose Air Base and we have rescue aircraft standing by. We are aware of your potential threat status. We will try the radio ship distress alarm across all frequencies just in case the *New Kobe Maru* is on another frequency." Within seconds the international alarm for ship in distress came across loud enough to wake anyone followed by, "Pan-pan, pan-pan, pan-pan *New Kobe Maru, New Kobe Maru, New Kobe Maru.* Change course, change course, change course. You are heading for a stationary drill rig. Change course now." No response. The call was repeated in Korean and Japanese, and twice in English, the international language of the sea.

Another ten minutes passed. They could make out the red and green navigation lights of the *New Kobe Maru;* it was bearing down directly on them.

Lieutenant Chouda called over the PA, "Drill Boss to the communications room. All non-military personnel to assemble in the mess hall." A few moments later, Si Matsumoto, the drill boss entered the room and Lieutenant Chouda said, "Get all your people and the researchers into Escape Pod One. Just in case. It looks as if we have a ship intentionally heading for us with intent to ram. If it gets within ten miles, I'll give the signal to launch. After you launch, get well away from the rig. Head toward shore."

A few minutes later, they heard jets overhead and Ensign Ucchi said, "Chitose advises two fighters have arrived and have the ship on their radar. One's gaining altitude to release an illumination flare." Within seconds the sky was bright as day and they could make out the outline of the ship approaching them. They saw the jets come to almost sea level with their landing lights on, and make a pass on the ship. "Lead pilot reports no sign of life aboard." They watched as the jets returned on a pass and saw tracers fired across the bow of the *New Kobe Maru.* With their landing lights on, they made a pass at low level coming in from the bow over the wheelhouse. "Lead pilot reports no one visible in the wheelhouse.

They have been authorized to attack and request us to hold off our missile defense until they have made a run."

"Roger that."

The jets came around and, from a mile in front of the bow of *New Kobe Maru*, the lead jet fired two missiles into the wheelhouse. The explosions were easily visible to those watching on the rig. Lieutenant Chouda muttered, "How do you stop a large freighter that's that close? I doubt shooting up the wheelhouse will put it off course or slow it down if the auto pilot is set. It's coming bow on to us. We've got to shut down their engines or hit their rudder to change course, or both."

"Chitose advises pilots feel their missiles too small to do much damage. The vessel is double hulled. They say the jets will hold back for you to fire your surface-to-surface missiles."

"Roger that. Tell the surface-to-surface missile team to fire one missile directed at the base of the superstructure. And prepare another to launch targeting the main deck in the middle of the cargo area."

"Missile one away." Launched almost straight up, it seemed it took only a few seconds for the missile to make a tight parabolic arch down to smash into the *New Kobe Maru* at the base of the superstructure resulting in a large explosion. They waited and assessed the damage. The ship was coming ever closer, now ten miles away.

Lieutenant Chouda toggled the P.A. microphone. "Drill Boss launch Escape Pod One. Drill Boss launch Escape Pod One." He saw the escape pod slide down its rails, torpedo into the sea and bounce back to the surface. In seconds, its engine started and someone within began to steer it away from the rig toward shore.

"Chitose advise the pilots are making a low pass from starboard over the superstructure." A few seconds later, the jets' landing lights were visible. One jet flew low over the front of the superstructure while the latter came across the stern. "Chitose advise the pilots report significant damage to the superstructure base, possibly penetrating into the engine room. Second pilot reports no change in propeller wash or rudder. The vessel is still underway. They will stand off for your next missile launch."

"Launch second missile. Prepare third and fourth for base of the superstructure." The second missile fired and shortly found its mark midway on the deck of *New Kobe Maru*. The sizable explosion from the missile was followed by a much bigger explosion sending a fireball two thousand feet into the sky. The jets returned and one passed over the damage while the second passed over the stern.

"Chitose advise second missile opened a middle hold and seems to have ruptured the hull on port side. They think the ship is taking on water. The ship is still making way but has slowed a bit. They await your next missile."

"Fire missiles three and four." They were quickly away and found their marks at the base of the superstructure." The jets made another assessment pass.

Ensign Ucchi, looking at the radar said: "Vessel is slowing, now doing thirteen knots. Distance is seven miles. Chitose advise last two missiles penetrated hull below the superstructure. The engine room is on fire. They request you cease fire as they want to attack the rudder to see if they can alter the ship's course."

"Roger that."

"Five miles, sir."

They watched as the two jets came low and released their remaining missiles toward the rudder of the *New Kobe Maru*. Although they could not see the impact, they could see the flashes from the missiles scoring. After a few minutes, Ensign Ucchi reported, "Sir, there's a slight change in course. Ship continues to slow, now doing eight knots. Chitose reports the jets will gain altitude and set another flare. Four miles, sir."

"Good! We're not safe yet. Order the last two missiles to target the mid deck again. Let's see if we can break it in half and sink it."

The last two missiles from their surface-to-surface battery were quickly on their way, almost straight up and straight down, penetrating the deck of the *New Kobe Maru*. They didn't need the jet pilots' assessment of the damage as they watched the ship heave in the middle and separate into two pieces. The explosion set off secondary explosions in other tanks, resounding in another huge fireball and a shock wave that shook the rig. They watched as the stern section sank quickly, severed end sinking and stern rising, with the engine still turning the propeller. All that remained from it was a flaming pool of oil drifting with the wind and tide toward the rig.

"Chitose advise the stern section has sunk and bow section has lost momentum and is sinking. They also note the near empty cargo holds of the vessel give it a lot of buoyancy and are hard to penetrate as the vessel is double hulled."

"Fire all anti-aircraft missiles directly at the hulk." The missiles were not designed for such a close-in and low trajectory but it was worth the risk. They were away shortly, one after the other managing to score hits on the drifting hulk but to little avail – like firing rifle bullets at a tank. "Advise Chitose and HQ we are abandoning the rig as a precaution. Advise we are out of missiles."

"Bow section now less than two miles sir and drifting toward us with the tide and wind."

He toggled the P.A. system, "Now hear this, now hear this. Good shooting but the bow section is drifting toward us. We will abandon the rig temporarily. All hands aboard Escape Pod Two. All hands aboard Escape Pod Two." He turned toward Ensign Ucchi, "Let's go."

"Chitose advises another pair of jets will be overhead in thirty seconds," said Ensign Ucchi as he signed off with Chitose and HQ. "Their mission is to sink the bow section."

Escape Pod Two launched successfully and was soon headed toward shore with the remaining personnel from the rig, well out of the way of the drifting hulk. The two newly arrived jet fighters attacked, aiming at the severed section of the hull, reasoning it would be the weakest point. In two passes, the jets used all their missiles but did not seem to do much damage except open a hole which spewed oil that caught fire. The hulk continued to drift down upon the rig and soon the sound of screeching metal could be heard in the Escape Pod Module as the hulk tangled with the rig. This was followed twenty seconds later by a huge explosion followed by a shockwave that rocked the escape pod over on its beam ends. The hull sank within two minutes taking the rig with it. Methane gas began roiling up from the ruptured pipeline and wellhead when the tangled mass of metal landed upon it. The burning oil residue from the near empty holds of the tanker proved a volatile mix, igniting the methane resulting in a massive fireball before it settled down to burn like a huge torch where the gas rose from the sea.

Chapter 35

Hector, along with Peter Thorpe, Chief FBI Agent attached to the US Embassy in Ottawa, accompanied Roger Martin to RCMP headquarters to meet with Inspector René Poole, a twenty-year veteran of the RCMP, in charge of the Serial Crime Investigation Division and Sergeant Jack Ruggan, the officer assigned the file on the murdered researchers. After small talk about their favorite hockey teams and the polar Canadian weather front raising havoc by bending down deep into the eastern USA, Hector began. "René and Jack, thanks for making the time to see us."

"No problem," said René. "I gather you've been making some good progress on what we call the murdered researchers?"

"Yeah. It's time to share some information. I gather you've been building a case on the perpetrator of the murder in Newfoundland?"

"Yes. When we put some attention to that murder, so did the Newfoundland Constabulary. Cooperation's been very good and the results have been positive. The Constabulary got a tip that a local underworld figure was spending lots of money and we had an undercover officer get close to him. He was bragging that he had graduated to "the big time." He practically told the undercover officer everything about it. The guy was so proud he had been selected for a contracted hit. We traced his newfound wealth to an international bank transfer into his personal account. The originating bank was in Lagos, Nigeria. He claimed the first deposit was poker winnings from his time on an oil rig in Nigeria and the second was accumulated salary from his time over there – can you believe it?"

"Not the brightest light bulb?"

"Nope. He had worked on an oil rig in Nigeria but it was over three years ago. Anyway, the Constabulary hauled him in and he eventually confessed. But he would not give up who contracted him or why."

"That   figures."

"He was apparently contacted over the phone by an intermediary who gave him a number to call. He used a cheap cell phone and threw it away in the ocean as he had been instructed to do once the job was done. He didn't keep the number. But we know the call was within Canada as the phone was not set up for international calls."

"Is there enough for a solid case?"

"We have his confession supported by what he told the undercover officer, plus we matched a pair of pliers in his truck tool box to the severed brake line. I think so. We can nail him but not whoever hired him. However, we haven't got anywhere on the other researchers' deaths."

"For what it's worth," Hector replied, "at Roger's request, we helped trace the money flow. It does route through a reputable Nigerian bank but the originating account is in Nevis in the Caribbean. It traces back to one Mr. Paddy West of Extraction Inc., a Calgary-based firm. In turn, funds were transferred into it from an account in Curacao from the Global Association of Refiners and Petroleum Producers."

Jack said, "That makes some sense."

"Right. But that information is not for use in court. Nor is it to be mentioned to your oversight committee. We have other information, built with contributions by the Japanese and Russian governments and our own people in the FBI, that traces the other murders and attempts back to this Paddy West of Extraction Inc."

"How solid is it?"

"We can place Paddy West's movements in the same cities and at the times when the murders occurred in Winnipeg, San Francisco, Anchorage and Toronto. Regrettably, we have nothing from the bomb fragments gathered from the Anchorage lab nor do we have any cell phone records or intercepts. The Japanese have a stronger case – almost. They have confessions that he hired two Yakusa to blow up the lab and do the hit and run on one of the professors in

Hokkaido. But those who confessed were executed by the Yakusa leadership as they had acted against Japanese best interests. So, that may be a little difficult to bring against Mr. West in a Canadian or American courtroom. There is no linkage, so far, associating West with the destruction of the drill rig in Sapporo.

"Here's a bio we did on Paddy West. He's ex-S.A.S. He profiles out as a high-level sociopath. I also included details of our tracing of his movements." Hector handed out copies of the file to Jack, Roger and René.

After they had both digested the file, Hector began. "Our Homeland Security people had a supposedly unrelated correlation bounce up when they were tracing Paddy West's movements. It may be of interest to you. You can verify it yourselves, but it looks as if our Mr. West was in Ottawa when your Senator John Marshall died."

"Merde! Merde! Merde!" said René.

"Yeah. He flew into Ottawa from Curacao, having changed planes in Miami and Toronto. He was there a few days, then flew on to Calgary the day the body was discovered. Here are the details."

"Time for him to scout out things, then do the deed," said Jack after reading the details. "This gives us a different perspective on that event. Mr. West is S.A.S trained – he's very capable of unarmed murder and staging the event to look like an accident."

René said, "We have to tread carefully. What could be the motive?"

"That man had many enemies," Jack mused. "IF Mr. West did a hit, who hired him? And why? Is it linked to the other deaths?"

Hector said, "All very good questions. There could be an association with the turmoil ensuing from the termination of the research, as the good senator was instrumental in that."

"Like, did he know too much? Could he have been a potential embarrassment?" said René. "That centers on the oil interests and the PMO or both. Merde!"

Jack said, "We need to access his files and we've got to build solid probable cause to do that. This will take a while and we'll have to keep it below the radar of the Oversight Committee."

"From what we've learned," Hector said, "I think it's easier to begin by looking at Mr. West and his relationship to the big oil interests. We've been doing that and may be able to help out as we've had some luck following money flows."

"What if we talk with the executor of Marshall's estate?" asked Jack.

"Delicate. But worth a try. Merde!" said René.

Chapter 36

Once again, Professor Iawama, his team members and his dean were gathered in the university's board room. Also present were Keisi Fujimoto, university chancellor, and the same three people from the Japan Oil, Gas and National Metals Corporation, Mr. Sei Matsumoto, president, Messers Uchi Watanabe and Ken Iebe, both directors. A special guest, Mr. Kiyoshi Uma, a director in the Secret Service, was also present. Mr. Uma was speaking.

"The seamen on the *New Kobe Maru* drove their lifeboat to the port of Huani and called the police and Coast Guard. It took them eight hours from the time they launched, so the action was all over by the time they reported in. Apparently, the terrorists disabled all the signaling equipment, even lights. All of their crew is accounted for. Only one person, the First Mate, was killed when he tried to shut down the engine. His body has not been recovered but is presumed to be in the wreckage of the ship. Only two of the terrorists did not wear head covering but only the deckhand who was in the wheelhouse saw them. He gave us a description and two known Al Qaeda terrorists have been identified. The rest of the terrorists were fully covered and did not speak around the crewmembers. Two bodies, apparently of the two terrorists who attacked the wheelhouse, have been recovered and we are in the process of identification. They seem to be Arab. It is presumed most of the terrorists left the ship the way they came but left two jihadists aboard to ensure the ship reached its target. The fighter pilots report they saw someone on the bow by the anchor winch just before the bow blew up."

Professor Iawama said, "Al Qaeda?"

"Yes. Our government received an e-mail whereby both Al Qaeda and our own ALEPH cult, the people responsible for the Sarin gas attack in the Tokyo subway, shared the credit. The source seems valid. It may be that the ones who kept their faces covered were Japanese and ALEPH members. They would have an easy time coming ashore and blending in when they finished their mission. The Americans report picking up some conversations of Al Qaeda leaders discussing preparations for an attack of this nature but they weren't sure where it would take place or when. For now, our

177

government is taking this at its face value and is blaming the incident on them. We are planning a suitable retribution. At least it's a good excuse to round up many of the ALEPH cult we've been observing in Japan. ALEPH claims over forty thousand members and affiliates outside of Japan and there is considerable overlap with Al Qaeda."

"But?"

"Yes. We are still investigating. It is quite possible the oil interests are really responsible."

"Where did they come from?"

"We're not sure. Likely by sea but all commercial shipping has been accounted for. It is possible they launched assault craft from land."

Mr. Matsumoto said, "Thank you. Now, let's hear the status of the rig and production. Professor Iawama?"

"The bow section of the *New Kobe Maru* destroyed the rig and landed on the wellhead and pipeline. The pipeline to shore was ruptured and gas flowed before the automatic shutoff at the wellhead triggered. We also had backflow from the gas in the pipeline on the side running to the shore. It stopped when a backflow valve triggered. These valves were developed by our people in collaboration with the Arctic team members from America, Canada and Russia. These, by the way, we have applied for patents on. In all, we estimate we lost ten thousand cubic meters of gas."

Mr. Matsumoto said, "It was burned as it was released into the atmosphere? What about the oil spills from the ship?"

"That wasn't too bad. Basically the holds were empty, just residual oil in the bottoms of the tanks. But because of that, the tanks were a volatile mixture of air and fumes causing greater explosions. Some oil did escape and some of it burned. Most was diesel and gasoline, not bunker or raw oil. We estimate the spillage at less than half a million liters. It burned well but there is an oil slick and we feel it can be contained and retrieved fairly well."

178

"Most important then, has the test well proven successful? How many cubic feet per day have you been able to flow?"

"We predicted approximately one hundred thousand cubic meters a day, but we achieved one hundred forty thousand cubic meters per day. We are successful. Once we have cleared the debris from the wellhead and positioned the replacement rig, we will step out with seven to ten more wells drilled at that site. Our problem is the need for infrastructure in pipelines and storage tanks ashore and for a plant to clean and compress the methane into LNG for ocean transport to take the gas to our major port cities."

"Excellent! All of you have done well. Despite the loss of the rig, you have proven the process and the potential for Japan to become self-sufficient. We will quickly bring in another rig and drill more wells. We must now pay more attention to the delivery and storage infrastructure. This is a high national priority."

Kiyoshi Uma spoke up. "The protection we provided for the rig was inadequate. The military will be improving the defenses, including homing torpedoes launched from the rig, from the air and from two high-speed coastal patrol vessels which will be on picket duty around the rig at all times."

Chapter 37

Jack Ruggan had made an appointment to meet Peggy Lamonde at her law firm. Peggy's administrative assistant, Donna Tremblay, led him into a boardroom and offered him coffee. A minute later Peggy Lamond entered and introduced herself. "Sergeant Ruggan? I'm sure you won't mind but I've asked Donna here to stay and take notes. As well, our managing partner, Jack Haskell, will join us. Ah, here he is."

After introductions and exchange of business cards, Peggy said, "Sergeant, you mentioned over the phone that you were reviewing the death of John Marshall. Both Jack and I are executors of his estate. You have us curious. Has something new developed? How can we help you?"

"Well Ms. Tremblay, you know I'm not at liberty to reveal much but I can advise we still have an open file on this."

"Can you at least give us a reason why the file is still, as you say, open?"

"Well, you are aware of the uproar over the deaths of the Arctic researchers?"

"Of course."

"One of those deaths, that of professor Mahoney in Newfoundland, has been proven to be an assassination. The perpetrator has been apprehended and there is a solid case. As he had no known enemies, we're taking a serious look at the deaths of the other two Canadians and, tangentially, Senator Marshall is linked as he was instrumental in getting the PM to terminate research funding. We are probing all linkages."

"Oh!"

Jack Haskell asked, "What do you want from us? Do you have something specific or are you on a fishing trip?"

"At this stage, call it a fishing trip. Is it plausible to you that his death may have been assisted?"

"Do you have at least one shred of evidence from the death scene that he may have been killed?"

"No. Not at this point in the investigation. In addition to Dr. Mahoney, three of the researchers, one in San Francisco, two in Canada, died in what at first were interpreted as accidents but could have been murders. There were two near misses badly injuring researchers – hit and runs – in Japan and Russia. Both of them were proven to be assassination attempts. There was a lab bombed in Alaska that killed an FBI agent who was protecting one of the Arctic researchers. We are convinced there is or was a plot to eliminate the researchers. "

"So, you're digging deeper," Jack Haskell commented. "As executors of the estate of Senator John Marshall, we have some responsibilities. In particular, his Last Will and Testament specifies we are not to release any of his papers if he passed away naturally."

"Interesting. Are you in possession of a lot of documents?"

"A significant number. We have reviewed them. But, of course, we must keep the contents confidential."

"Of course. However, may I ask if you discovered anything that would directly correlate to his death?

"You're aware that Senator Marshall ah, traded in knowledge?"

"Yes. That's come up."

"There is always the possibility that someone wanted to ensure Marshall kept a secret. But I can assure you, in our review we found nothing that stood out. Nothing that would trigger the covenant to release the material to the police."

"What would you need in order to release the documents?"

"If you prove he was murdered, we are authorized to provide you with the documents."

After Sergeant Ruggan departed, Peggy said, "Jack, I'm surprised you revealed the bit about the covenant."

"CYA, my dear, just covering our asses and building a little insurance. You never know what the leadership of our glorious political party currently in power may try to do about our possessing the files. Who knows? They may even try a break-in like Watergate."

"Or worse. I agree they're acting as if their power has gone to their heads."

"Next step – CYA with the PMO."

Chapter 38

Joyce Withers was known as a tough nut, a hardened, wizened, brilliant, seasoned, award-winning investigative journalist who "scared the hell" out of her journalistic targets. She was cranky. Demanding. Probing. Untrusting. Accurate. Her juniors at the *Toronto New Tribune*, one of Canada's leading newspapers, respected her but considered her a cranky fossil and tried to stay clear. At age fifty-seven, journalism and the pursuit of a big story was her only life since Ben, her husband of twenty years, had passed away ten years ago. Her two daughters, one in Sydney, Australia and the other in Cape Town, South Africa, were seldom in contact.

She had some of the old skills of journalism: she could punch a keyboard at one hundred twenty words a minute error free and she took flawless notes in Pitman shorthand. She had managed to keep up with technology, mastering computer word processing and spreadsheet software, data base trolling, cell phone tweeting and texting. One friend commented she could have made a great trial lawyer as she was tenacious when she got a lead, ever probing, always seven to ten steps ahead when questioning people. Her journalistic skills had won her and the paper many awards for in-depth reporting and had generated a fair share of lawsuits which she and the paper inevitably won.

Roger Pearson had reached Joyce on her cell phone as she was walking to her car in the newspaper's parking lot. After the usual pleasantries, he said, "Joyce, looking for something interesting to sink your teeth into?"

"Roger, can we meet? I don't trust cell phones."

"OK, see you soon. Bye." Roger hung up. Joyce looked at her cell phone, shook her head and continued walking to her car. She was not surprised to find Roger sitting in the front passenger seat.

This must be pretty important to get Roger off station to come to Toronto. She knew he was still attached to the Canadian Embassy in Washington. She climbed into the driver's seat. "Roger, aren't we mysterious today? You must have something good!" She started the car and put it into gear. "Where to?"

"If you can drive me to the airport, we can talk on the way."

"Sure. What's up?"

"Joyce, there's an interesting connection that may be worth a story. Sort of a follow-up to the furor in the House of Commons Question Period about Senators Rule, Lamont and Marshall. Looks like more argument that Senator Rule has a severe case of conflict of interest. More than just the cancellation of the methane hydrate research. Apparently, he was instrumental in cutting back on funding to the Ministry of Fisheries and Oceans to an alarming degree and there's a feeling something serious is behind it. Many people are getting concerned that he's on the Security and RCMP oversight committees as they feel he should be investigated along with the cancellations and cutbacks."

"Nice. You know, this whole issue of senators being appointed and not elected, of being allowed to sit on boards of directors and even run their own businesses stinks to high heaven. I'd love to try to help sway public opinion to clean that all up."

"You'll have to verify it, but the RCMP are linking Senator John Marshall's death to the deaths of the methane hydrate researchers. The one killed in Newfoundland was definitely killed as a contracted hit. You know about the three attempted murders, hit and runs in Japan and Russia and a research lab bombed in Alaska in which an FBI agent assigned to protect the researcher was killed. These have all been determined to be assassination attempts. The RCMP are likely going to be trying to access information held by the PMO that relate to the senator and the cancellation of the research and his ties to the big oil interests. Looks as if the senator may have been brokering some other fixes too.

"You'll find some material in an envelope on your back seat. That'll help you get started. Lots of references, dates, names, files etc. You should take a close look at Senator Manfried Rule as he holds a lot of control over the RCMP and may be stifling their ability to conduct a fair investigation. He's certainly on the payroll of the oil industry. Surprisingly, much is public record but no one has bothered to link the dots. You could make a case of blatant conflict of interest. You know what to do."

"I look forward to it. I'll have to run the idea past my editor, Ray Bonspiel, but I'm sure he'll love it."

"Great! I'd advise you to be a little wary of the big oil interests though. They can play rough."

"No problem."

Joyce had just finished explaining her project concept to her editor, Ray Bonspiel, who said, "OK Joyce, go for it. I like it and I'm sure the editorial board will love the concept. You've just filed that exposé on high priced vitamin pills that'll run over six issues. Right now, anything I had in mind to assign to you can be fobbed off to someone else. I expect something within a week, though – at least the first installment of a series. Also, try not to make too much work for our legal department."

"Ray, you know I always have my facts – solid unquestionable facts."

"Yeah, facts end a lawsuit but it doesn't stop them from trying. Have fun and keep me informed."

Joyce began by reviewing the incomes of Senators Rule, Marshall and Lamont then expanded her review to cover all senators. This was easy to obtain as the government's transparency policy required all Members of Parliament and Senators to reveal their incomes from all sources. Although a matter of public record, few people bothered to review them. Joyce's analysis revealed a number of senators were sitting on corporate boards of directors but the ones drawing by far the greatest incomes from that had been Rule, Marshall and Lamont. The majority of their incomes came from oil exploration companies and those supplying the oil industry. Her first exposé began to gel in her mind and she was soon burning up the computer keyboard with a five-part series raising the question of conflict of interest. She questioned why Senators Rule and Lamont should be allowed obvious conflicts of interest such as sitting on the Senate Oil Transport Review Committee and

185

the Oil Extraction Environmental Standards Committee while receiving huge incomes by sitting on the boards of directors of oil companies. A review of their voting and committee transcripts revealed constant support for oil industry interests. This led to questioning why they were instrumental in requesting the PM to cancel the Arctic methane hydrate research, suggesting that it was an act designed to eliminate potential energy competition.

As a final piece of that series, she explored the deaths of the Arctic researchers, citing the Newfoundland murder and events in Japan, USA and Russia and revealing that the RCMP was now investigating the deaths as suspicious. Her piece was explosive, inferring that the oil industry was ruthless and questioning whether the senators were involved in the deaths and whether Senator Marshall's death was suspicious.

Chapter 39

When the "Mayberry" team felt they were ready to do a full-scale test of the system they had developed, Ivan and Una organized an ideal location high in the Russian Arctic. "Pee...where?" asked Norma.

"I thought I'd get that question," exclaimed a smiling Una. "Pevek. It's about 640 kilometers, say 400 odd miles, inside the Arctic Circle. It's a seaport that's seen better days but is now getting a new lease on life as a military base for Arctic outreach, as a shipping hub for new settlements being established along the Arctic coastline and as a research center. Our prime minister and president consider it a strategic port in Russia's new Arctic policy to exploit the resources, use the seas as a transportation system, and ensure that the Arctic remains a zone of peace and cooperation and to protect the Arctic ecosystems. We have quite a concern that China is trying to stake out a claim for part of the Arctic.

"It also has a lot of permafrost with embedded methane – both on and off shore. For us, the location of Pevek is good – on the east side of Russia, like us. It has a good all-weather airport so we can get to it readily by air. It's on the coast in the East Siberian Sea not too far from Wrangel Island which serves as a delineation point separating the East Siberian Sea from the Chuckchi Sea – that's the sea on Alaska's North Slope."

"So we'll not be too far from Alaska?" mused Stephanie.

"By jet, not too far."

"That'll help," said Hayden. "Once we prove up the process in Pevek, we're to build a smaller-scale more commercial version in Alaska and invite the world to view it."

"Yes. Pevek will remain top secret – away from prying eyes and hopefully out of reach of our enemies. Russia has a major Arctic research center there. Access to Pevek is restricted. It's a great place to house the prototype model."

"How big is this place and what will the accommodations be like?" asked Marie.

"It's not Mayberry. It's Russian. Not counting the military base, which is twenty miles out of town, the population peaked at thirteen thousand back in 1989 but is just growing from four thousand. It's expected to grow past five thousand in the next two years. Housing is the traditional Russian apartment blocks – you know six to eight stories with a mixture of layouts, depending on your level of employment. Each of us can expect a large furnished two- or three-bedroom apartment with housekeeper/cook. There's a new supermarket and a number of restaurants. Heating is from a central heat and electricity plant, presently fired with coal from nearby coalfields.

"The port was originally established to ship coal, tin, uranium and gold from local mines. It even had a role as a Gulag. Until the late 1980s, tin and uranium were extracted by prisoners in the Gulag system. There were two large Gulag camps, "North" and "West," which supplied uranium and tin – the camp buildings and graveyards are still there outside the city. Nowadays, there are no prisoners. Workers elect to work in the Arctic because of the incentives of higher pay and living allowances, better retirement and holiday perks etc."

Robert said, "Una, you mentioned a military base. Is it very big?"

"Fairly big. Let's say it's growing quickly to brigade strength. With Russia's new Arctic policy to maintain a military presence in the region, Pevek is a port of call for nuclear submarines and ships on Arctic patrol. The airfield has an air force base that has been enlarged. The army has established two brigades of soldiers specifically trained for Arctic combat and one of the brigades has been assigned headquarters in the Pevek area. We'll be well protected as they will take on our security. "

"It sounds good," commented Stephanie. "How long will we be there?"

"We will remain based here in Mayberry but team members can fly in to Pevek for the testing. Maybe stay up to a week or so at a time. Our engineering technicians will handle construction. This

188

prototype is pretty straightforward – just drill into the permafrost to release the gas, move it to storage and clean it, then transport by pipeline to the power plant. It's been pretty easy to convert one of the boilers at the power plant to be gas fired. We can concentrate now on "packaging" the process to serve a smaller scale village, with automation separating out and harvesting the impurities, and also substituting for diesel fuel in internal combustion engines."

Carl said, "And, of course, the race is on to patent everything possible. We're making good progress with applications. We've got momentum. Things are moving right along."

"We're very fortunate to have such a great cadre of technicians – machinists and engineers – helping to bring our ideas into prototypes very quickly," commented Robert. "Things have moved along very quickly and smoothly."

"It helps to have an unlimited budget," replied Uri, "and that's thanks to the Willard Institute and the endorsements of the president and prime minister of Russia and of the Japanese government."

Hayden said, "I like the Japanese way of looking at this. We're at war and we're going to win!"

"There's one thing I've learned about isolated and growing locations in Russia," said Ivan, with a smile and a twinkle in his eye. "Bring your own toilet seat, bathroom cleaner, soap and toilet paper. They're in short supply."

"You're kidding?" asked Robert.

"Nope."

Chapter 40

Saint Lucia was a good place to hide, to grieve, to think, to plan. He had found an excellent upscale resort situated on over a hundred acres of hilly beachfront near the international airport that been highly rated both for luxury and catering to his kind. He had isolated himself in a luxurious cottage that afforded privacy and great room service well away from the main hotel. But, after four weeks of sun, sand, surf and solitude, the experience was wearing thin.

Richard Brooks had come to the resort a few days after he had been fired from his job as personal executive assistant in John Marshall's Senate office. He understood that his job had ended with the death of John Marshall but was still steaming from the way it had been handled.

He vividly recalled the day. He had shown up at the office at his usual time of eight a.m. He had the daily business of the office well organized by the time Adrian Carlyle, a representative from the Prime Minister's Office and Judy Forsque, Chief Clerk of the Senate clerical staff, barged in with four uniformed security guards in tow. Judy informed Richard that Senator John Marshall was dead and they were seizing all files in the office. He was also informed that his employment and that of the rest of the office staff terminated on the death of John Marshall. He would receive two weeks' severance pay. Under the watchful eyes of two security guards, he was escorted out of the office with his few personal items and was banned from re-entering the building. Within minutes, his whole life had changed.

He had been shocked and numbed by the totally unexpected death of John Marshall. They had been together for over seven years and had been close – discretely close. Lovers. Co-workers. Confidants. At John's insistence, they keep their love affair secret. At the office, professionalism between boss and personal secretary was the rule. There had been no behavior that alerted the staff to their relationship. Meetings after work were always clandestine – rarely John's condominium, not that frequently at Richard's apartment in Ottawa. More often they met in an apartment John had financed for

Richard in a pro-gay quarter of Montreal where they always arrived separately. Locally, they were never seen publicly together. Perfect decorum and separate bedrooms prevailed when they traveled together on business. They would holiday in areas favored by the gay community, such as Palm Springs, San Francisco, Key West and St. Croix, but they always travelled separately and on different days to their rendezvous. John was older by fifteen years and the dominant partner. John the mentor. Richard was the ever efficient and obedient assistant, always covering John's back in senate and business affairs.

Richard missed John. It took over two weeks before his grieving began to transition into seething anger. His brooding led to a plan to embarrass the PMO and the Senate. He had lots of ammunition as he had gleaned a private file of machinations orchestrated by his mentor which he kept squirreled away in a safety deposit box. John had continuously given him documents and audio and video tapes of transactions for safekeeping – a "back-up set in case of emergency" as he called it. John had told him there was always the chance someone would "do him in" and the files were his to use to get even if that ever happened.

John Marshall had also provided for Richard. The Montreal apartment was in Richard's name and it was debt-free. Also sitting in a safety deposit box was a little nest egg of over a million dollars – untraceable and undeclared cash. John had told Richard he was not included in his official Last Will and Testament as the official residue of the estate was to go to the law school at his Alma Mater university. Richard's legacy was the contents of the safety deposit box.

John Marshall's death, in Richard's eyes, was likely not accidental. He felt the police investigation into John's death would only be cursory – swaying toward ruling it accidental as that would benefit the political masters. As one who was in on all John Marshall had been up to, Richard was convinced his lover had been terminated. John had been getting too greedy with the big oil interests. Then again, he was also getting too demanding with the PM and threatening to reveal some muddy secrets. Yes, he was killed to shut him up. Had to be. Now, the question was how to enact revenge – and make some money doing it. Slowly, carefully weighing pros and cons, testing angles and developing contingencies, his revenge started to take shape. Number one target: the PMO.

Chapter 41

Joyce was getting into the driver's seat of her car parked at the newspaper building when she noticed an envelope on the passenger seat. It had her name on it but nothing else. She opened it and found a note and some biographies. She read the note:

Joyce,

You have the opportunity for a scoop (see, I know how to get your rapt attention).

Thelma Kenny, CEO of the Willard Institute in Washington, D.C. (Telephone: 202 541 0202) is expecting you to call to arrange an exclusive interview with the Canadian Arctic researchers who have been in hiding. That is: Robert Berubé and his wife Marie; Norma Jensen and her husband Carl; and Peter Melville. I have enclosed current biographies on all of them for your interview preparation. Also enclosed is a description of the Willard Institute and a bio on Thelma Kinney as I suspect you will also want to interview her.

The researchers will remain in hiding but you will be in contact by video link from the board room of the Willard Institute.

Thelma has only one rule. You cannot ask where they are, nor are you to speculate where they are. This is for their safety.

Have fun with your scoop!

R

"Well," thought Joyce, "now for some more fun. Thank you, Robert."

After clearing the project with her editor, Roy Bonspiel, she contacted Thelma Kenny and was invited to visit the Willard Institute in Washington, D.C. to set up and conduct the interviews.

At their first meeting, Thelma and Joyce bonded well. Thelma explained the mandate of the Willard Institute and how and why they were sponsoring the researchers and pushing for patents on the technology. At one point Joyce said, "So the Willard Institute is not solely altruistic but also in this for the patent revenues?"

Thelma smiled. "Of course! Patent revenues help sustain our researchers and finance scientific advancement. We're into many things, some of which do not pay off – or may be many years away from commercialization. We often fund what can be considered "pure" research. We also have the funds and mandate to sponsor unbiased looks at major issues, such as global warming, ocean pollution, etc. Bear in mind, we share the patent proceeds with our researchers. Some are now multi-millionaires.

"The methane hydrate research overlaps two areas: commercialization and global warming. The abundance of methane hydrate can fuel the world for centuries and it is a fairly clean gas. It's tricky to extract but can be most beneficial. On the other hand, global warming is releasing it from the ground and oceans at an alarming rate, increasing global warming. And that process will only speed up with greater global warming. That can threaten our entire existence. We want to raise the alarm about the threat of global warming. That's why we're sponsoring a paper to be presented to the United Nations by our researchers – we've got some solid research and astounding data that must be brought to the attention of the world."

"Can I quote you?"

"Yes. In fact, I'll go you one better. I've seen some samples of you being interviewed on TV concerning some of your previous exposés. You're good at it. Would you like to do a video recording of this sort of discussion and your interviews with the researchers to go along with your written work? That will come in handy when you are interviewed on TV. We have our own TV production department who would help with the technical parts of the presentations and editing. Once you publish your series, I can help you get on some of the national news channels, even some international ones, including in Canada. Our PR department could work with you to build publicity – such as guest appearances on national TV morning shows."

"Oh, my! My paper will do the same exposure thrust in Canada. I often do TV and radio interviews after an exposé. Video material of the interviews would be excellent! Yes please! I prefer unedited material or control of the editing. How long do you think this would take?"

"You'd better tell your editor you'll be away for three to four weeks."

In that time, Joyce was able to build a five-part series which ran daily in the *Toronto New Tribune*. This quickly led to guest appearances on the national news of the Canada Broadcasting Corporation, Canada's largest broadcaster, the BBC and three of the big American networks. Video clips of her interviews were received with excitement by the broadcasters. She interviewed well. Two-thirds of Canada's population – a huge audience, almost unprecedented, had seen her on TV.

She managed to make the front page with her first article when it headlined:

Fear
Arctic Researchers Afraid to Return to Canada

When she interviewed Robert and Marie Berubé, Norma and Carl Jensen and Peter Melville, they reiterated that they felt their lives were still in danger, especially if they returned to Canada. They were happy to pursue their research and were making good progress. They described the patent application process, noting they had met with strong, but not unexpected opposition from competing researchers from the oil industry but had been successful. Joyce played up the fact that the patent process benefited the Willard Institute and the Russian and Japanese partners that Canada had lost by cancelling their research funding.

Chapter 42

Manfried Rule and Christine Lamont were meeting over cappuccinos in a coffee house near the Houses of Parliament in Ottawa. Manfried said, "An interesting thing came up in the Security Oversight Committee this morning. The FBI informed our security personnel in Washington that they have the Arctic researchers sequestered away in a safe house in the Virginia countryside. They're all there for a two-week meeting with the Willard Institute patent attorneys. Apparently, the Canadians will be interviewed by Joyce Withers while they're there. She's going to be doing an exposé directly linking the oil industry to the deaths of their associates and detailing corruption within the senate and PMO. Apparently, they'll be naming names."

"Really? Did you find out the location?"

"Yeah, in Shenandoah National Park on a small lake surrounded by mountains. Lake Bailey. About a hundred miles from Washington D.C. Apparently, the place is pretty remote, nestled up a box canyon in the Blue Ridge Mountains about fifteen miles in from Skyline Drive which is a scenic drive running the ridgeline of the mountains. It was built in the Depression as part of a New Deal make-work project. The army used it as a conference center but it was taken over by the FBI in the nineties. They call it Camp Samuel."

"I'll pass it on."

Hector was on the phone with Sanford. "Well Hector, it didn't take long for that story about the researchers meeting with the patent attorneys to get action. We've intercepted Christine speaking to Chairman Van Der Zalm. He, in turn summoned Paddy to Curacao."

"I suspect Paddy will organize and probably lead an attack team?"

"We've intercepted him contacting five of his key men. He's pulling them out of their base in Nigeria. Looks as if an oil company has given them a lift to America on a corporate jet that's filed a flight plan to Raleigh, North Carolina. He's going to have to act fairly quickly – that should be to our advantage."

"He'll want to scout out the terrain first."

"Yeah. Our people have been alerted. They'll lay low. It's your show."

"The FBI will handle it from arrival in Raleigh."

"Great! I'll be keeping our Japanese friends in the loop."

Chapter 43

Once again, Jack Haskell was meeting over lunch with John Roberts at the club. After being served the entrée, the Prime Minister's Chief of Staff opened the discussion. "You said over the phone this may be a bit urgent? What is it?"

"We had a visit from a Sergeant Ruggan of the RCMP. They're looking at John Marshall's death in relation to the deaths of the Arctic researchers."

John, in process of sipping a spoonful of clam chowder, began choking and gagging. From behind his napkin, he spluttered, "Oh shit! How did that happen?"

"The death of the scientist in Newfoundland is an open and shut murder case. They're sure it was associated with the attempts on scientists in Japan, Alaska and Russia and the deaths of the others in Canada and the United States. The common linkage is the Arctic research. As Marshall was instrumental in getting you to cancel it, they're sniffing a correlation."

"Shit!"

"I have a problem... No, WE have a problem! As executor of Marshall's estate, we're obligated to turn over his files to the police if they determine his death was murder."

"Shit!"

"The local police did a cursory examination of all the contents in John Marshall's safe, computer and filing system as part of their crime scene investigation at the condo where he died but they released all that to the estate when they decided he wasn't murdered. We have his files and computer from his apartment and safety deposit box in Kamloops. We've got that tucked away in a safe place."

"Good!"

"But your people ransacked his Senate office and took his computers and all his files from there."

"Yes. We have control of it. Some of it is quite volatile. But I doubt if he kept too much in his office. You probably are in possession of much more. Problem is that too many people know we did that so there would be a stink raised if that stuff was destroyed."

"It could be subpoenaed by the courts."

"There'd have to be a pretty good reason. Even if the reason goes public, there'd be a huge stink. We'll have to try to stifle it – I hope nip at the oversight level."

Chapter 44

Lowering his binoculars, Paddy thought, an interesting challenge, but not anything he hadn't handled before. Leaving the rest of the team at a farm outside of Raleigh, he and Stan Thomas had taken on the task of scouting out the Lake Bailey conference center. They were lying on a ridge overlooking the two-story main building situated about two hundred feet up a path from a dock on the lake. They estimated it held at least a dozen bedrooms on the second floor. The roofs of some seven duplex cottages nestled around the main building were visible among the pine trees. They noted a parking lot in front of the main building at the end of the paved road leading in from Skyline Drive, some seventeen miles to the west. The lot held half a dozen cars. Earlier, they had passed a gate and gatehouse with two SUV's parked behind. The gate was in a ten-foot-high chain link fence that stretched across the narrow valley, climbed the canyon walls and ran along the ridgeline encircling the property. They had noted it was electrified but had managed easily to skirt around it.

The lake was at the end of the box canyon. It was narrow, about quarter mile wide and a mile long, surrounded by near-vertical canyon walls on three sides. They had taken the time to scout it out and found the canyon terminated at a cliff at the eastern end of the lake with a three-hundred-foot waterfall that was a photographer's dream. A small stream emptied westward from the lake weaving a serpentine path and sharing the floor of the canyon with the road to Skyline Drive.

They had counted three security personnel patrolling the grounds. Add that to the two on duty at the gatehouse equaled five on any shift. They looked around and identified the guards' bunkhouse midway between the gatehouse and the lodge. Judging by the cars in front of it, it looked as if there might be another five off duty. They estimated four housekeeping personnel, a cook, assistant and two maids. They weren't sure how many FBI personnel would be inside with the targets but they assumed at least two.

Chairman Van der Zalm's comments guided their planning. The researchers were gathered with their patent attorneys. This was a crucial point in their patent applications – a good time to foul them up by eliminating both the researchers and the patent attorneys. Yes, the work could be duplicated but there would be a major delay. Objective: seize their work and incapacitate them. Seize computer memories and documents for the industry's own researchers and patent attorneys to win the patent race. If Joyce Withers was present, kill her.

Having scouted the terrain, the tactical plan was starting to gel. They would return to Raleigh and develop their assault plan. While both were lying prone on the ridge looking down on the buildings, they were startled by a loud voice behind them. "FBI. Don't move! You're surrounded." Both froze. The voice again, "Hands on your heads. That's it. Don't move!" Two FBI agents in SWAT gear rushed up and proceeded to handcuff each. The search for weapons revealed nothing but a camera and wallets which were confiscated. Paddy and Stan were pulled up into a sitting position facing a small semi-circle of FBI agents in SWAT gear. One of the agents, possibly the lead one, while waiting for an agent to finish rifling through the wallets, said, "You're trespassing on FBI land. What are you doing here?"

Paddy came up with a story. "We were hiking through to photograph the waterfall. Then we walked this way and discovered the buildings below. We're taking a rest break and   were wondering what they were for."

The agent examining the wallets said, "A Cecil Smith and Mr. John Jones both from Houston, Texas. Not too original." The lead agent snickered. Paddy and Stan snuck a quick look at each other, puzzled.

"Well, we know you better as Mr. Paddy (Patrick) West and Mr. Stan Thomas of Extraction Inc. Mr. West, you were recently in Curacao. And Mr. Thomas, you flew into Raleigh on a private jet yesterday from Port Harcourt, Nigeria. We've had you under observation. Oh, by the way, we've picked up your buddies on the farm near Raleigh."

"Are we being charged with something? I want a lawyer. I know my rights," said Paddy. This was echoed by Stan.

201

The lead agent, Mark Spencer, said, "Well, Mr. Thomas may be charged with trespassing on FBI restricted ground, to begin with. Perhaps murder conspiracy along with your buddies – even sabotage. But we have something special in store for you, Mr. West. You'll be going with those two gentlemen." Two men in SWAT gear came forward, lifted Paddy to his feet. With each securely holding an arm they led him toward a helicopter that had just landed about five hundred feet away. Paddy was shoved into the passenger bay, secured by seat belt and leg shackles and whisked away.

A month later. US Air Force Base, Langley, Virginia

With Dave Green driving and Jerry Wong in the back seat, the black government-issue SUV entered a hangar isolated at the far end of the airfield. Inside, a Bombardier 8000 Executive Jet was parked, with four men standing by the stairway. Jerry had noted a perimeter guard of at least eight well-armed men radiating out from the hangar – likely fellow CIA personnel keeping security tight. The aircraft had no insignia and no national flag. Dave drove the black SUV right up to the jet's stairway. Tadao Suzuki and Sanford met Dave and Jerry at the plane's stairway. Tadao introduced them to the two men he had with him, Mishi Matsumoto and Sei Tadano. An unconscious Paddy, handcuffed and legs shackled, lay in the cargo bay of the SUV. Dave popped the back door latch. Jerry, Mishi, Dave and Sei reached into the cargo bay and quickly transferred Paddy aboard the aircraft.

Sanford turned to Tadao and said, "In a way, I'm glad you're taking him off our hands. It saves a messy trial. We interrogated him, of course, and I've sent you the transcripts of that. You may be able to get some more out of him but I think we did a pretty good job. What are you planning to do with him?"

Tadao, thinking for a moment, said, "You've done so much for us and we are most grateful. Well, let's say we Japanese take Mr. West's interference very seriously. He's been very destructive of that which we consider of strategic importance. Let's say, we are at war and he's considered a major enemy and threat to Japan. He'll get what he deserves and we'll send a message to his employer. First, we'll take him to a secure location for further interrogation.

Then, we'll use him to send a message to his employer. We have our traditional ways."

"That sounds good to me."

Chapter 45

A courier service delivered a package to the PMO addressed to the personal and private attention of John Roberts, Chief of Staff. It was signed for and eventually found its way to John Roberts. He opened it and found a cheap, disposable cell phone, a small but good quality voice recorder and an envelope bearing the instructions: *Play the recording first, then open this envelope.* John called his office assistant who was in the outer vestibule guarding the door to his private office and asked her to ensure he was not disturbed until further notice. He then played the recording. The voices of those on it were easily recognizable.

"Don't talk to me about conflict of interest! There's nothing in the rules saying I can't receive money as a member of a Board of Directors while serving as a senator. I'll not resign from the Senate. It'll take a scandal to do that and I'll pull you all down with me if it comes to that."

"How much cash would you want if the party paid you to resign?"

"At least five million plus the usual Senate pension... And an ambassadorship to London."

"That's too rich."

"And don't give me this shit about signing the order to rescind the research funding. The party got a five million dollar donation and you two split a million that was sent to your offshore accounts in Mauritius. That's just good business. It's obvious "big oil" got a little carried away trying to eradicate the researchers. That's not our fault. Mind you, we could make a few dollars by putting a cap on the murder investigations."

The PM's voice: *"That's going a bit far, screwing with the judiciary. You've attracted a lot of attention. We've got to do something about the perceived conflict of interest."*

"I'll resign from my directorships, if that'll satisfy you. But then that should be applied to all Senators."

"Right, we can bury a study toward that end in a committee for at least a year. That's a way to shelve it for now. In the meantime, we've got damage control to worry about."

The tape was accompanied by a short note containing the numbers to offshore bank accounts of the party, the PM and John Roberts and the sums deposited in each resulting from that deal. As well, the note said, *You will want to talk with Mr. Smith on the untraceable cell phone enclosed. He will call shortly.*

With a knot in his stomach, John Roberts called the Prime Minister's executive assistant and asked her to clear time for the PM to have an immediate meeting with him. "It's best if he comes to my office." As luck would have it, the PM was just finishing a meeting and was able to drop in a few minutes later.

"You look white," he said. "What's up?"

John once again asked his executive assistant to give them some privacy, then turned to the PM. "You've got to hear this. We've got a major problem. The ghost of Senator John Marshall is starting to haunt us." He played the tape then showed Eugene the note.

Eugene read the note. "By giving us the banking coordinates, this guy is showing he really knows everything. Shit! Can we buy him off? If so, for how long? What else will he want to gouge us over?"

"I guess we have to await his phone call and find out."

"In the meantime, let's move our money to new bank accounts and try to kill the money trail. You've got to let the party's management team in on this. It affects one of the party's secret accounts as well."

Chapter 46

Setting up the prototype in Pevek went smoothly. All the team members made periodic visits to help expedite the project, but overall, the work was well and speedily handled by the technicians Una and Ivan had selected. A drill crew tapped a bed of permafrost containing significant methane hydrate. Following the methodology developed by the Japanese, Peter, Vanessa and Hayden oversaw design and construction and soon had a productive well. In turn, the raw gas was piped to a storage facility newly built on the outskirts of Pevek, where test-scale equipment had been installed to "sweeten" the gas by removing moisture, separating out impurities, then storing the "cleaned" gas. The cleaned methane gas was then piped to fire a boiler at the central steam plant producing heat and electricity for distribution throughout the city. At the insistence of the board of directors of the Willard Institute, the impurities extracted would not be dumped into the environment but further refined into useful and marketable by-products, such as sulfur, ethane, propane, carbon dioxide, nitrogen, and hydrogen sulfate. Residue of chemicals used in the refinement process would also be recycled. By-product water would be purified for domestic consumption.

In the middle of winter, all were present at the plant for a little ceremony when the boiler was lit for its first use of the methane gas. Things went as planned. The firing of the boiler was almost an anticlimax. The system would be heavily monitored and occasionally tweaked over the ensuing months. The main concern would be to ensure a continuous flow of gas up the wellhead and to provide adequate storage and separation. After six months, the system would be ramped up to a full production scale with better wellhead flow and refinement of the marketable by-products. Careful monitoring would lead to the development of software to automate the system.

Back in Mayberry, in addition to assisting engineers in designing a full-scale plant to clean the gas and refine impurities, the team was moving out well in other directions such as adapting internal combustion engines to run on the gas. This field of carburetion – fuel-injection expertise – had long been dominated by Italian technology but the team improved on that work. Russian engineers contributed to the advancements by coating cylinders in ceramic to cut friction. They also introduced sodium-filled valve stems to help keep consistent temperatures (a technology in common use with their armored military vehicles) and a cobalt-chrome-tungsten alloy to coat valves in order to provide a hard surface and minimize wear.

Time was spent on ensuring the gas would flow from storage to use at low temperatures without solidifying. Eventually, a simple and economical method was perfected based on removing moisture.

At a review meeting, Robert summed up. "We've proved the process. We have a working prototype of one boiler contributing to heating and lighting a fair-sized city in the Arctic and we will soon convert other boilers at the steam plant. The process is more economical and less polluting than coal. It is less potentially dangerous than the twelve nuclear plants they have put on barges and placed at new villages in the Arctic. Our Japanese partners are producing from a deep offshore marine environment and are looking forward to quickly offsetting their dependence on imported oil. Now, our next challenge is to scale down and automate the process to work reliably for a small Arctic settlement with little maintenance required."

"Now that's a real challenge," remarked Hayden. We've got to write and design a lot of software and built servos to automate and add in redundancy and, oh, yeah, be able to work in severe climatic conditions."

"You've got the idea!"

"Plus," chimed in Norma, "we must not pollute the environment. We have to produce useable, marketable products from the residue – just like our model in Pevek."

"Look at that from another point of view," said Carl. "If we teach the villagers to properly handle and package the assorted residue products, they have something to sell. That would be very attractive for the truckers hauling goods in over winter ice roads, as it gives them something of value to transport out rather than going south empty."

Peter said, "I can see a lot of work for our patent attorneys. There'll be a lot of innovation in this area."

"Amen. It'll be fun!" said a smiling Vanessa as she squeezed Peter's hand.

Chapter 47

At seven-thirty that evening, John Roberts was still in his office. He jumped, jerking his feet off his desk when the cell phone finally rang. "John Roberts," he said, as confidently as he could.

The voice on the other end said, "Mr. Roberts, how are you?"

"Concerned. Who are you and what do you want?"

"For now, a token of your sincerity. Half a million dollars – US dollars, not Canadian. I want it delivered offshore to a numbered corporate account in Mauritius."

"What do we get for this?"

"My silence, of course."

"Will you turn over all documents?"

"I can but you will never know if I kept a set for my personal protection."

"That's pretty loose. How can I guarantee your silence? Perhaps you'd come to work for us?"

"You mean, a senatorship like you gave John Marshall to buy his loyalty?"

"Or an ambassadorship. Whatever."

"Yeah, right! An ambassadorship to some godforsaken third world country! Dropped somewhere and forgotten. You guys don't treat people very well. With the Senate under fire, I doubt if you could get away with an appointment either. Fuck you!"

"Think it over. I'll keep the offer open. We want your loyalty and your silence. John Marshall may have conned his way into a senatorship but he served the party well once he was appointed. He was a great fund raiser."

"He also brought in a lot of deals from which you, the PM and the party benefited."

"This is true. We miss him."

"He was giving you some problems though."

"Yes, but nothing we felt couldn't be ironed out with further negotiation."

"That's long enough for this phone call. I'll let you think over my request. First, I want half a million. Your offer of an appointment is interesting but that would come after you have shown your sincerity by depositing half a million. I will call again tomorrow afternoon with the banking coordinates for my bank in Mauritius." The phone went dead.

John put the phone down on his desk. Four other people were in the room: the PM, Fred Archer, from Acme Security, a large, private investigation firm under contract to the party, Ernie Kowalchuk, and André Robadeux, both senior executives, Chief Financial Officer and Secretary, of the Unity Party. Fred had tapped the phone and was fiddling with the recorder, about to play it back.

The PM said, "John, I only heard your side of the conversation but I like your approach."

Fred played back the recording. When it finished, John Roberts commented, "He wants half a million US sent to a corporate account in Mauritius. I suspected he was someone close to John Marshall who would know how we buy party loyalty; that's why I offered to recruit him."

Fred said, "Interesting that he didn't try to disguise his voice. We can try to match his voice. We'll start with those known to be close to Marshall – associates, etc." Fred played back the entire conversation then contacted his office where the cell phone call was being traced. They reported the call was from a pay phone in the central train station in Ottawa. "I doubt if he'll call from the same place twice."

André Robadeux, after giving it some thought said, "You know, that voice is familiar. Fairly cultured. Middle-aged."

Ernie Kowalchuk, Chief Financial Officer of the party, commented, "He seems to know his way around offshore banking. Mauritius is one of the few tax havens that maintains customer privacy. No one can look into account ownership. I doubt if he'd keep the funds there. He's probably using a numbered account registered to a numbered corporation somewhere else and will probably immediately transfer the funds when they arrive in Mauritius. At least, that's the way I'd do it."

Fred said, "I'll get back to the office and start my people tracking the voice. In the meantime, if he calls, you have the recorder attached to the phone. It's set to turn on when the phone rings. Let me know if you recognize the voice."

After Fred left, the remaining four helped themselves to drinks from the credenza bar. André said, "If we pay, he'll just be back for more." All agreed.

Robert had poured himself a fifteen-year-old single malt scotch on the rocks. He took a sip, then swirled the ice in his glass. "If we don't pay, it'll probably be all over the media in a day."

Sipping on a beer he had poured into a cut crystal glass, André said, "We've got to identify him first. We've got to stall until we do that. John, you might have hit a nerve with the offer of an appointment, maybe you can play with that some more – if only to stall him." All agreed.

"And if he doesn't play along?" asked Robert.

Ernie, nursing a mineral water, looked at the ice cubes in his glass and said, "Then we'll put on the gloves – but first we've got to know who we're dealing with."

A little after noon the next day, Fred Archer called André Robadeux. "Your man is Richard Brooks. He was John Marshall's executive assistant. From what we have discovered so far, he took the loss of John Marshall very hard. They might have had a

211

relationship. I've got people developing a biography on him. Should have a nice package on him by late this afternoon"

"Excellent work. I thought that voice was a bit familiar. Yes, I agree. That's him. We're scheduled to meet at the PMO again this late afternoon, just in case this guy, Richard, calls. Will you advise the others of the name?"

"My pleasure."

That evening, the group was together again awaiting the call. Fred had provided each with a three-page biography on Richard. After each had digested the content, Eugene was the first to speak up. "So, they were secret lovers! I would never have guessed. Talk about discreet!"

John Roberts rubbed his chin. "Can we use that to our advantage?"

"Best not to tip our hand and let him know we're aware of it," said Fred.

A few minutes later, the cell phone rang and John answered. "Yes?"

"Mr. Roberts, you've had some time to think over my demand and to talk it over with the PM and others. Are you willing to comply with my modest request?"

"I have indeed conferred with others. Your demand is possible but we want assurance you will turn over everything – so that the material will never see the light of day. And we do not want to be constantly milked for more over this."

"I see. My fee would be higher, much higher."

"Have you given any more thought to coming over to our side – to work for us?"

"As a senator? As an ambassador?"

"We were thinking more of an ambassadorship but one acceptable to you. Not one of the front line positions, such as London or Paris but one that would be comfortable."

"Such as?"

"Perhaps St. Thomas? St. Lucia? Trinidad?"

"I don't know…I'd need to give it more thought."

"Remember, John Marshall kept his secrets when we made him a senator. It worked out well for him. We had a healthy mutual respect and he was very productive for the party. You could do the same. Come over and work with us – for the good of the party."

"You know, it's an interesting thought. Only problem is that an ambassadorship will probably end when your party's thrown out of office."

"Likely true. We have to work together to preserve the integrity of the party in the eyes of the electors. More reason for you to show loyalty to us."

"I'll have to give it more thought. What about a senate appointment?"

"You know the climate right now. Do you think we could get away with an appointment?"

"Mmmm."

"We can also consider a senior level bureaucratic position in the government or one of the government corporations."

"Reasonable pay but a lot of work. I don't know. Let me think on this."

"It's Friday now; why don't you take the weekend to mull this over, then get back to me. Say, Monday? Same time?"

"I'll do that." The line goes dead.

Fred called his office to see if the trace was successful. After a brief conversation, he hung up. "Same thing. Called from a public phone. This time at a department store. We didn't have time to organize surveillance before he slipped out of his apartment. But, we have a surveillance team waiting for him when he returns. We've also got a team watching his apartment in Montreal. The teams have orders to observe but not pick him up."

"John, I think you've got him dangling. Think he'll accept a deal?" asked André.

Ernie Kowalchuk jumped in. "We'll have to wait and see. In the meantime, my people will prepare a contingency plan. Eugene, John, the party will take care of it."

Chapter 48

An exhausted Prime Minister Eugene Rogers flopped onto a sofa in his office after braving another session of Question Period in the House of Commons. He had been peppered relentlessly about questions raised by Joyce Withers in the *Toronto New Tribune.* "John, I can't stonewall much longer," said the weary PM to John Roberts. "We have to do something about Rule and Lamont – maybe even look at some reform measures for the Senate."

"That Joyce Withers certainly lit a raging fire of public opinion against what is perceived as Senate corruption. The latest opinion poll has us down another seven percent in public approval and it's still falling. We're at the lowest confidence level ever."

"There's rumor afoot that some back benchers are calling for my resignation, wanting a No Confidence vote."

"The party whip should be able to keep that quiet. But there's still the possibility one or some of the backbenchers may opt to leave the party and cross the floor to sit independently or join the opposition. That would be bad. We've got to get a handle on how serious that is. If we lose some, others may follow and we lose our majority to govern. Worse than that, the party members may be after my resignation."

"Yeah. We've got to act – do something seemingly positive in response to public outcry and we've got to pacify the backbenchers."

"Do something or be perceived to do something about the issue of conflict of interest by senators?"

"I doubt if just striking a committee to review the matter would satisfy very many. It would bury things for a while though."

"To after the next election where it could be tabled and forgotten?"

"I doubt it. Public outcry is too strong. We should be seen as moving to clean up the perceived corruption. The Senate will have to bring in new rules against active conflicts of interest. But the public is clamoring for the heads of Senators Rule and Manfried – let's throw them to the wolves."

"How? Call in the RCMP to investigate?"

"That too. First, let's get Senate to suspend them. Let's immediately get them off the committees they sit on like RCMP and Security Oversight and any relating to the energy and environmental sectors. Also Fisheries and Oceans. It would probably be difficult to get them to resign from the Senate without a suitable incentive."

"Like an ambassadorship to London, Rome or Paris?"

"Yeah. We've done that before. But that's probably not sufficient. They're earning big bucks working for the big oil interests."

"They've also brought us and the party some good income. Remember?"

"Right. But we've got too much at stake with the Chinese to have the government collapse before that deal can be done."

"Amen brother! Amen."

The next day, as a surprise revelation in Question Period when confronted once again about the perceived corruption of Senators Lamont and Rule, Prime Minister Roberts rose to respond. "Honorable members, last night, both Senator Rule and Lamont, at my request, have resigned from all parliamentary committees. I have today requested the leader of the Senate to examine the question of conflict of interest in depth and to provide recommendations on how to avoid such conflicts in the future."

This was followed by an uproar in the house as members shouted and pounded tables with their fists. Pandemonium erupted in the press gallery, with some clamoring, pushing and shoving for the exit to the hall where they could file in-person voice and TV reports, while others had their heads down texting the news to their superiors. Some of the veterans paid close attention to the turmoil on the floor, waiting for the second shoe to drop. After what seemed like a few minutes, the leader of the opposition rose and was recognized by the Speaker of the House. "Mr. Speaker, would the Honorable Prime Minister elaborate if he feels the matter warrants investigation by the RCMP?"

"The Leader of the Senate is empowered to do so," replied the PM.

Chapter 49

Richard decided to spend the weekend at the Montreal apartment. He had a lot of thinking to do. Could he trust these guys? Would he like a minor ambassadorship? Something about the ambassadorship angle was appealing. St. Thomas or St. Lucia were tolerant of gays – after all they were gay travel destinations, weren't they? Maybe he could have some fun there. But how long would an ambassadorship last with an unpopular government that could soon fall? Maybe best just to milk them for all the money he could get up front. A senatorship would be nice – John Marshall would be proud of him. But how difficult would it be for the PMO to pull that off? At least that would endure past the present government.

The apartment walls were closing in on him by Saturday night. He felt a little lonely. Time to get out and get some action. He dressed in his best leather pants and jacket with a pink silk shirt undone past the second button, making sure to have a portion of his yellow handkerchief showing in his back (right) pocket to signal that he was submissive and liked watersports. He walked a short block to his favorite bar, Le Club Arc-En-Ciel (The Rainbow Club) on Sherbrooke Street. At eleven-thirty in the evening, the bar was just starting to get busy. Its clientele were the LGBT set, mainly gay men but there always were some lesbians and transvestites, both singles and couples, or party groups. Richard eased up to the bar and ordered a Labatt's light beer. When he was into his second beer, a man, similarly dressed in tight black leather pants and aqua-colored silk shirt under a black leather vest, moved into the seat beside him and said "hello." Richard noted he had a yellow handkerchief in his left vest pocket, signaling he was a dominant and into watersports.

Richard returned the greeting. "Hi, I'm Richard. You're new here? Haven't seen you around before."

They shook hands. "Yeah, I'm Steve Hartling. From Vancouver. I come here a couple of times a year on business, sometimes on vacation. Are you local?" Steve was about Robert's age. A little taller by two inches and a very fit-looking two hundred pounds. Richard thought he had a pretty handsome face with a neat moustache matching his crew-cut black hair.

218

"Well yeah, local in a way. I have an apartment here. But I work, or used to work that is, in Ottawa. I split my time between here and Ottawa." It didn't take long for Richard to reveal he had been Executive Assistant to Senator John Marshall, his lover and mentor, and that he was bitter over losing his job upon the Senator's death. Steve was a good, empathetic listener. Over the course of the evening they became good friends. Steve said he was an executive at a shoe wholesaler. Richard made the first move. After getting a signal from the bartender – a right-handed "OK" – indicating Steve was known to him and safe, Richard made a move. "I like the color of your handkerchief. Would you like to come to my place? Maybe we can put all the beer we've had to some good use?"

Steve swallowed his beer and put the glass down on the counter. "OK." He called the bartender and paid the tab for both of them. "Let's go."

At Richard's apartment, they both had another beer and eventually moved to the bedroom standing together beside the bed embracing, slowly exploring, helping each other undress between French kisses and gentle fondling. Richard was pleased. "I love it that you have shaved off all your body hair. Mmmm. Shall we shower together? I want to soap you down."

Steve was dominant but considerate and knew how to pleasure his partner. Eventually, bondage and breath control was brought in only after they agreed on signals to say when it was excessive. Richard had lots of toys to work with as John Marshall had been heavy into BDSM as the Master.

Steve stayed over Sunday, and left mid-morning Monday, saying he had promised to visit the head office of one of his suppliers. They agreed to meet for dinner that evening at Le Coq d'Or, Steve's favorite restaurant. Richard had enjoyed the visit. He was exhausted. Completely drained. It had been a long time since he had coupled with someone of equal energy, stamina and creativity who brought him to orgasm so many times. His favorite had been bondage in the large Jacuzzi-style bathtub.

Time away from Steve gave Richard time to think. Finally, he took the metro across the city, bought a prepaid cell phone at a drug store and placed a call to John Roberts, telling him he now wanted five million dollars within twenty-four hours. He was not interested in an appointment either as senator or ambassador or whatever. He was tired of talking it over. He would call again in eighteen hours with the banking coordinates.

After Fred played the phone call back, John Roberts said, "Well, gentlemen. Now we know where we stand."

"OK," said André. "We have a contingency plan for this. John, Eugene, time for you to ease back from this and let the party take over. Time for you to build deniability. Go home to your families and try to relax. We'll take it from here." The cell phone was turned over to Ernie Kowalchuk. It was reasoned the finance man should be the intermediary if Robert called, as he could review details of transferring funds offshore.

Chapter 50

Richard arrived at the restaurant first and was seated. Steve arrived shortly afterward sporting a new look. "Steve, wow! You look different! What happened to the moustache and where's your hair? I didn't know you wore glasses."

"Well, you know, I felt like a change. I took my contacts out. Been wearing them too long. Bald makes me look sexy, doesn't it?"

"I'll say!"

Dinner at Le Coq d'Or was magnificent. Richard had poached Atlantic salmon and Steve had lobster. Steve insisted dinner was his treat. He ordered an excellent expensive French Chardonnay and toasted their friendship. Conversation was light with Steve talking a lot about his visit to the shoe supplier and the new models soon to be in the stores. Steve paid the bill with cash. By taxi, they made it back to Richard's apartment about ten o'clock and were soon naked on the bed nestled in a tender embrace. After a gentle first round, Steve asked, "May I tie you up?"

"Sure. What've you got in mind?"

"Oh, let's start with the ben-wa balls and go from there." Steve soon had Richard on his stomach with hands and feet tied to the bedposts. Shortly into their play, Steve's cell phone interrupted. "Ah, nuts. I've got to take that call, it's probably someone from the west coast – you know the time difference is three hours earlier out there. Sorry. Don't go away." Picking up the phone, leaving Richard tied up, he got off the bed and went into the front room. Richard could hear little save for an occasional monosyllable like "OK" or "good."

He was soon back. Richard recoiled hard when he was first struck. "Ouch! That hurt! What the hell are you doing? Time out. Time out! I don't like this! Stop! Stop!" Steve had a whip in his hand and was furiously pummeling Richard's back and bottom. He was drawing welts and blood. He only stopped momentarily to jam a ball gag in Richard's mouth and cinch it tightly. Finally, after about

221

a hundred heavy strokes of the whip, Steve said, "All right asshole, where're all John Marshall's documents? If I don't get them, you're gonna die a very slow and painful death. Nod if you're ready to talk." He whipped some more. "Not interested in talking yet?" He stopped after another dozen heavy strokes when it looked as if Richard was losing consciousness. "I'm gonna take a break to search your apartment. Then I'll be back with more."

Richard passed out in total agony. He was painfully brought back to consciousness with Steve rubbing salt into the wounds. That stung like hell. Steve removed the ball gag and Richard tried to talk but found his mouth too dry. Steve helped him sip some water, then Richard managed to gasp, "Find anything?"

"A little. I've gone through your computer, clothes, file cabinet and drawers – even your car parked downstairs. I've found a safety deposit box key and you'll tell me the location and how to access it. You'll bring me the contents."

"I will not!"

"Well, indirectly you will. I'll keep you alive until I get the contents."

"Wha?"

Steve produced a hypodermic needle containing diphenhydramine, the basis of many antihistamines, a great, potentially lethal sedative, and stuck it in Richards butt. "You'll go out for a while. See you when I need you."

A few minutes later Steve answered a knock on the door and let in Brent "Smitty" Smith, a chubby older man, an expert at theatrical make-up, who was carrying a small suitcase. Smitty said, "How's the patient?"

"Not wanting to cooperate. He's got a high threshold for pain. Seems to like a bit of it but I've pushed past that level. I've found a safety deposit box key though. The boys who ransacked his Ottawa apartment also found one and records showing the location of a bank nearby. I've found some files on an account in a bank just a few blocks away. Likely it's that bank where he has another box.

We can wake him up later and make him talk. Meantime, you can do your thing making a mask of his face."

They turned Richard over to lie on his back. As a precaution, they retied his arms and legs to the posts. "OK. Take off his hood and I'll get started."

A few hours later, the first imprint had been reversed into a pliable rubber mask. Smitty touched up the coloring and looked at Richard. "Not bad if I do say so myself! We're all ready for the new Mr. Richard Brooks."

"Right now, he's covering for me in Ottawa. He'll be along in the morning. In the meantime, let's get Richard talking to pin down the location of the safety deposit boxes and other possible stashes."

Steve brought out another hypodermic kit and proceeded to inject some serum into Richard's left arm. Richard came up to semi-consciousness and they began beating and questioning. In a few minutes they had two safety deposit box numbers and locations, one close by in Montreal and the other in an Ottawa suburb. After getting what they wanted, assured he had no other safety deposit boxes, they put Richard back to sleep, then crashed out themselves on overstuffed chairs in the living room to rest till the morning.

At eight a.m. after they had breakfast from what they found in Richard's kitchen, their third man, Dan LaPoint, arrived. He had been selected both for his impersonation skills and the similarity of his physical appearance to Richard's. Dan spent half an hour practicing Richard's signature and got pretty good at it. In the meantime, following some color photos the surveillance crew had taken of Richard, Smitty selected some of Richard's clothes and laid them out for Dan. Smitty helped Dan put on the mask of Richard's face. Dan dressed, and after some touch-up and a wig, Smitty said, "Perfect!"

Steve left Smitty to watch Richard and drove Dan to the bank. Dan took an empty briefcase with him and easily passed the cursory scrutiny of the clerk on duty at the safety deposit box vault when he presented Richard's ID and signed a pretty good impression of Richard Brooks. With the help of the clerk with the bank's key, he opened the vault and took the box to a private booth where he transferred the contents to the briefcase, returned the box to the vault, collected his key and left.

Back in the car, he said, "Piece of cake. Next stop Ottawa." Steve drove him to General Aviation at Montreal's Mirabel airport where a charter jet was waiting to whisk him to Ottawa's MacDonald-Cartier airport for his visit to the next bank safety deposit box. Fred met him at General Aviation in Ottawa and traded an empty briefcase for Dan's full one from Montreal.

Steve returned to Richard's apartment and relieved Smitty. Richard would be his and his alone. He dosed Richard some more with serum and settled down to catch some sleep until he got word that Dan had cleared out the box in Ottawa. Four hours later, he got the "all clear." Fred had assessed the contents of the material gleaned from the boxes and was very happy. On the phone, Fred said, "You're sure he didn't have any other material stashed away?"

"No sir. I went around that a few times. No more safety deposit boxes."

"OK. Over to you to finish up. See you soon."

Steve began his first round of sanitizing the apartment by wiping down all surfaces with bleach, soap and water to remove fingerprints. He vacuumed and washed the floors. He would do Richard's bath and bedrooms twice. He would change the bed sheets and wash the originals after Richard was taken care of to reduce the chance of a CSI detecting body fluids. He poured large amounts of lye down all drains to help destroy hairs trapped in them. He loaded the dishwasher and turned it on. He would empty it and put away the dishes before he left.

He then carried Richard into the bathroom and laid him face down on the tile floor. He filled the tub with hot water. Holding Richard's hand to a glass to leave fingerprints, he poured a half tumbler full of whiskey down Richard's throat and placed the near empty glass close by at the side of the bath. He dumped Richard in the bath face up and held his head under until he drowned.

Once again, he scrubbed the bathroom, living room and kitchen for prints. He stripped the bed. The sheets were soaked with Richard's urine. He was thankful there was a rubber sheet underlay or he'd have to do something to the mattress. He put the linens in the clothes washer and added considerable detergent with bleach, made sure it was running and remade the bed with fresh linens. He wiped down Richard's leather garments, ropes, hood and rubber toys and bed sheet with a bleach-soaked cloth, dried them and put them away in one of the dresser drawers. He emptied the dishwasher and put away the dishes. He emptied the vacuum cleaner dust canister into a garbage bag then washed the canister, the heppa filter and rotary brush and inspected the vacuum tube from brush to dust canister, taking the time to pick out wayward hairs with a pair of tweezers. Steve had worn old clothes and rubber gloves for this part of the operation. He now changed into his street clothes and bagged the cleanup clothes. He would throw them and the garbage in a dumpster on the other side of town when he left for Ottawa.

At ten o'clock in the evening he slipped out of the apartment with the garbage bags, got into his car parked two blocks away and headed home to Ottawa. Once out of Montreal, he pulled into a rest stop and tore off the rubber skullcap he had worn to trick Richard into thinking he was bald. His hair could breathe again. The cap had been sweaty but it helped cut down on the chance of leaving some hair behind for the crime scene investigators. He had decided to leave Richard's laptop and everything else in place in the apartment. He had backed up the laptop's files onto a thumb drive – good enough.

The fetid, decomposing body of Richard Brooks, the loner, was discovered ten days later when neighbors complained about a strange smell. Police found they had a difficult case with minimal forensics. However, they placed the time of death sometime late Monday evening or early Tuesday morning. Perhaps it was excessive BDSM sex play that caused the death either during or after the play. Accidental? Murder? Not sure. Perhaps he had run a bath to try to recover from his BDSM episode, took a stiff drink with him to the bath, passed out from the alcohol and the heat, slumped down in the large tub and drowned. The scenario was an all too common occurrence – easy to jump to that conclusion. It was easy to rule that his death was accidental.

Chapter 51

Sergeant Jack Ruggan was in Inspector Poole's office. They had brought their self-serve coffees to a round worktable with four chairs. "Jack, now that the PM's taken Senators Rule and Lamont off all standing committees, are you concerned about anyone else running interference for the PMO on the Security Oversight Committee?"

"No sir. The rest of the members have all been vetted and come up clean – no conflicts. So far, no news about a replacement for Manfried Rule, though."

"Well, let's move quickly and call for access to the papers of the late Senator John Marshall that the PMO confiscated. I've advised the Security Oversight Committee that we are continuing to investigate Marshall's death. I talked with the Chief General Council and the Assistant DA of Public Safety in the Department of Justice and they in turn cleared it with Stephen Rains, their appointed Minister of Justice. We have the green light for a subpoena. I don't think Mr. Rains thinks there is anything to the issue."

"OK."

Next day.

Sergeant Ruggan was on the phone with Inspector Poole. "I presented the subpoena to John Roberts but he stonewalled me by turning it over to the PMO legal department who are declaring the material to be confidential – state secret. Our lawyers have met with their lawyers and they're taking the matter to court for a ruling. It looks dead in the water for at least a few weeks."

"Figures. It'd be better if we could specify certain materials. Dates, times, e-mails from whom to whom and the linkages we are searching."

"Yeah, we could do with a break like that."

Chapter 52

Eileen Brooks Taylor was devastated. She and her brother Richard had always been close. He was seven years older and had always been the big brother. Not in a macho way but sensitive and caring, funny and always there for her. She was determined to find out why he'd died.

She was getting a little impatient waiting in the lobby of the *Toronto New Tribune* when a woman approached and called her name. "Mrs. Taylor? I'm Joyce Withers. Thank you for coming." Joyce looked around the very public lobby and said, "Let's go up to my floor. I've got a conference room reserved for us."

Once seated in Conference Room 7A, and after serving Eileen coffee and a sweet bun, Joyce came to the point. "Eileen, you said on the phone that you had some material in your possession relating to the methane hydrate Arctic researchers' murders and you were afraid to go to the police? How did you acquire it?"

"My brother was John Marshall's Executive Assistant at the Senate. They were also lovers."

"I see. Your brother's name?"

"Richard Brooks." She pulled a tissue out of her purse and dabbed her tearful eyes. Near hysterics, she said, "He's dead! He's been killed! Now they're both dead!"

Placing a comforting hand on Eileen's arm, Joyce waited a few moments, then gently said, "What happened?"

"After John Marshall's death, Richard was depressed – in mourning, I guess you could say. But he was really upset about the way the government fired him immediately after Marshall died. He went away for a few weeks to think things out. To St. Lucia. We're close – very close. There was no one left on our family but me and him. I'm married to a wonderful guy and we live in Seattle with our two teenage children. Even though we're on the other side of the continent, Richard and I spoke on the phone once a week – long conversations. When he came back from St. Lucia he sent me a package of documents, even some CD videos and tape recordings. He told me to rent a safety deposit box and put them in it. That this was his insurance because he feared John Marshall had been killed and that someone might be after him to tie up loose ends. He even sent me a copy of his will and the phone number for his executor/lawyer."

"You should go to the police."

"Richard didn't trust the police. He felt there was a cover-up about Senator Marshall's death – that they'd only turn the documents over to the Prime Minister's Office. I chose you as you've been writing very strongly and effectively about the conflicts of interests of those senators mixed up with the oil industry getting the Arctic research cancelled. I've seen you on TV many times talking about it. I have documents showing they were paid to do it and that both the Prime Minister and the party in power were paid off."

"I see. So what do you want from me?"

"I want you to reveal these documents."

"Let me review them. Did you bring them with you?"

"Yes."

"OK. Let's do a quick sort, then read."

After a few minutes, Joyce looked up from the document she was reading. "My God! This is incredible! You've got to go to the police. But I recommend you go directly to the RCMP officer in charge of the investigation of the serial killings of the Arctic researchers. I'll arrange it for you. But first, let's copy all these. You and I will do that together – I don't want others sniffing at this. That way, we can keep the pressure up on the investigation." All the while she was thinking, *Another scoop.*

"Good."

Joyce took Eileen and her materials to the copy room. Luckily, it was empty. They entered and Joyce locked them in. While Joyce was copying the files with Eileen helping, she placed a call to Ottawa to Sergeant Jack Ruggan. Joyce persuaded him to come to Toronto to interview Eileen, arguing that her life might be in danger. After a little persuasion on Joyce's part, ("Get your sorry ass down here right now or you're going to see a hell of a lot of embarrassment when I go to press with the first part of this story") Ruggan said he would catch a commuter flight and be there around four p.m. The meeting would be at Joyce's office. Finishing the copying with a few hours to kill, Joyce commandeered the Conference Room for the rest of the day. She called up the paper's head of security and had him send a person to guard the door to ensure privacy and protection for Eileen. They called out for sandwiches and settled in to reading everything again, taking notes. Joyce ran to her desk and brought back a recorder and her laptop computer. After playing one of the tapes she found in the package of documents, she called in a technician, telling him to copy all the tapes but to do it in front of her in the conference room. Once that was organized, she began an in-depth backgrounder interview of Eileen – going deep into the human interest side of her relationship with her brother, his gay persuasion and his relationship with Senator Marshall.

Joyce phoned her editor to advise him she was onto something hot. When he was filled in, he agreed to hold front page space in the morning edition for her. With Joyce typing at full speed, Eileen kept busy making arrangements to see the executor of Richard's will and for Richard's cremation. The executor reported he had notified the banks and credit card companies and discovered something unusual. Richard had visited each of his safety deposit boxes on the day just before his death, and removed all contents. His Ottawa apartment appeared undisturbed.

When Sergeant Ruggan arrived with his boss, Inspector René Poole, Joyce had sent to press her first story of what she envisioned as a ten-part series. After introductions, Joyce took charge of the meeting and asked Eileen to explain why she was present.

After getting Eileen's explanation, Inspector Poole spoke. "Madam, I am so sorry you and your brother have little trust in the police. I can understand your point of view. But, let me assure you, the RCMP is independent from the influence of Parliament – as is the Canadian judicial system. If what you claim to be revealing and incriminating material sheds light on the murders of the Arctic researchers, then it is very important to the case Sergeant Ruggan is building. From what little you have revealed so far, there could be a corruption case against members of Parliament and the Senate and the Prime Minister's Office, even the leadership of their party. This could be explosive. Will you surrender your documents to us for examination?"

Joyce intervened. "We've agreed you may examine them here. Now. After, if you can give us assurance that the material supports indictments either for corruption and/or murder, you may take the documents. However, I have copies and I have full rights to expose them at my discretion."

A shocked and emotional Sergeant Ruggan blurted, "You can't have that! We need time to build a case. We need to keep the documents confidential until court."

Joyce gave an insincere smile. "Bullshit! If I write about this and expose some documents, it's out in the open. The shit's hit the fan. The public will be clamoring for action. It'll make your job easier. You won't be under pressure from the Parliamentary Oversight Committee to let it slide."

Inspector Poole thought a moment, waving Sergeant Ruggan to silence when he was about to speak. "No sense getting hot about this until we've seen the documents. May we read them please?"

Sergeant Ruggan and Inspector Pool took time to read carefully. Joyce then played one tape for them, one where John Marshall wanted an ambassadorship and mentioned pay-offs. When it finished, Sergeant Ruggan and Inspector Pool looked at each other. Ruggan gave a nod and Inspector Poole spoke. "The material about the Arctic researchers is most important. Of course, so are the other examples of pay-offs. We can use it immediately to subpoena the PMO for corroborative documents, demand surrender of the late Senator Marshall's files and lay charges of corruption. The tapes are significant – to say the least. We have enough here to get a search warrant of the PMO and even the Senate and party offices. Joyce, can you sit on this stuff for a few days? At least not mention the specific documents in our possession? We need a little time to follow money trails. Perhaps you have enough material to work around this for now?"

After a long and reflective pause, Joyce said, "I'll grant you that. I plan to start with Eileen and work on the angle of her brother's death and his relationship with John Marshall. That might light a fire with the Montreal police to make them look a little closer at Richard's death. Then I'll work back through Senator Marshall's dealings. BUT I want exclusive on this, no leaking to other media types or I'll broadside you publicly with all sorts of detail. I want to be informed in advance when you're about to serve a warrant on whom and why. OK?"

Inspector Poole frowned and thought for a few moments. "OK. Deal. Please never quote me but there are times when it may be advantageous for the press to get involved. Mrs. Taylor, thank you for bringing this to our attention. In addition to the Ottawa side of this investigation, I will instruct our Montreal office to assist the Montreal Police with their investigation. These documents indicated that Richard's death was probably murder. It is interesting that he visited both his safety deposit boxes on the Monday before his death."

After taking a statement from Eileen, they took their copy of the documents and left. Joyce turned to Eileen. "I guess you're the one to tie up Richard's loose ends. Are you going to go to Ottawa?"

"Yes, I'll fly up in the morning. I have an appointment with the executor of the estate and I've got to close up his apartment, get it ready for sale. Same with the one in Montreal."

"I think you're a little safer now that you've dumped everything on the RCMP."

Joyce had one of the newspaper's security personnel escort Eileen and check her into a good hotel, courtesy of the paper. She called for another guard to escort her to the main safe where her copy of the documents would spend the night locked away.

The editorial staff had gone creative with the headline. The morning paper's front page main headline was:

Cover-up?
Senator Marshall's Lover Murdered
Was Senator John Marshall Also Murdered?

By Joyce Withers Toronto New Tribune

At first glance, the death of Richard Brooks, Executive Assistant to the late Senator John Marshall, looked accidental. A second guess might infer a crime of passion in Montreal's gay community. The festering, semi-decomposed and mutilated body of Richard Brooks was discovered in his bath in his apartment, in a trendy area of Montreal's Sherbrooke Street popular with the LGBT community. Evidence pointed to accidental drowning or a crime of passion involving BDSM sex. Police assumed it was a crime of passion. Was it murder or, perhaps, accidental death?

A battered and bleeding Brooks had been in a full bathtub consuming hard liquor and may have passed out and drowned. However, someone had wiped the entire apartment clean. The ever-efficient Montreal police quickly cleared the case by determining accidental death – presuming the sex partner cleaned up the scene to avoid implication.

Richard Brooks's sister has confirmed he was gay. He had an apartment in the trendy Le Village Gay quarter of Montreal popular with and accommodating to the LGBT community. Did he have an affair with Senator John Marshall? Yes, according to his sister, Richard Brooks and John Marshall had a solid but discreet relationship for the past seven years. They were a monogamous couple. Richard told his sister it was unlikely anyone in the Senate office was aware of the relationship as they were "very proper and professional" at work, were never seen together in Ottawa and seldom socialized in Montreal. His sister claims John Marshall gave Richard the money to buy the Montreal apartment mortgage-free. It was a hideaway for their affair.

Could Richard have been murdered or accidentally drowned in a gay one-night stand with a new, casual partner? Maybe. That's what the Montreal police think. It's easy to think that way.

However, new evidence has come to light that suggests murder for a cover-up and hints that the death of Senator John Marshall may well be related and not accidental. Richard was in possession of incriminating documents from Senator John Marshall's activities that some people would not want made public.

In the meantime, the RCMP have taken an active interest in the death of Richard Brooks and Senator John Marshall.

Joyce filled some space with interview details about Eileen and Richard and built a bio of Richard. She ended her piece with *Stay tuned...*

Trying to sleep in after spending most of the night writing, Joyce was awoken by an eleven a.m. phone call from Ray Bonspiel, her editor. "Congratulations! You're raising hell again! I took a look at what you wrote last night for the next two issues and ran it by the editorial board. Our owners are feeling a little pressure, but their response is, and I quote: "Tell her full speed ahead. You've got 'em by the balls. Squeeze hard!"

As she lay in bed trying to get back to sleep, Joyce's phone rang again. "Joyce, its Sergeant Ruggan to advise we are serving a subpoena and search warrant on the PMO. We're targeting files, both paper and electronic, likely in the possession of John Roberts."

"I was thinking of a story on the Arctic research cancellation."

"Very timely. Bye."

Chapter 53

Hector and Sanford were meeting in Hector's office. Sanford commented. "Joyce Withers is doing well. She's got the PMO and the party executive on the run."

"That's an understatement! Our liaison agent with RCMP in Ottawa says the RCMP would like to arrest John Roberts. He may take full blame and Prime Minister Eugene Rogers will try to slide away from the mess but there's enough evidence to nail them both, plus Senators Rule and Lamont, the Unity Party Secretary and CFO." Jack Ruggan's not yet revealing they have the money trails. That'll be a trump card. They won't move until they have a completely solid case with huge evidence and witness redundancy."

"And that's just the stink around the Arctic research scandal. Can you imagine what'll happen when the RCMP reveal they have charges pending on at least seven other incidents of bribery?"

"Yeah, I gather Inspector Poole is keeping some aces in the hole. He doesn't want to lay all charges at once. I'd love to see him hit them on the China deal though."

"Maybe Joyce can help there. Sort of force the issue with a story in the *Toronto New Tribune*."

"If done right, that should be a final blow to topple the PM and his government," said Hector. "It's not as easy as it looks. Their government structure is different than ours. All the judiciary is in the Ministry of Justice and that's tightly controlled from the office of the Minister. And, as you know, the Minister of Justice is also the Attorney General of Canada and that is a political position with the Minister appointed from the Members of Parliament. It's always a senior post in the Cabinet – the inner circle of portfolio Ministers of the party in power, currently the Unity Party. All the work is done by the civil service with the top position being Deputy

Minister. Then, the various divisions each have Assistant Deputy Ministers heading them.

"Currently, the Minister of Justice/Attorney General is Steven Rains. He, like Prime Minister Rogers, is from the West. He apparently got appointed as a pay-off after he dropped out of the race for Prime Minister at the leadership convention and agreed to endorse Eugene Rogers. He was a major contender for the leadership. Apparently, he has a lot of loyal and influential followers in the Unity Party and it's rumored he's being held in the wings as the heir apparent to replace Eugene Rogers."

"Ah. That might be helpful!"

"Maybe. The civil service side of the Ministry of Justice is extremely professional. Informal soundings with some of the top echelon indicate some unrest at the corruption they are sniffing or sensing in the Unity Government but they say the Unity Government – that is the PMO – feel the Department of Justice must not be tampered with. It must be considered above reproach."

"Interesting."

"Yeah, it stems from the basic roots of the Unity Party. They're all for law and order and a sense of judicial fairness."

"But some favors are for sale?"

"Not in the Judiciary. At least they haven't stooped to that yet."

"What's involved in shutting down this government?"

"If they 'lose confidence' – as they call their ability to govern – the government has to dissolve. As the government is running technically at the approval of the Head of State – Queen Elizabeth, in this case – her representative in Canada, the Governor General, can step in and, like an umpire, call the game. In Parliament, the Speaker of the House, as an appointee of the Governor General, can do that if the party in power loses its majority. An election has to be called unless the MPs can cobble together a coalition of MPs and petition to be the party in power."

"So, they could be forced to call an election?"

"Yeah. Not like our system where you have to grin and bear it between fixed election dates."

"Correct. There may be periods of time when the governance of the country is in the hands of the senior bureaucrats until an election and they're technically answerable to the Governor General."

"This should be interesting."

Chapter 54

Summer in Curacao, June through September, is the monsoon and hurricane season. The day had started well. Sunny, a cloudless sky that yielded in the early afternoon to dark clouds and wind-driven rain as a heavy weather front moved in. By three p.m. streetlights were on and swaying with the wind gusts. Rain was heavy, torrential, near horizontal, filling the streets and flooding the storm drains. Leaving the office with the doorman holding an umbrella over him as he ran to his car, Chairman Van Der Zalm managed to duck quickly into the back seat of his chauffeur-driven Mercedes. He greeted Domenick, his driver. "Looks like the weatherman was right! We're going to be hit hard with this storm."

"Yes sir! Dey say we can expect de winds to fifty knots but it should be over by early morning."

Chairman Van Der Zalm noticed a DHL shipping box, about eighteen inches square, beside him on the back seat. "What's this box?"

"I don't know sir. It's addressed to you personally. I picked up from the office mailroom where it was delivered a few minutes ago. The mail clerk and I were having coffee and she asked me to make sure it got to you as she knew you'd be going home early."

"OK." He examined the shipping bill of lading. It was from the cigar store in Havana, Cuba where he purchased his hand-rolled cigars. Nothing unusual. But he couldn't remember ordering anything recently. Well, with time to kill in heavy traffic, may as well open it. After undoing the tape and opening the lid, he pushed down through the popcorn foam and felt something solid. Pushing away the Styrofoam stuffing, he found something round and solid wrapped in a clear plastic bag. With two hands, he pulled it out of the box, noticed a strong rancid-metallic smell where something dark was oozing out of the bottom of the plastic. He took a closer look then realized he was holding the grotesque head of Paddy West. Screaming, he dropped it like a hot iron and clamored to get as far away from it in the confines of the back seat as possible. He

237

was clawing at the door handle, trying to escape for what he felt was an eternity.

Domenick jammed on the brakes when he heard the first scream, then pulled the car over to the curb and released the door locks. Still in panic mode screaming, frantically clawing at the door handle, Chairman Van Der Zalm finally flung open his passenger door, hurled himself onto the pavement on hands and knees and began to retch. Domenick came up beside him in the driving rain. "What's the matter? What's the matter? You OK?" Chairman Van Der Zalm continued to retch and could only point to the severed head on the floor in the back seat.

Chapter 55

True to his word, Inspector Poole had the Montreal Regional Detachment of the RCMP serial crimes unit light a fire under the Montreal Police Department. RCMP Corporal Frank Garneau was working closely with Montreal Police Department homicide detectives Sergeant Marc LaSalle and Detective First Class Marie Dubois. He briefed them on the serial killings file of the Arctic researchers, including what had been discovered by Japanese, Russian and American counterparts. Once the linkage to Senator John Marshall and his influence peddling on behalf of the oil industry was explained, Montreal Police Department re-opened the case. Corporal Garneau was authorized to make all resources of the RCMP available to detectives LaSalle and Dubois. This resulted in them jumping at the offer to use the RCMP forensics lab and personnel for a second look at Robert's apartment as their own resources were stretched thin. The lead CSI from the original Montreal Police team that examined Richard's apartment was frustrated to find the scene wiped clean. She welcomed the chance to look again. A team of six tore apart the apartment centimeter by centimeter. Dismantling sink, toilet and bath drains finally produced some hairs and a partial print was lifted from one of the sex toys (an enema kit).

Sergeant LaSalle and Corporal Garneau re-interviewed the bartenders at the Le Club Arc En Ciel and found one, Guy Marschant, who remembered Robert visiting the Saturday night. He also remembered Steve. "Sure, I remember him. He's one of you. He flashed a badge and slipped me a hundred bucks to vouch for him with Richard."

Sergeant LaSalle was puzzled. "What do you mean?"

"He said he was a detective. He showed me his badge – Ottawa police, if I remember right. Said he was on an assignment here."

After getting a good description, Corporal Garneau asked, "Do you have CCTV here? Maybe you got him on the video?"

"No, sorry. This is a discrete place. You know the clientele we cater to."

They canvassed the neighborhood looking for places that had CCTV surveillance, but found nothing.

A few days later, Frank Garneau telephoned Marc LaSalle. "Good news on the DNA on the hairs. Most were Richard's but we have two foreign ones. We've run through the DNA bank and found a match. Partial fingerprint also matches. This guy's not a felon but was recently in the military – that's why we have the DNA on file."

"And, you're going to drag this out and keep me in suspense? Who is it? And where is he?"

"All right. His name is James Skinner. Last known address is Ottawa. Served in the Canadian Army for ten years, in the Airborne Commando corps – you remember the one that was disbanded because they were too rough for peacekeeping and had very violent, read sadistic, initiation rites?"

"Yeah, I remember."

"I've "acquired" his service record and psych profile – don't ask how. He was discharged for sadomasochism. He's a pretty heavy-duty sociopath."

Do you have a line on his address and current occupation?"

"Yeah, he has an apartment in a trendy part of Ottawa. He works, supposedly, for a security firm out of Hull, Quebec called Acme Security. And guess what? Acme Security just happens to have a client in the form of the Unity Party in Ottawa."

"What comes around goes around, eh?"

"Next question, do you want him extradited from Ottawa or wherever we find him? Do you think you have enough on him? Can you get your District Attorney to sign off on extradition and an arrest warrant?"

"He's certainly a person of interest – and the only one for now. If not for murder or manslaughter by excessive BDSM or whatever, he is possibly the one who destroyed the traces and can be charged with interfering – even if Robert Brooks died naturally. Yes, of course."

"Let's get it done then."

With the assistance of the Ottawa and Hull police, the RCMP found and arrested Jim Skinner, alias Steve Hartling. By the time he was arrested, his moustache had grown back in. He was brought to Montreal and confronted with the evidence. He was identified by the bartender as the person who had been with Richard that Saturday night. He "lawyered up" – Acme Security provided him with one of the best lawyers money could buy. With his lawyer present, he claimed that yes, he was with Richard that Saturday night but not Sunday or Monday. He had spent Saturday night with him but left for Ottawa at noon Sunday in time to make a dinner engagement that evening with a client.

Fred at Acme Security had covered the bases. He provided an affidavit that Jim Skinner was at his desk in Ottawa for the entire week, that Jim had entertained clients in Ottawa on the evenings of Sunday, Monday and Tuesday. Credit card receipts signed by Jim Skinner and client statements were produced to prove it. Jim's lawyer hired a private investigation agency in Montreal who discovered that Richard had dinner at Le Coq d'Or Monday evening with a bald man wearing glasses who paid the bill in cash and left a generous tip. Due to the alibi, the Montreal police were forced to drop Jim as a person of interest as they placed time of death late Tuesday evening or early Wednesday morning. They searched for the man who had dinner with Richard Monday night but struck out.

Police were still puzzled as to how and why Richard accessed his safety deposit boxes both in Ottawa and Montreal on the Tuesday before his death. They concluded he must have gone home to Ottawa, then returned to Montreal on the Tuesday. There was a sufficient time gap between the visits to the safety deposit boxes to allow for travel by car between the two cities. Police found the boxes to be completely empty. Why? What was in those boxes and

241

where did the contents go? There was no trace of the contents, assumed to be incriminating documents similar to what Eileen Brooks turned over to the RCMP.

Chapter 56

The senior partners of Marshall, Garneau, Haskell, LeMonde, Saganaw and Jones were in their conference room. Jack Haskel was presiding. "I called this meeting because I got word today that the RCMP are laying corruption charges against Prime Minister Eugene Rogers, John Roberts, and some of their party's executive, as well as Senators Rule and Lamont. This is all stemming from documents that turned up in the possession of the sister of Marshall's executive assistant. She went to the police and the media with them after her brother was killed."

"There goes the ball game!" commented Pierre Saganaw.

"Yeah, we've been backing the wrong horse," said Randolph Jones. "At least we've had some great business while it lasted. But you can be sure the new party that comes to power will have their own favorite law firms."

Ever practical, Jack Haskell said, "We've got some things to consider: 1) Do we wish to distance ourselves from them? or 2) Do we offer our services for their defense? For one? For more than one of them? and, 3) What do we do about the documents entrusted to us by John Marshall? The RCMP will want them."

A pensive Peggy Le Monde said, "These are not mutually exclusive."

"Elaborate please," said Pierre Saganaw.

"Well, if we take on the defense of one or some of them, we do have Marshall's files. I bet what we have is more complete than what found its way to the sister. It may give us an inside advantage. Another thing – if we keep it buried, the political party leadership may be grateful when they're able to resurrect themselves."

Pierre said, "Or, we could hold that over their heads to get some favors whenever they rebuild. Mind you, that may be a long time coming."

"We must not lose sight of the Will's covenant," Haskell reminded them. "If the police deem foul play – read murder – we are obligated to turn the documents over to them."

Inspector Poole accompanied Jack Ruggan to the conference room in the offices of Marshall, Garneau, Haskell, LeMonde, Saganaw and Jones, where Peggy LeMonde greeted them and offered coffee while the other senior partners came in. Peggy handled the introductions once all were present and Jack Haskell welcomed Inspector Poole. "Inspector Poole, this is a pleasant surprise! I take it by your presence that this matter has made some headway?"

"I presume you're referring to copies of some of John Marshall's papers that we have acquired. Yes, we are making progress. The papers have been most revealing and charges are justified in many instances. In turn, this is leading to searching for more documents. You know, corroboration. Filling in gaps. Other leads."

"I'm sure. And, of course, we have a very complete set of John Marshall's documents. We do not want to be obstructionist. However, we are under the covenant of his Last Will and Testament to surrender them only if you deem his death not to be accidental. Has anything changed in that regard?"

"This is perplexing. First, I must ask you to maintain that which I am about to say in absolute confidence. Are we agreed on this?" He produced a tape recorder from his jacket pocket, elaborately turned it on and tested it. Satisfied it was working, he looked at each person in turn starting with Jack Haskell, stating their name and asking the question. Getting agreement. "Good, let it be noted for the record, all of you have agreed that the following is in complete confidence. You must appreciate that this investigation stems from the murders of the Arctic methane hydrate researchers and that this stretches into Japan, Russia and the USA, involving police and national security personnel of those countries. We have information that leads us to conclude that Senator Marshall was murdered and it was linked to the deaths and attempted murders of the Arctic researchers."

Jaws dropped around the table. Peggy Lamonde held her temples as if she had just acquired a massive migraine. Pierre Saganaw muttered, "Merde!" Randolph Jones rubbed the back of his neck. Jack Haskell interjected. "Do you have sufficient proof to go to court?"

"Unfortunately it's not that easy. The Japanese and Americans acquired and verified a confession. However, the murderer was later executed by the Japanese."

Jack Haskell said, "As long as you can assure us that you deem Senator Marshall's death to be murder, we must honor the covenant of his last Will and Testament. We will surrender the boxes to you herewith."

"Thank you!"

Sergeant Ruggan called in a forensics team to enter the law firm's safe with Peggy Lamonde and take possession of the files. Peggy was careful to point out the seals and provide a notarized log detailing when, where and by whom the documents had been inspected and re-sealed. After they departed with the files, Peggy, Jack and the senior partners once again met in the conference room. Jack Haskell said, "I think this is for the best. This way, we've covered our asses with the RCMP. We've followed the covenant to the letter. The PMO was already under fire due to the papers the RCMP acquired from the sister of Marshall's lover."

A bemused Pierre said, "Besides, we have copies. There's nothing stopping us from defending one or some of the accused."

"Just wait till the RCMP review all the files," Peggy mused. "They'll have enough to nail the PM, the PMO and the party executive to the wall."

Randolph Jones said, "We should start seeking some new business."

Chapter 57

Christine Lamont had returned to her Senate office after sitting through a boring committee reviewing funding for Canadian artists. After pouring a cup of coffee from the credenza coffee pot, she had managed to settle into her sofa, kick off her too tight shoes and put her feet up on the coffee table, when her executive assistant, Janet Murray barged in. "There're two policemen out there demanding to see you."

Sergeant Jack Ruggan and Roger Pearson were escorted in and introduced themselves. Christine said, "RCMP and CSIS?"

Jack Ruggan, taking a recorder from his jacket pocket, said, "Correct. We'd like you to listen to a tape." He placed the recorder on the coffee table and turned it on.

> *"Mr. Van Der Zalm? It's Christine Lamont."*

> *"Ah, Senator Lamont. It's always a pleasure to talk with you. What news do you have for us today?"*

> *"Apparently, the methane hydrate Arctic researchers are gathering at an FBI safe house in the Virginia woods in Shenandoah National Park. They're at a small lake, called Lake Bailey. It's about a hundred miles from Washington D.C. Apparently, the place is pretty remote, nestled up a box canyon in the Blue Ridge Mountains about fifteen miles in from Skyline Drive, which is a scenic drive running the ridgeline of the mountains. The FBI call it Camp Samuel.*

> *"They'll be there for at least ten days working with patent attorneys of the Willard Institute and then they will be interviewed by Joyce Withers and, possibly some TV network journalists. I understand Joyce Withers will be linking the murders of their colleagues and the cancellation of their research directly to the oil industry. She'll be naming certain individuals.*

"Thank you Christine. It's always good to hear from you. Also, thank Senator Rule for me. Look at your offshore account in a few days.

"Thank you Chairman Van Der Zalm."

Jack Ruggan turned off the recorder. "Even without names mentioned in the conversation, your voice is very clear. We've verified it by voice recognition software. And, we know Chairman Van der Zalm as the head of the Global Association of Refiners and Petroleum Producers located in Curacao. Roger, would you please show Senator Lamont what you have found?"

"Certainly." Roger handed a piece of paper to Christine which she read, her hands began to shake and she turned white in shock.

"How did you get this?"

"It's none of your business. You can't deny that's your offshore bank account in St. Kitts. You can't deny money has been deposited to it. We've traced some of the money transfers from an account indirectly belonging to the Global Association of Refiners and Petroleum Producers."

"What do you want?"

"We've recorded more of your conversations with Chairman Van Der Zalm. We feel we can make a case against you as an accessory to at least three counts of murder. There's the deposit of one hundred thousand dollars around the time of the deaths of the researchers plus deposits linked to some of your phone conversations with Chairman Van Der Zalm. We have interesting material from the files of Senator John Marshall that implicates you as well. Also, there was an attempt on the lives of the researchers in Camp Samuel – you led the assassin to that. That's accessory to attempted murder. Add to that the pay-offs you received from the Global Association of Refiners and Petroleum Producers – a clear trail to the cancellation of the Arctic methane hydrate research – and we have corruption in the first degree. You're cooked. We have charges pending in Canada and, of course, the FBI wants you as accessory to murder and conspiracy to murder. We have more –

some of your other payoffs have a clear trail as well. You can come quietly or we can go to the press. How would you like to play this?"

"What do you have in mind?

"Would you like to be a witness for the prosecution? We may accept a plea bargain if you wish to provide us with more information. However, you may wish to resign as a senator first."

"Interesting. May I call my lawyer? I'm sure we can work something out."

"You may. You should also be aware that another team is arresting Senator Rule as we speak."

"Are Prime Minister Rogers and John Roberts aware of this?"

"Not yet."

RCMP Interrogation Room C, Ottawa Headquarters

Senator Christine Lamont was escorted into Interrogation Room C. She accepted a cup of tea and a donut while awaiting the arrival of her lawyer. Inspector Poole gave Christine a half hour in private with her lawyer, Janet Dumont, then knocked and entered. He placed a recorder on the table, turned it on and tested it, stating the date and time and who was present. When satisfied, he began the conversation. "Madam Dumont, permit me to review why we invited Ms. Lamont in for further questioning."

"You played her a recording of a conversation and showed her a financial paper trail. I question if they could be used as evidence in a Canadian court."

He played the recording, let her read the paper outlining the offshore money trail, then began. "We had a warrant for the wiretap. It's legal. The financial paper trail came to us from the American National Security Agency – the NSA. It's part of their normal snooping. We could subpoena it as we have a bi-lateral agreement for sharing information like that."

"You have more?"

"'Fraid so. Yes, a lot more concerning Ms. Lamont's gaining financially from her conflict of interest with the oil industry. Then there is the matter of the deaths of the researchers and the fact that she benefited financially from that. We understand she received a hundred thousand dollars to keep quiet about the deaths. That implies she may have been in the forefront of the plot to kill them. Anyway, we feel we can tie her into the murders as an accomplice – albeit unwitting."

"Although there are no rules prohibiting senators to gain from consulting or memberships on boards of directors, what do you want? "

"Her complete cooperation. We really seek bigger fish. We suggest she resign from the Senate forthwith, then assist us in return for reduced charges."

"No. Not reduced charges. All or nothing. If she turns witness for the prosecution, she gets immunity."

"That will depend upon what she reveals to us and how we may utilize it."

They took a break for Christine and Janet to confer privately, which gave Inspector Poole the opportunity to join Sergeant Ruggan in Interview Room F where a discussion was underway with Manfried Rule. When he returned to Janet and Christine, Janet spoke. "OK. We want an immunity agreement now covering both murder conspiracy and all other possible charges and she will tell you everything about her experiences in the black art of influence pedaling and others she knows who have been involved. This is in consideration that you will not go after her offshore bank account. She will resign from the Senate immediately."

"You lose the bank account and consider yourself lucky, as there is lots of room for corruption and tax avoidance charges, etc. Consider there are many additional charges waiting for you. We're concerned with criminal cases, especially murder and corruption. Excuse me for a few minutes while I prepare an immunity agreement. As you know, we include a clause that your client is not to disclose any information to others. Perhaps you will best use the time for preparing a letter of resignation from the Senate?"

The immunity agreement was modified and rewritten a few times in the back and forth of negotiations, but by early morning both parties had agreed and signed off. The Senate resignation letter was reviewed and signed. Inspector Poole allowed Christine the dignity of phoning the Senate leader and reading the letter to him. It was then e-mailed and officially hand-delivered to the home of the Leader of the Senate. A press conference was scheduled for ten o'clock that morning where Christine would meet the press and read her resignation letter.

Inspector Poole reconvened the interrogation. "Ms. Lamont, as you now have immunity, can you shed any light on the death of Senator John Marshall? We know you and he and Senator Rule were paid to get the PMO to cancel the research. We have the paper trail and some recordings."

"Yes, we arranged it. We were well paid. We were all very upset when we learned the researchers were being killed off. We hadn't bargained for that! We were just involved in getting the funding cancelled. I complained to Chairman Van der Zalm and he sent one hundred thousand dollars to my offshore account. I understand he did the same for the others. However, John took exception. He wanted more, much more. He told us he had demanded ten million as he hadn't bargained on the murder of the researchers. He said we should do the same but I, for one, was too afraid of the Chairman to go up against him."

"I see. Was the PMO involved in this?"

"John told us that the PM, the Unity Party and John Roberts were all paid for the cancellation of the research. But, I'm sorry. It's hearsay in a court of law. However, John was also pissed that the PM had asked him to resign from the Senate. He was swearing he wasn't going to go quietly – that he would make public some very dirty secrets. He also wanted to be paid out – both five million cash and an ambassadorship to a prestigious country."

Inspector Poole took a few minutes to privately call Joyce Withers, catching her in bed, and informing her that Christine was resigning from the Senate forthwith. He declined to elaborate on why Christine had been pulled in for questioning.

RCMP Interrogation Room F, Ottawa Headquarters

Senator Manfried Rule was placed in Interrogation Room F. He was offered some coffee, tea or water and he selected bottled water. He was told that Senator Christine Lamont had also been picked up for interrogation and was in another interrogation room. He was then left alone awaiting the arrival of his lawyer.

Sergeant Ruggan gave Senator Rule a few minutes with his lawyer, Ken Janson, then entered and, after introductions, began. "I want you to hear a recording from a warranted wiretap where you get honorable mention." He played the recording.

"Mr. Van Der Zalm? It's Christine Lamont."

"Ah, Senator Lamont. It's always a pleasure to talk with you. What news do you have for us today?"

"Apparently, the methane hydrate Arctic researchers are gathering at an FBI safe house in the Virginia woods in Shenandoah National Park. They're at a small lake, called Lake Bailey. It's about a hundred miles from Washington D.C. Apparently, the place is pretty remote, nestled up a box canyon in the Blue Ridge Mountains about fifteen miles in from Skyline Drive, which is a scenic drive running the ridgeline of the mountains. The FBI call it Camp Samuel."

They'll be there for at least ten days working with patent attorneys of the Willard Institute and then they will be interviewed by Joyce Withers and, possibly some TV network journalists. I understand Joyce Withers will be linking the murders of their colleagues and the cancellation of their research directly to the oil industry. She'll be naming certain individuals."

"Thank you Christine. It's always good to hear from you. Also, thank Senator Rule for me. Look at your offshore account in a few days.

"Thank you Chairman Van Der Zalm."

"You'll note, Senator Rule, that you were mentioned in that conversation."

Ken Janson jumped in. "So, what's your point? Are you arresting my client on a flimsy comment like that?"

Sergeant Ruggan then passed a piece of paper to Manfried Rule. "You may be interested in this."

After a few seconds to read and comprehend the paper, Manfried commented in a shaky voice. "How did you get this?" Ken Janson snatched the paper from Manfried and began reading. After reading and rereading it, he said, "I want some private time with my client please."

Sergeant Ruggan left the room and took his recorder with him.

In private, Ken said, "Is this financial paper trail of transactions to an offshore bank account yours?"

Weakly, Manfried said, "Yes. How did they get it?"

"Let's find out." He went to the door, knocked and when it was opened by a guard, asked for Sergeant Ruggan to return.

When Sergeant Ruggan returned and turned on his recorder, noting date and time, Ken said, "Although I doubt you could use this information in a Canadian court, my client and I would like to know how you obtained this information."

"Let's say, for now we consider that material corroborative and that we have established significant evidence from other sources that may lead to a number of charges. However, the recorded conversation I played for you leads to a charge that we consider to be in the forefront."

"What is that?"

"Conspiracy to murder. There was an attempt on the lives of the researchers in Camp Samuel – you led the assassin to that. By the way, the lead assassin confessed to the plot and that he was hired by Chairman Van der Zalm. You identified the location of the researchers and passed that along – for financial consideration, I might add – to Ms. Lamont, who, in turn, passed it on to the Chairman and he acted upon it by commissioning the assassination plot. "

"Are you charging my client?"

"Not yet. We're still building the case. It'll come in due time. We're also looking at conspiracy charges against your client associated with the murders of the researchers – at least the ones in Newfoundland, Toronto and Winnipeg. We've been working with the FBI and they're looking at your client for involvement in the death of one of their researchers in San Francisco and the bombing of a lab at the University of Alaska and the subsequent death of one of their agents. By the way, the FBI obtained your client's offshore banking information – legally, I might add – and shared it with us. Mr. Rule, you're free to go – for now, but we've alerted Border Security you're not to leave the country, and Homeland Security has put you on their Watch List. And, oh, by the way, we've seized your offshore bank account."

Chapter 58

Joyce met with her editor and explained her next project. He was excited but nervous. "You've got to vet everything – and I mean everything – through the legal department. I'll assign a senior lawyer to you. And, congratulations – for the duration, you have twenty-four-hour security. Lady, you're treading on dangerous ground."

Joyce began her new series revisiting Senator John Marshall.

It Was Murder – Not Accident
Senator John Marshall Murdered
Hit Man Confesses

The RCMP has been advised by intelligence officials in Japan and the US that a person apprehended and in Japanese custody confessed to killing Senator John Marshall. The individual has an extensive history as a contract hit man who had come to the attention of intelligence services in many countries. Why would a hit man be paid to kill Senator John Marshall? Who did he alienate? What was he up to when he was killed?

The mystery deepens when you consider that Senator Marshall's executive assistant, Richard Brooks, died "accidentally" shortly after the murder of his boss. It must be noted the hit man claimed he was not involved in that. RCMP and Montreal police both feel the death of Richard Brooks was not accidental and treat it as an open investigation.

A review of John Marshall's papers provided to the RCMP and your newspaper by Eileen Brooks, the sister of Marshall's executive assistant, have revealed a number of activities that could have led to trouble. One notable example was his involvement in the cancellation of the Arctic research funding which his papers reveal was instigated by the oil industry. But that is only one of many examples of his manipulations.

The RCMP spokesperson advises that the killer's confession revealed his employer but that and the name of the hit man will remain confidential, as further investigations are pending.

Chapter 59

You can get anything you want in Las Vegas – providing you can pay for it. Sheik Mustafa Bin Rizal felt it was time for a little relaxation. He had spent a business week in Curacao as his nation's representative on the Board of Directors of the Global Association of Refiners and Petroleum Producers. His corporate jet, a customized Boeing 767, brought him and his entourage to Las Vegas – one of his favorite spots for R & R. His secretary had secured the penthouse of his favorite hotel right on the strip, had arranged for a high stakes poker game and, of course, his favorite treat.

The poker game had been good. He was only down eight hundred fifty thousand and might make it back in tomorrow's game. Right now, he was in bed with his treat. He thought the boy couldn't be more than thirteen or fourteen. He was a white kid with blonde hair and blue eyes, clean complexioned, well groomed, with a developing build – possibly from one of the former Soviet states. The boy had been well trained in delivering sexual pleasures and he had very good manners to boot. Mustafa was enjoying the boy and half thinking of buying him from the escort agency to take home.

With curtains drawn, the bedroom was dimly lit, providing good ambiance – dark but with sufficient light to make out the boy's features. Out of his peripheral vision, Mustafa thought he caught a glimpse of a black shape emerging from behind a curtain as the curtain moved. He stopped caressing the boy, began to turn his head more toward the movement and was beginning to sit up when a force pinned him to the bed. He looked toward the force just in time to see a man-shaped black form raise a sword with two hands and begin to swing down. That's all he saw as his head separated from his body in one clean slice. The boy was decapitated half a second later.

The ninjas arranged the bodies on the bed. Torsos in an embrace. Heads on pillows facing each other but with a one foot separation from their torsos. After taking pictures, they left by the window as silently and invisibly as they had entered. The bodies were only discovered in the late morning when a butler arrived with breakfast and the head bodyguard, Mohamed Salim, entered the bedroom to ask if Mustafa wished to eat.

After surveying the carnage, Mohamed Salim exited the bedroom, closed the door and forbade anyone to enter. He then called the Sheik's senior brother, Prince Abdul, in Saudi Arabia, to report the death and seek instructions. Eventually, considerable sums exchanged hands with hotel security and management and the owner of the escort agency that had supplied the boy, ensuring their silence and assistance. The bodies were flown to Riyadh for disposal.

A few days later, Chairman Van Der Zalm received a DHL envelope – again from his cigar source in Cuba. Heidi Zuder, his executive assistant, brought it to him at his desk. "What is it?"

"Just an envelope. I opened the outer envelope and there's another inside. I didn't open it as it's addressed to your personal attention."

"O.K…" He carefully examined the DHL envelope, noting it had originated with his cigar supplier in Cuba. Finally he extracted the inner envelope. It was thin, big enough to hold a couple of unfolded sheets of paper. He then said, "Take it down to security and have them open this carefully. There is no thickness to indicate a foreign object in there but, you know, there could be a poisonous powder or something."

Gingerly holding the envelope, Heidi left. She returned an hour later with Lars Linden, Chief of Security, who was holding the envelope. "We examined the envelope. It contains photos – some are very unpleasant photos. I've examined for fingerprints and other traces but found nothing."

Lars handed the envelope to Chairman Van der Zalm who took out the photos and gasped at the one on top as he realized what he was viewing. He felt weak in the knees. With his hands shaking he said, "I was aware that Sheik Mustafa Bin Rizal died by decapitation in Las Vegas but I was not aware of the boy. That's horrid!"

He shuffled through the collection of photos. In addition to the grizzly photos of the bodies, there were half a dozen photos taken locally. One was of the Chairman getting into his car with Domenick, his driver holding the door for him. His hands started shaking more so when he realized there were photos of his bedroom and office. The message was clear. They were coming for him.

"Sir, I presume this is associated with the head of Mr. West that was sent to you?"

"Absolutely. Someone, I believe the Japanese government, is sending us a message in no uncertain terms telling us to leave their methane hydrate project alone."

Still shaking a few minutes later, Chairman Van der Zalm suffered a massive stroke and was rushed to hospital. He never recovered sufficiently to return to work and accepted early retirement.

The Executive Committee of the Global Association of Refiners and Petroleum Producers agreed that the Japanese were sending them a message and decided to avoid any dirty tricks in future. There was some division in their ranks, with a couple of members deciding to approach the Willard Institute and the Japanese government to see if they could license the extraction process. The majority of the directors chose to continue contesting patent applications and advancing their own research.

Chapter 60

John Roberts rushed into Eugene's office. "The RCMP arrested Christine Lamont and Manfried Rule!"

"What? When?"

"I just got word. Looks as if they were picked up simultaneously, less than an hour ago."

"Oh, shit! What are the charges?"

"It doesn't look as if they've been charged yet. Apparently, they've been hauled in for questioning concerning the Arctic methane hydrate research cancellation and the deaths of the Arctic researchers. Both have requested lawyers."

"Well, I can see charges of influence peddling. But how do they relate to the deaths of the Arctic researchers?"

"You've got me there. I guess we'd better find out."

It was a little after 12:15 a.m. when Manfried Rule was able to awaken John Roberts at home. "John, I'm sorry to be calling so late."

"I heard you were arrested by the RCMP. What happened?"

"They let me go – for now. They're building a case. They're trying to pin me for a murder conspiracy!"

"What? What've you been up to?"

"It's concerning the Arctic methane hydrate researchers. The FBI broke up a murder plot to kill off the remaining researchers when they were meeting with their patent attorneys. The ringleader was arrested and he confessed."

"So, how're you implicated?"

"I'm accused of divulging their location. I passed on the information to Christine and she told the Chairman of the Global Association of Refiners and Petroleum Producers."

"Sounds innocent enough."

"Except they also have proof I was paid for it."

"Oh."

"What should I do? You've got to protect me. The party's got to protect me. I've been loyal and reliable. And, I've also earned you and the party good money."

"Yes. Yes. But we've got to think of what is best for the Unity Party right now. I'll talk it over with the PM and the party executive and get back to you in the morning."

John Roberts managed to snatch a fitful sleep until being awoken by a call from Christine Lamont just after six. "Christine! Where are you?"

"I've just been released by the RCMP."

"I spoke with Manfried. I understand this was concerning a murder plot on some of the Arctic methane hydrate researchers?

"Yes. I'm afraid I can't say anything more about it. I'm calling to advise that I've resigned from the Senate. I'm holding a press conference at ten this morning. I'm not mentioning why I'm resigning."

"We'll miss you – but you're doing the best thing for the Party."

Next day at 10:30, after many discussions with Eugene Rogers and the Unity Party leadership and after viewing the press conference at which Christine Lamont announced her resignation, John Roberts met with Manfried Rule and Ken Jansen in his office at the PMO. "I'm not surprised she resigned," he said, rubbing his right temple to try to soothe his roaring headache. "You say the FBI's building a case as well?"

"Yeah." Ken Janson was nervously rubbing the back of his head. "We're dealing with two jurisdictions – probable cases in two countries – involving Christine and Manfried here. There's potential for a stink in both countries. You may be able to put a damper on something just involving Canada but not so easy crossing the border."

"Manfried, I talked this over with the PM and the Unity Party executive and we've reached a decision on what's the best path for the Party." He went over to his desk, picked up a piece of paper and handed it to Manfried.

After he read it, he passed it to Ken to read. "So, you want me to resign too?"

"Yes. We feel it's for the good of the Party. In light of Christine resigning, we feel it's even more pressing that you also resign. Now."

"But I've been loyal to you and the party. You can't cut me loose."

"Your resignation from the Senate is needed. Now."

"And what if I refuse?"

"The PM will publicly ask for your resignation."

"Then some damaging information against you, the PM and he Unity Party may come to light."

"It's not nice to threaten. We know you've been loyal. Trust the Party. Resigning from the senate is an honorable thing to do. You know the party executive will try to do its best for you."

"Will you let me confer with Ken for a few minutes privately please?"

"There's an empty conference room you can use. I'll ensure you aren't disturbed."

261

When they returned a few minutes later, Manfried handed John the signed paper. "Here's my resignation. I trust you'll advise the Senate Leader and the PM."

"Yes. We'll announce it publicly during Question Period.

Chapter 61

One of Sanford's researchers noticed some press releases emanating from the PMO that were taking a favorable slant toward China's willingness to partner with Canada's Department of Fisheries and Oceans for some ongoing research projects in the far north. Of particular note was a memorandum signed by the PM of Canada and China's President when the President recently visited Canada granting China rights to conduct research in Canada's Arctic waters to explore ocean currents, conduct hydrographic surveys and assess global warming. Buried deep in one of the releases was a comment that Canada had agreed in principle to permit China to establish a permanent research station on Ellesmere Island. Apparently, according to the researcher, the agreement received little notice in the Canadian media.

Sanford organized a meeting with Hector, Roger Pearson and Martin LeRoy. To begin the meeting, he handed out copies of the press releases and backgrounder info gleaned by the researcher for all to read. Martin LeRoy was first to comment. "So, it's starting."

"I'll get full details on all this and pass it on to Joyce," said Roger. "The length of the proposed lease of the research station site and the numbers of people the Chinese are planning to locate there could be explosive when exposed. It's time to reveal John Marshall's sordid hand in facilitating this."

"Good idea!" said Martin emphatically.

Joyce jumped at the material and soon had another exposé grabbing the front page.

China Sell-Out?
Canada Giving Ellesmere Island Away?

The government of Canada has apparently been negotiating to cede substantial control of Ellesmere Island to China. It is well known that China wants a piece of the Arctic, not only because the open ocean shipping lanes are becoming feasible as the ice cap melts, but also for the abundant mineral wealth that lies beneath the sea and on our Arctic islands. China has approached Denmark to purchase some remote islands but Denmark has refused. China then upped the ante and offered to purchase Greenland but this was also declined. At the UN, along with the United States and a number of other countries, China has protested Canada's claim to some Arctic passages, declaring they are international waters.

Thin Edge of the Wedge?
Lease or Buy?

*Canada's Prime Minister Eugene Rogers recently signed a friendship protocol with China's President Xi Xiue to write an agreement permitting China to establish an Arctic research station on Ellesmere Island, Canada's most northern landmass. If ratified in its draft form, the agreement would give China a 99-year lease on half the island and permit up to **one hundred thousand Chinese nationals** to reside there.*

*It must be noted, Canada has a weather station on Ellesmere Island with **only five full-time personnel** over the winter months. Needless to say, Canadians would be outnumbered. Is this really just the thin edge of the wedge leading to a complete Chinese takeover of Ellesmere? What does Eugene Rogers have in mind? Is he thinking of selling out to China? What about the mineral wealth on Ellesmere and in the surrounding ocean? Will China claim that? Take it or buy it? What could Canada do if China just took the island once they outnumbered us?*

Is Eugene Rogers negotiating to sell Ellesmere? It's not without precedent as that's how our American friends grew rapidly with purchases of Alaska and Louisiana.

A few days after Joyce's first article appeared, Sanford met again with Hector, Roger Pearson and Martin LeRoy. After pleasantries, Martin was the first to speak. "The official opinion poll shows that the Canadian populace are not at all happy with the Ellesmere Island deal. The Members of Parliament are getting swamped with calls from their constituents opposing the sell-out. Confidence in the Unity-led government is now in the bottom teens – that's unprecedentedly low. The public is not happy. The opposition is having a field day in House of Commons Question Period. We're getting word that some of the backbencher MPs of the Unity Party are very nervous. Some are already talking with the opposition about possibly crossing the floor of the House and siding with the opposition."

"Is it time for the blockbuster?" That was almost a rhetorical question from Sanford.

Roger smiled. "Our people have spoken with many of the senior federal bureaucrats, including their leader, Rob Vaughn, Clerk of the Privy Council. They know there's corruption within the Unity Party; they've seen it and are fed up with it. They'd like to see something happen. They can't speak out but they're so fed up, they can point to some areas that would lead investigative journalists to the manure piles. In fact, we've developed quite a file already."

Hector asked. "Time for Joyce to seek gold in the dung heap?"

"Yeah. Joyce already has copious stuff from Marshall's files. Time to turn over the manure."

Chapter 62

Sergeant Ruggan was meeting with Inspector Poole and Eileen Gerber, a representative from the Ministry of Justice. They were sitting at a small circular table in Inspector Poole's office. They had reviewed all files they had received from the sister of Richard Brooks and from the lawyers for the estate of Senator John Marshall. Inspector Poole asked, "Well, Eileen, what do you think?"

Eileen, a fifty-something robust short person with a brilliant mind and always-positive personality, was a twenty-five-year veteran and a senior prosecutor in the Public Safety Department. Her specialty was "difficult" or "delicate" cases. "This is appalling!" she said. "It opens a very sensitive can of worms."

"Uh, oh," said Ruggan. "Does that mean we should let this slide?"

"Absolutely not! BUT when we build a case or cases – I can see multiple names to be indicted – we must be extremely solid on each count. For the good of the country, we can't let blatant corruption at the highest levels slide."

Inspector Poole rubbed the back of his neck. "I'll have to take this higher up the totem pole."

"I already have, with the Chief General Council. He gave the green light and will connect with your superiors. We do have the problem that it's unprecedented in Canada to arrest a Prime Minister. Also, consider that he is the one who selected the Minister of Justice – it could even be considered a coup attempt if the Minister goes against the PM. Until we are totally prepared, we should try to avoid bringing this officially to the attention of the Minister of Justice."

"Better to get the PM to resign first?" asked Jack.

"The senior executive in the Unity Party will sacrifice Eugene Rogers and replace him in a heartbeat if it gave them a chance to survive as the party in power."

"Better if the Unity Party lost their ability to control the government," said Inspector Poole.

Eileen smiled. "Their control will implode if seven more MP's cross the floor. The Unity Party would lose its majority to govern and the other parties would be unlikely to see a coalition as beneficial."

Jack said, "I know just where to start."

Chapter 63

Timed to coordinate with the day of Inspector Poole's presentation to the Security Oversight Committee, Joyce pulled out all stops and her editorial board once again gave her the front page of the morning edition.

Ellesmere Island Sell-out
Senator John Marshall Paid to Broker a Deal
By Joyce Withers, *Toronto New Tribune*

RCMP investigation has corroborated documents acquired from the estate of the late Senator John Marshall revealing his role in brokering a deal that would see China purchasing Ellesmere Island. Documents reveal Chinese emissaries paid John Marshall an up-front fee of ten million US dollars for his "facilitation" services. A senior investigating officer of the RCMP stated: "Senator Marshall's paper files and e-mails are quite detailed. In addition, we have verified the money trail. Senator Marshall received the money in an offshore account in a tax haven country. We note that three deposits totaling nine million dollars from that account were subsequently made by Senator Marshall to other numbered offshore accounts. That trail will merit further investigation."

It is fair to assume that the ten million dollars in facilitation money was split between accomplices partnered with John Marshall. Who would be possible recipients? One can only assume it would be people who could make the deal happen.

What Price Ellesmere?
John Marshall's papers reveal that China at first offered two hundred billion US dollars for Ellesmere Island but this was countered by the Prime Minister's Office (PMO) asking one trillion. At the time of Marshall's death, negotiations were ranging between three hundred fifty billion and five hundred billion US dollars. His papers also reveal he was expecting a ten percent brokerage commission for closing the deal, a fee that was still

268

under negotiation at the time of his death. If payment followed the pattern of the initial "facilitation" payment of ten million, which was split between John Marshall and three unknowns, the four recipients would be splitting between thirty-five and fifty billion dollars. That makes the deal a pretty "high stakes" game for the facilitators – whoever they may be. Of course, Canada would benefit by three hundred fifty to five hundred billion US dollars to pay down our debt and possibly create a heritage fund, but do we know the value of Ellesmere Island?

The mystery deepens. Why was Senator John Marshall killed? Who are his partner-beneficiaries in the Ellesmere Island deal? What is the value of the natural resources on and around Ellesmere Island to prompt the Chinese to pay so much? What do they know that we are not privy to? Is this related to the PMO's decision to cut off funding for our Arctic researchers and suppress or destroy their research? We, the Canadian people, except for a very few who may benefit from brokering the deal, are being treated like mushrooms.

Chapter 64

The Security Oversight Committee was chaired by Senator Leon Kirschner. Fortunately, he was not implicated in any of the papers and additional vetting found he was clean of any wrongdoing. The Committee comprised ten members, four Senators and six MPs (Members of Parliament) including the Minister of Justice/Attorney General, Steven Rains. Two senators and two MPs were not from the Unity Party. After a private meeting between the Commissioner of the RCMP, the Chief General Council and Senator Kirschner, a special meeting had been called two hours before Parliament was scheduled to begin daily session. No one had been told the purpose of the meeting. While awaiting the start of the meeting, most gossip focused on Joyce Wither's article on Ellesmere Island that had come out that morning.

Inspector Poole presented the case. He began by revealing some material from Senator John Marshall's files, such as the recordings, e-mail and paper memos relating to the cancellation of the Arctic research funding. The final item was revealed in two steps. First he showed the money trail of the transfer of funds from the Global Association of Refiners and Petroleum Producers in Curacao to the offshore accounts of Senators Marshall, Lamont and Rule, both concerning the cancellation of the research funding and hush money after the story came out about the deaths of some of the researchers. It was noted that both Senators Rule and Lamont had been arrested and charged. He finished by saying, "The money trail and memos show a definite link with the Prime Minister, his Chief of Staff and two senior members of the Unity Party. In the one example, funds from the Global Association of Refiners and Petroleum Producers were transferred into offshore numbered accounts belonging to them."

One of the Senators raised her hand. "You have given us one example. I presume you have more issues like this?"

"Yes. We have found many – let's say, "incidents." Another example is a definite money and paper trail showing that Senator John Marshall, with the PMO and the Unity Party leadership, accepted payment for their own gain to facilitate the possible sale of Ellesmere Island to China."

After considerable thought, Stephen Rains spoke up. "At first, I was quite upset that you and my own people had kept me in the dark on this. However, what you have laid out is a matter most serious and cannot be ignored, stifled, swept under the rug, whatever you want to call it. I certainly have had no part or benefit from their dealings. The corruption in the PMO is horrific. You have my complete blessing to proceed with the filing of charges against them. I hope you can recover some of their ill-gotten gains.

Inspector Poole thanked the Attorney General for his support and advised that they had managed to freeze all the offshore accounts they had so far found. The committee members looked at each other or at the papers in front of them in stunned silence.

Concurrent to Inspector Poole's presentation in the Security Oversight Committee meeting, Sergeant Ruggan and Eileen Gerber were holding a meeting of their own. They had invited a select list of uncorrupted Unity Party MPs, all backbenchers, and the leaders of the opposition parties to a boardroom at the Ministry of Justice where they made an identical presentation, finishing by advising that charges would soon be laid. Again, there had been no forewarning. Invitees were not told the reason for the meeting except that an urgent issue was pending. Twenty-four of the thirty-one invited were present. No one was allowed to leave the room during the meeting and all cell phones were surrendered to an officer at the door.

After Joyce Withers' expose came out in the morning paper, John Roberts, Eugene Rogers, Ernie Kowalchuk, and Andre Robadeux were huddled in the PM's office to plan counter measures. Their first concern was to move their offshore funds to new accounts. They had settled on a choice of banks on the island of Mauritius where it was alleged the banks could still provide secrecy but they were encountering some problems setting up new accounts. They had been alerted to what took place in the Security Oversight Committee by one of the members who had been present but this was only after the meeting ended. They did not have time to react before Parliament began its afternoon session. A quick check revealed that the RCMP had indeed frozen some of their offshore bank accounts. Eugene Rogers chose to miss Question Period to try to move some other accounts before they were seized. He refused to accept phone calls from Steven Rains.

When Parliament opened that afternoon, one after another, nineteen Unity Party MPs from the backbenches – members of the "Outer Circle" of the government who had not been favored with ministerial positions and who had not been participants of the payoffs – left the Unity Party and crossed the floor to sit as independents. At that point, Marc La Grande, the Leader of the Opposition, rose and addressed the Speaker of the House.

"Madam Speaker, by my count, the Unity Party no longer has a majority. In fact, I count they are eleven short of a majority. I respectfully ask that this government shall be declared to cease and that the Governor General be so informed." This was met by a roar of applause and desk thumping by the opposition and independents. A very flustered Madam Speaker rose. "I am satisfied with your count and I agree the Unity Party no longer has the majority of MPs needed to govern. This session of Parliament shall cease forthwith."

Members of the media in the press gallery were astounded. Pandemonium ensued as they scrambled to file the news. Interviews with many of the MPs who crossed the floor revealed an even bigger story.

Chapter 65

Eugene Rogers interrupted the very tense discussions in his office to take an urgent phone call from Madam Monique Richileu, the Speaker of the House. With no time for pleasantries and urgency in her near hysterical voice, she said, "Eugene, you lost your majority to govern. Your government is dissolved! Nineteen Unity Party MPs crossed the floor to sit as independents. What's going on?"

Eugene began to shake. He shouted into the phone as he put it on speaker for the others to hear. "What? Impossible. We had no warning! Say that again. I've put you on speaker phone."

"I had no choice but to close Parliament as you have lost your majority. Nineteen Unity Party MPs crossed the floor to sit as independents."

John Roberts said, "Oh, my gawd!"

Andre Roubideaux jumped up, his hand hitting his forehead. "Mon Dieu! We're next!"

At that moment, Eugene's executive assistant barged in. "The RCMP are here and have served a warrant. They want all our files and all of you!"

She was lightly pushed out of the way by a uniformed RCMP officer, Corporal Jules Real, who entered the room with four other officers. "Gentlemen, you are all under arrest. The Office of the PMO has been placed in trusteeship by order of the Governor General. We have warrants for all your files, including your personal files. Currently, the Unity Party offices and your homes are also being searched."

A stunned John Roberts managed to speak. "What are the charges?"

Corporal Real responded. "We'll go into them in detail at headquarters but we have quite a list of charges, multiple counts, ranging from accessory to murder to accepting bribes and benefiting from use of public office."

Corporal Real then turned to Eugene Rogers. "Mr. Rogers, before going to RCMP Headquarters where you will be formally charged and booked, I am instructed to take you to the residence of the Governor General where he awaits your formal resignation and that of your Unity government."

Chapter 66

Joyce was prepared for the news that the Unity government had collapsed. As the backbenchers who had crossed the floor of Parliament revealed their reasons and grabbed the evening news headlines with the corruption story, she polished her "bombshell," as she called it, because it was sure to capture the nation's attention in the morning edition. She vetted the story with her editorial board and the newspaper's lawyers, then sent it to press. She scored the front page again:

Prime Minister Arrested
PMO Raided by RCMP, PM Resigns
By Joyce Withers, *Toronto New Tribune*

Yesterday, RCMP exercised a warrant to arrest the Prime Minister of Canada along with six senior executives of the Unity Party. After nineteen Unity Party MPs crossed the floor, the Speaker of the House dissolved the session of parliament. RCMP escorted PM Rogers to the residence of the Governor General where he offered his resignation.

The RCMP also seized documents and computer hard drives from the PMO and the homes of John Roberts, Eugene Rogers and six senior executives of the Unity Party.

RCMP were searching for corroborating evidence of documents that came into their possession from the files of the late Senator John Marshall showing collusion and bribery. Under-the-table-payments, amounting to millions of dollars, were apparently made to the Prime Minister and key Unity Party members during secret negotiations to sell Ellesmere Island to the Chinese. "Corroborating evidence" is the correct term as the RCMP now have in their possession two sets of documents from the files of the late John Marshall which have led to more materials and statements from some of the collaborators. It will be interesting to learn if the PMO, which reputedly had similar records of e-mail and other documents, had retained them or purged their files in an attempt to destroy evidence. The PMO had seized all files in

275

Senator John Marshall's Senate office and it will be interesting to learn if they had been retained or destroyed.

Corruption goes deep in the PMO. RCMP have unearthed a paper trail revealing that China has been negotiating secretly with the PMO to purchase Ellesmere Island, Canada's northernmost island in the Arctic. Bribe money has changed hands. A PR plan has been uncovered designed to convince Canadians to say yes.

Documents seized included a "Social Media Marketing Plan" outlining a six-month, two-hundred-million-dollar media campaign designed to sway public opinion in favor of the deal before proposing it to Parliament. The documents also contained verification of a money trail of bribery payments from the Chinese government to the Unity Party, the PM and his Chief of Staff. An unnamed government source would not go on record but stated: "These guys would sell their mothers if they could get a cut of the deal. Regardless if the sale would have netted large dollars for the Canadian government coffers, a positive point and a way to eliminate our deficit, these guys were only doing it for the commissions going to their offshore tax haven personal bank accounts. After eleven years in office, these birds became very rich and contemptuous of what is for the good of Canada. They were only interested in what made them richer."

This was followed up the next day with the headline-grabbing expose:

Secrets Sold to China
By Joyce Withers, *Toronto New Tribune*

Documents seized in the RCMP's raid on the PMO and Unity Party headquarters corroborate corruption at the highest levels of the PMO and the Unity Party. In preparation for the sale of Ellesmere Island to China, the PMO transferred files to the Chinese government from the Department of Fisheries and Oceans revealing the latest hydrographic surveys and data revealing oil, gas and mineral deposits. It is interesting to note that personnel in the Department of Fisheries and Oceans had been mystified why

276

the PMO directed them to destroy all files pertaining to studies in and around Ellesmere Island but the motive seems to have been preparation for transfer of real estate to China.

Epilogue

The Point Barrow radar station was perfect for their testing. Located on a point of land famous as the farthest northern point of the United States, Point Barrow is also known as the point of delineation of two of the Arctic seas, the Chuckchi Sea to the west and the Beaufort Sea to the east. Nearby, there is a memorial marker for aviator Wiley Post and entertainer Will Rogers who died there in an airplane crash in 1935. The Point Barrow Distant Early Warning (DEW) radar station was established in 1957 and has been actively providing long range radar surveillance ever since. It morphed into the modern North Warning System (NWS) in 1989 and modernized again in 1998, highly automated with a small maintenance staff. It is maintained by the 611th Air Support Group and is under the control of Elmendorf AFB, Alaska. In addition to being an active main station for the NWS, due to its abundance of surplus facilities and an excellent airfield, the site now hosts the Global Atmospheric Watch, an atmospheric monitoring station.

The site is remote. The military consider it relatively easy to guard due to lack of hills or vegetation – which makes it also a very bleak landscape. It is some 5 miles southwest from Point Barrow, a city of 4,200 souls.

The site is on permafrost, as evidenced by the undulating boardwalk that shifts during the months of surface thaw. The permafrost has significant quantities of methane hydrate, making it a perfect test bed.

As the site is in close proximity to some of the oil fields of the Alaskan North Slope, a number of the oil exploration companies have offices in "downtown" Point Barrow. Sanford and Hector, in consultation with Ruth Dempsey of Homeland Security and Caroline Weston of State Department, had agreed on the site. Thelma Kenny of the Willard Institute was reluctant at first but eventually came around to the idea. Sanford thought it was "like waving a red flag in front of a bull" – perfect.

Base security was beefed up. More electronic security systems were installed around the perimeter of the base and in all buildings. This included the relatively new low frequency underground cable system designed to monitor footsteps and vehicle movement. Thirty additional security personnel were brought in. Employees were sworn to secrecy. Personnel were informed that e-mail and cell phones were monitored. All were confined to base until rotated out to "the lower 48," restricted from visiting the town or talking to locals. All civilians flying in to the airport were carefully screened in advance and under surveillance as they went about their business in the town. Special attention was given to oil field workers.

Equipment was flown in from "Mayberry" on commercial air freighters directly to Point Barrow where technicians proceeded with drilling into the permafrost, assembling the extraction and containment infrastructure, and converting engines to run on methane. The goal was to have all engines on the base run on methane. This ranged from the diesel generators providing electricity and heat to snowmobiles, trucks and cars. Within two months, the model Arctic village was running entirely on methane generated from the bed of permafrost beneath it. It was time for the reveal.

The Willard Institute had choreographed the press conference on a grand scale. Key senior investigative reporters and camera crews had been gathered from the major world media networks, along with journalists from the world's most influential presses, such as the leading magazine on economic issues. All were brought in by chartered flights. Joyce Withers received special treatment, accompanying Thelma Kinney on the Willard Institute's private jet.

Robert Berubé, Stephanie Lees as well as Hayden and Ikumi Kincade were present for the big moment. Norma, Ivan, Peter and a very pregnant Vanessa stayed in Mayberry. Robert led the press conference which, after a general introduction, was followed by a tour and demonstration of the equipment and a question period. Stephanie and Hayden assisted in the demonstrations and stepped in to elaborate at question period.

Robert's careful collaboration with Thelma and the PR department of the Willard Institute was reflected in his opening speech at the press conference:

279

Ladies and Gentlemen,

Thank you for making the journey to one of the most remote places in America. This location for our technology unveiling was selected because it is in the high Arctic, reflecting both opportunities and environmental concerns.

Today, you are here to see the product of an opportunity realized. That is, the harnessing of that which is found in abundance here. Buried in the permafrost is methane. Methane in great quantities. So far, research has identified significant quantities in the polar and sub-polar regions – enough to fuel the world for the next three hundred years. Think of that. Enough to fuel the world for the next three hundred years.

The methane, or natural gas as you may wish to call it, burns cleanly and is far less polluting than hydrocarbons such as gasoline or diesel. As you know, natural gas has been mandated to fuel vehicles in many of the world's most populous cities, such as Bangkok, Singapore and New Delhi, and the conversion has dramatically improved air quality.

The methane contained in permafrost is tightly held and difficult to extract. It is in the form of methane hydrate which, simply put, is methane gas trapped in ice. Permit me to demonstrate:

(There was a pause while Robert reached into a plastic cooler and extracted a large chunk of ice. He took a barbecue igniter and proceeded to light a corner of the ice. The ice began to drip while burning. Photographers clamored for good positions to film the burning ice.)

You can see the flame burns clean. The drops coming off the ice are water. The by-product of burning methane hydrate is basically water.

This demonstration makes things look simple, but I can assure you that the act of safely wringing the methane out of the methane hydrate mix in a commercially viable way has proven difficult. A successful methodology developed in the Canadian Arctic by a team comprising Japanese, Russian, American and Canadian researchers has now been refined into commercialization. Japan is successfully extracting methane from offshore methane hydrate deposits in waters one kilometer deep. Russia has successfully tapped land-based methane hydrate in permafrost: the gas is now providing all the fuel needed for heat and electricity for a city of seven thousand people located above the Arctic Circle. Russia is quickly moving to fuel other cities this way.

You are here to review the technology that has been adapted to provide all the fuel needed for a small Arctic village. Think of it. Fossil fuel would no longer need to be transported at great expense to a remote Arctic village. All their fuel needs would be generated from their local permafrost. This, in itself, is remarkable, but it is only a start. Eventually these technologies will service fuel needs around the world.

These achievements met with significant resistance. Forces have opposed this technological development not only in the courts by challenging patent applications but also at the cost of lives through assassinations and attacks on individual researchers, labs and equipment. The opposition has played rough.

For example, Dr. Stephanie Lees, here of the University of Alaska, had her lab bombed, a tragedy in which her FBI security escort was killed. Stand up please, Stephanie. For those who wish, she will be available for interviews later.

In Japan, terrorists used a pirated oil tanker to crash into and sink the drilling platform of the first producing well. Thankfully, no lives were lost on the drill rig.

Three Canadian researchers and one American were killed by what was determined by police to be assassinations. As well, there were two attempted assassinations, one in Japan and one in Russia — fortunately the people targeted survived their injuries.

Political influence eliminated Canadian research when funding was removed and research files destroyed — a product of lobbying by the oil industry.

Lately, most opposition has been in the form of a patent race with world-wide patent applications by this research group being challenged in the courts by representatives of the oil industry. They have deep pockets. Fortunately, this research group, a syndicate of the Japanese and Russian governments and the Willard Institute, also has deep pockets – and excellent lawyers. We have overcome all lawsuits against our patent applications to date and see the same for the future. We have many, many more patent applications to come.

We'll save questions in this area for later.

Now, let's look at this equipment we asked you to come and see. We will take you for a tour and explain the process. But first, a general description.

Harvesting the methane begins with drilling into the permafrost and releasing, in a controlled way, the methane hydrate, then piping it into a storage tank. From the storage tank, the gas is "scrubbed" – impurities and water are removed. The processed methane is stored until needed, then transferred by pipe or filling pump to the engines it drives. All of this is automated. At the ground level, monitoring and maintenance is simple. Monitoring data is also sent by satellite to a central computer on a continuous basis. Equipment maintenance is simplified with replacement modules. Modules, such as circuit board chips needing repair, are flown out to a central repair facility.

The process is environmentally correct as all by-products, such as sulfur, ethane, propane, carbon dioxide, nitrogen, and hydrogen sulfate, are separated and captured. Water is purified for other uses. Residue of the chemicals used in the refinement process are completely recycled.

By-products, both in quantities and types, vary with the geography but, as mentioned, are commonly sulfur, ethane, propane, carbon dioxide, nitrogen, and hydrogen sulfate. Each is separated and packaged for export. This gives the village a new income stream by selling the by-products. They aren't perishable, so they can be sent out sporadically when transport is available.

You'll be able to learn more on the walk-through and demonstration.

All engines in this village, from trucks, quads and snowmobiles to diesel generators have been converted to run on methane. Obviously, there is less pollution. We have also mastered the technology to operate all equipment even in the coldest temperatures and harshest conditions.

I think I've taken enough of your time for now. We will be here for questions and individual interviews after the tour.

Thank you.